Praise for the Base Branch Series

"Megan Mitcham's books are well-paced, well-plotted suspense novels edged with stunning sensual intensity. Her lovers are cold and deadly--except when they are skin-to-skin. I can't wait for the next book in the series!"

- DELILAH DEVLIN
New York Times and USA Today bestselling author

"Nail-biter all the way to the end."

- Michelle, MsRomanticReads
Adult Romance & Erotic Book Reviews

"This is a fresh and exciting story with lots of great characters."

- 5 Star Amazon Review, Enemy Mine

"Megan now joins my elite team of must read authors. I fell in love with her work in *Enemy Mine*, and it just gets better the more I read."

- TNT Reviews

BOOKS BY MEGAN MITCHAM

BASE BRANCH NOVELS
ENEMY MINE
JUSTICE MINE
STRANGER MINE
WARRIOR MINE
DANGER MINE - July 2015
PRISONER MINE - January 2016
SURVIVOR MINE - April 2016

BUREAU NOVELS
FOR ALL TO SEE
PAINTED WALLS - October 2015

BLACKLIST SERIES
VERSIONS
VIRTUES - 2016

BOX SET
HEARTS IN DANGER - June 2015
benefiting The American Heart Association

ANTHOLOGIES
ANTICIPATION
CONQUESTS - 2015
ROGUE HEARTS - 2015
SEX OBJECTS - 2016
COWBOY HEAT
HIGH OCTANE HEROES
WILD AT HEART VOLUME II
benefiting Turpentine Creek Wildlife Refuge

Enemy Mine

Base Branch Novel #1

Megan Mitcham

Copyright Warning

Published By MM Publishing LLC
Edited by Lacey Thacker
Cover Design by Deranged Doctor Design

Enemy Mine
All Rights Are Reserved. Copyright 2014 by Megan Mitcham
First electronic publication: October 2014
First print publication: October 2014

Digital ISBN: 978-1-941899-00-7

Print ISBN: 978-1-941899-01-4

To Mom for reading to me. To Dad for making me read. To Art & Kay for re-igniting my love of books.

Chapter One

Sloan stood in the shadowed ink of night. Swirling wind whipped her ponytail. Thin strands tickled her cheek, but did not obstruct her view. The rest of her body mimicked the statue perched at the center of the penthouse balcony. Unlike the bare-breasted figure, Sloan wore black from the tips of her unruly mane to the soles of her combat boots. Beyond the sculpted stone balustrade and the steep drop of the building she'd scaled, the National Mall glittered like a diamond on America's hand. The view from the luxurious Pennsylvania Avenue condo drew people from all across the globe. Yet, she paid it not a glance. Her eyes locked on the scene unfolding on the other side of the dwelling's massive glass wall.

Complications one and two.

A woman, her curves crammed to overflowing in a sparkling white cocktail dress, tugged a man into the ultra-modern living room. Everything inside the premium abode glistened, from the glass chandelier to the alabaster granite beneath the woman's five-inch stilettos. The man swaggered after her swaying hips. His narrow chest puffed with a fifty-fifty mix of ego and vanity. They stopped at the wet bar and the two nearly became one. His lopsided grin mingled with a sneer. He curled around her, his broad body molding to her lush backside. He blanketed one tweed-covered arm over her shoulder. The other crept its way up her buxom hip. As the gown fell to the floor, bare skin rewarded the man's endeavor.

Agitation tickled the back of Sloan's neck for a split second before she gridlocked the useless emotion. She hadn't been given time to perform reconnaissance. Too bad. So, she'd been sent out alone with less than reliable intel. Just as well. The task remained the same. Retrieve all information from Madame Tracy Walters' laptop. Sure, stealth was preferred. The empty dwelling she'd been promised would've made it much easier. Yet, as was often the case when negotiating covert ops, plans changed. Waiting for the occupant and her guest to leave wasn't an option. Her commander had stressed this assignment dealt in time-sensitive material. Speed was priority.

If you can't go in the front door due to heavy security, you find a back door. Or, in this case, a balcony. If you can't go in the balcony, you find a window. Taking one step backward, Sloan peered down the structure's side wall. While the condominium's street front facade arched and bowed with an artful design easy for climbing, the side street exterior slid down to the asphalt below with only a hand full of pocketed windows. None in safe reach.

The sharp thwack of flesh meeting flesh brought her head around. In the dark recesses of her mind, in memory scarcely visited, Sloan stood, eyes wide, as a thickly-veined hand connected with a beautiful woman's cheek. The woman's pleading eyes, amber just like her own, watered, but shed no tears. Blinking the image away, she met reality. Madame Walters pinned her client to the bar with a pointed elbow. Black slacks and tighty-whities hung around his thighs, revealing a blindingly white butt. A hint of red marred one tensed ass cheek.

Sloan swallowed rage that had nothing at all to do with the couple on the other side of the glass, and resumed her search. After a quick climb to the roof, she used a skylight to drop into a white marble bathroom thick with the scent Eau de Whore. Her tuck and roll left only a whisper of sound, quickly covered by a series of throaty pants emanating from the living room. The bedroom she entered dwarfed her own and boasted the largest bed she'd ever seen. The monstrosity suffocated in silky white linens. Sloan got the feeling the madame surrounded herself with white to mute all the impurities in her life. But, psychologist she was not.

Across from the bed, flanking an ornate mantel, were two doors. The first, a closet smaller than the apartment sized one she'd seen in the bathroom, brought a shock of color to the scheme. Bright red coated every surface. Paraphernalia of Walter's trade hung on the walls. Pulleys and eyebolts. Leather straps. Feathers. Floggers. Whips. Fake dicks of every odd shape, color, and size. Beads. Plugs.

My, what a thorough businesswoman.

Tracy Walters, previously Tara Walley, was a self-made woman. Coming from nothing, she'd quickly made a name for herself. Stripper, turned call-girl, turned entrepreneur. Tracy made her mark culling the most exotic and talented ladies in the land to service D.C.'s elite. But by going international and mixing it up in the world of high crime, she amassed a fortune. Now known not only for her bedroom abilities, but her ability to funnel drugs, women, and arms through several key continents, Madame Walters had earned the Base Branch's notice and Sloan's abhorrence.

Grunts and giggles moved closer, reverberating down the hallway through the open bedroom door. Without hesitation, Sloan returned the room to its innocent guise with a twist of the knobs. Two ground-eating strides brought her even with what she suspected was a home office, but the amorous pair rounding the frame prevented her from slipping through unnoticed.

So much for foreplay.

One side step enveloped Sloan in darkness behind the thick wood of the bedroom door. Ignoring every human instinct—fight, flight, blinking, breathing, scratching itches—she stilled. Only her heart stirred, as the two groped their way past her into the room. Walters unlatched the man's nipple from her bite and turned away with a rough giggle. Her heart-shaped bottom brushed the man's lap as she turned and swished to the goody closet. When she opened the door the light shown from the recesses, casting a spotlight on the bed.

Sloan took her first good look at the client.

Byron Graham, West Virginia's pristine good-ole'-boy and two term senator, practically salivated as Tracy Walters disappeared into her little den of iniquity. She returned with a fist full of leather and a wicked smile. The man poised to make a promising run for President of the United States during the next election moaned as his wrists, then ankles, were cinched into black restraints.

Well there's your foreplay. A little rougher than I'd imagined. But who am I to judge?

Sloan moved like a flower opening for the morning sun. Centimeter by precious centimeter, she eased her hand into the left pocket of her black tactical pants and retrieved a camera no larger than a flash drive. *Click. Click.*

The device made no sound, but the pictures it took were concussive enough to rock the east coast. Sloan captured the likely future president strapped to the end of a bed in a standing X with a ball gag stretching the skin of his mouth, while a world-renowned madame and war profiteer knelt before his dangling package.

Who the hell needed Nationwide on their side, when they had insurance like this?

No one.

Sloan could wave hello, walk into the office, remove the damning evidence from Tracy Walters' computer, and pirouette her way home with the pictures as leverage. Then again? If she tipped her hand, she could just as easily be taken out by a sniper's bullet as soon as she left the building. The stakes were that high. In reality, when weren't the stakes that high in her line of work? Dodging a sniper was definitely more trouble than waiting for these two to get distracted.

So, she waited and watched.

Voyeur much?

Sloan didn't think so. She'd need some level of sexual interest in the display before her, and she didn't have as much as one stiff nipple. She marked voyeur off her list of proclivities.

After twenty minutes of flogging, Sloan wondered whether or not Ryan, her male counterpart and friend, would have wood from this voyeuristic job. She ventured a positive guess. Not that it would have impeded his operation in any way. Hell, even a preacher would be shocked into watching. But the unfolding scene didn't rouse or revolt her. Perhaps her coworkers' jibes were accurate.

Ice. Annie Artica. Freeze.

When Graham was blindfolded and Walters was busy swallowing his cock, Sloan slipped into the adjoining room. City light bled into the space from a picture window. She easily discerned the glass desk which sat in front of a wall of shelves sprinkled with books, various ornaments, and artful nude sketches. Sloan locked both sets of doors and sat at the desk before opening the laptop and typing furiously for several minutes. As shrewd as Tracy was with a man's penis, she was even more so with her password protection.

Triumphantly, Sloan set the flash drive to accept duplicates of everything the computer held. She waited. Beyond the door grunts, whimpers, and slaps continued. The innocuous files flew across the screen. Sloan prowled the room for a surveillance camera. Finding none, she returned to the desk in time to read the name on one of the soaring files.

Lucifer.

Her heart bucked.

Chapter Two

Waiting sucked more cock than Tracy Walters. Usually, it didn't faze her, but Sloan had more important things to capture than the errant piece of cereal she chased around her bowl. Too bad she couldn't do a thing until given orders.

Suddenly, the glasses in the cabinet behind her head began to clink and rattle. The countertop vibrated in time with the *boom boom* of the thrumming bass creeping through the walls. Sloan cocked her head toward the microwave's digital clock. As it had for two years now, the red light flashed the twelve o'clock of neglect. Fixing it always seemed like wasted effort, and judging by 2-C's ever-dependable beats, the thing was only a couple of hours off.

Disinterested in the chase, Sloan carried the spoon to her mouth without the prize. The milk chilled her throat as she swallowed. Flipping the handle, she let the spoon hang there, her tongue nestled in the scoop. The last bit of grain pirouetted in the bowl.

The one that got away? The lucky one?

Sloan slid off the faux wood grain of the Formica countertop. With a finger, she dislodged the polyester running shorts from the crack of her butt, walked two small steps to the sink, and dragged the now warm spoon through her lips.

Staring at the Grape-Nut, she dumped the bowl's contents. "Nope," she said. "Not the lucky one."

The whitewash of milk stood in the stainless steel basin for several seconds before the ancient pipe relented to gravity's pull. Her hips didn't twerk with the beat, nor did her teeth grit in annoyance. Sloan simply washed the bowl, spoon, and water glass, dried them, then placed them in the pulsating cabinets and drawer.

Silently, she padded out the dark kitchen through the living room, running her fingers over various locks and latches as she went. In the pitch-black room, no interior lights blazed from the fluorescent fixtures above. Blinds, cinched tight, blocked curious eyes. Stubbing a toe on a couch or rapping a shin on the coffee table weren't concerns. She had neither. She did have a desk in the guest room, which had never housed a guest, but other than that, her bed and night stand were the only pieces of furniture she required, and she could find them with her eyes carved out.

In the bathroom, Sloan depressed the measly lock on the knob. The tinny sound echoed against the muted orange tile walls. Maybe that was another reason she never turned on the light. The color was about as pleasing to the eye as dog vomit. But no, aesthetics had nothing to do with it. Sloan removed the Sig from her waist holster and wiped the sweat from the grip with the side of her T-shirt before placing it on a homemade shelf. Just above the sliding door of the shower, the painted four-by-five strip of plywood blended in to the white of the wall. From under the hem of her shorts, she pulled thin, black-matte blades from sleek leather sheaths strapped to each thigh. The blades clanked as they settled onto the shelf next to the gun. Finally, she unzipped the pocket at the small of her back, retrieved a slender black phone, and then placed it with the weapons.

The tepid water beat onto her chest. She leaned into the deluge, letting it fleece the evening's dirt from her skin. Back alleys were filthy places filled with garbage of every variety. Turning around, she let the water pound some of the tension out of her shoulders. As she worked the bar of L'Occitane verbena soap, her one and only serial splurge, against her washcloth, the calming scent filled her nostrils. It smelled like what life should be. A spring morning after a cleansing rain. The nip of winter hanging in the air, but the promise of warmth just around the bend. The dream eased the remaining tightness from her muscles. In the dark, Sloan scrubbed the lather of bubbles over every inch of her skin, beginning with the arc of her neck, working her way down.

* * *

Clean, dry, and dressed in a white tank and grey cotton shorts, Sloan eased back the fluffy comforter and sat on the center of her bed. Blinds shut tight, the inky blackness lightened to grey in her bedroom with the help of the street light filtering in from the parking lot beyond her window. She placed the gun on the bed in front of her crisscrossed legs. One blade she hid under her pillow, the other under the mattress edge. She dropped the phone onto the nightstand, then opened the drawer.

A string of high-pitched curses permeated the wall behind her large wooden headboard. "*Humph.*"

What was it with people and their routines?

As she unrolled the cleaning kit she'd retrieved from the side table, the faint *boom* of 2-C's radio accompanied the nightly brawl of the couple next door. With deft hands, Sloan released the loaded magazine from the pistol and racked the slide, ejecting the round from the chamber. With the subject of every practice shot and dry fire in her mind, Sloan took aim in the center of his forehead, just a wrinkle above his greasy brow line, and fired. The firearm clicked impotently, but in her tenacious imagination the imaginary bullet exploded out the barrel and slammed into meaty flesh. *Whack.*

Too bad she hadn't gotten the real life chance. *Yet.*

While 2-A bit into the habitual two-timer with dirty words Sloan rarely thought, much less used, she methodically cleaned her sidearm. By the time she put everything away and nestled her head on the puffy pillow, the verbal firefight from next door was replaced by the excited voice of an infomercial salesman and rumbling snores.

Routines.

Sloan stared at the crack in the ceiling. The tiny chasm originated at the window frame, spreading upward through the wall and the plaster over her head. The width of the fissure was no more than that of a pin. Hardly ominous. Yet, it mocked her, how closely it resembled her life. A crevice devoid of anything real, filled only with work. The crevice had grown about a quarter-inch in length since she'd last laid here through the night, studying it until the sun had lightened the sky.

Why the hell did she keep this place? Not for the neighbors or the structural integrity of the building. The fact that the upstairs tenant could fall through his floor and crush her skull at any moment should give her pause. Was this decrepit apartment her sick attempt at normalcy? A routine?

No, since the word denoted things happening with regularity. Sloan had a variable existence, because Santa didn't come down the chimney on Christmas Eve with a sack of goodies, and God didn't appear in a blinding white puff of smoke to vanquish evil. She had this place because she occasionally had downtime from work, and park-bench-sleepers got arrested.

C'est la vie. And then you die.

No sooner had the thoughts run through her brain, than variability vibrated her phone.

Chapter Three

Twenty minutes later, Sloan turned the grey sedan she leased into a dull, dark parking garage. At this hour the lot and office building in downtown D.C. were nearly deserted. Dirty yellow fixtures set intermittently in the concrete walls did little to light the way. Sloan parked on the middle level and got out. Using the car's body and windows as a mirror, she scanned her surroundings for movement. With not so much as a stray cat riffling through the garbage cans, she ducked back into the car. When her hand gripped the slick leather of her briefcase, she heard them. Two soft footfalls. Before she could react, a masculine voice whispered from just beyond her door.

"Beat you."

She knew the voice and the satisfied smirk on its owner's face, nearly as well as she knew her own...well, the voice and face, not the smirk.

"Once, in how many years? I wouldn't get smug, but I know there's no stopping you," she said, turning to address the night's champion.

Ryan Noble shook his slightly shaggy mop of blond hair. "Nah. Na-uh. Twice. Remember the time —"

"Yeah, I remember the time I *was shot*. If you want to count it, go ahead. But how sad is that?"

His stupid smile nearly blinded her with its brilliance, and almost made her smile back.

They fell in step together, heading for the elevator. "Where the hell were you hiding, anyway? I looked everywhere. Behind the column?"

"A ninja never gives away his secrets."

Surprisingly, a snort of laughter shook Sloan's shoulders.

Ryan let loose a triumphant roar. "I made you laugh. Let's blow this joint and head to Vegas. I can't lose tonight," he said, shaking and rolling imaginary dice.

She pushed the down button on the elevator, and then shoved him inside when the doors opened immediately.

"You could never be a ninja," she said while punching in a code on the keypad of the elevator's emergency telephone. The doors closed and Ryan laughed again. "See," she added, with a Vanna White hand gesture at their reflections. "Look at you. You're like three feet taller and a hundred pounds heavier than your average ninja. And stealthy, you are not. I could hear those tugboats coming from Virginia," she added with a pointed finger toward his sleek, black leather shoes. "You couldn't keep your trap shut for five minutes, either. Even when you're in a room by yourself, you talk."

He folded thick arms over his chest and strained the seams of his tailor made suit. "Like you know a ninja. Besides, I snuck up on *you*, didn't I?"

"About that. I still want to know where you were hiding."

He made a show of clamping his thick lips between his teeth. Like that would last. Sloan decided to see how long he could keep quiet. She folded her arms across her chest and raised an eyebrow at his image in the smooth metal door. He turned his nose up.

Sloan studied their reflections. Both wore sharp fitting charcoal grey suits with white shirts underneath which their cover as lawyers demanded. The fabric, however, was the beginning and end of their similarities. At five-eight, one hundred thirty-five pounds of svelte muscle, with a butt and boobs that made bikini-wearing an X-rated, and therefore scarcely occurring, event, Sloan was far from scrawny. However, she could stand behind Ryan and vanish from sight.

Ryan was a golden boy, from the blood in his veins to the long list of his commendations. Like a gold coin, Sloan could test his genuine carats with a bite to the arm. Hell, his coloring even went along with the theme. Blond hair. Blue eyes. Glowing tan. Straight white teeth, plump lips, and dimples in the flesh beneath his strong cheekbones worked in unison to form a contagious smile. Other women had referred to it as sensuous. Fuckin' sexy had most recently been used to describe his face.

She could see it, but had never felt it. Their relationship over the years had developed into older-sister-little-brother roles. She'd be the adopted older sister, since they looked nothing alike.

Dark waves of hair brushed the tops of her breast pocket. Amber eyes stared back at her, the ink of her pupils matching her locks. Her skin was dark caramel. Her oblong face hosted big eyes, a petite nose, fishy kiss lips, and a sharp chin. While people called Ryan sexy, she got saddled with *interesting*.

She would never be mistaken for a white girl. Hispanic, maybe. Native American, on occasion.

Asian, if she did her make-up right. African American, if she played up other features. In truth, Sloan didn't fit any demographic, which came in handy in her line of work.

When the elevator came to rest she slid Ryan a look. All the color had drained from the border of his mouth, and the muscles in his neck strained from his continued effort to keep silent.

"Give it up," Sloan tossed over her shoulder as she exited the small space.

He growled back, "Never. Okay. Fine, you win. Damn it. You know me too well."

Yeah, she did know him, so well that somewhere along the way she'd grown to care for him. More than she cared for her own life most days. While she was damaged goods, he was unblemished and honorable, worth the sacrifice she'd make, if the necessity ever arose.

Quite a shocking realization, since she didn't care about much these days except doing the job.

After caring about so much, working for so long, fighting to make things right, she'd worn her iron will to a paper thin sheet. Numbness was her last line of defense. The only thing guarding her sanity.

Vail Tucker's stern voice ricocheted from deep inside his office, through the partially closed door, and off the concrete and glass of The Base's hallway. "Briefing. Conference room. Five minutes. Invaluable work, Harris."

"Thank you, sir," Sloan answered.

This covert special operations sector of the United Nations, known as The Base Branch, did not exist. At least, as far as the US government as a whole was concerned. Sure, everything they did the president and a fistful of top ranking military and agency guys sanctioned, but nobody, not even the first lady, knew of it. No one even whispered of it as though it were lore.

Together, Sloan and Ryan turned down the corridor away from the operations commander and their offices, heading for the designated location.

Ryan pulled open the heavy glass door. "After you."

Sloan rolled her eyes, but hurried through the entrance before he let the thing squish her for the offense. The large rectangular room was cold, literally and figuratively. Yet, it was more home than the dank apartment. Two long walls of naked glass and two short cement walls with massive flat screen monitors framed the space. In its center stood a long wooden conference table surrounded by twenty high-back chairs.

"So," Ryan began after they sat side by side on the far side of the table facing the door. "What'd he pull you away from tonight?"

He knew better than to ask about her mission, but why'd he have to ask about her night? She snapped her head around to meet his gaze. "Where were you hiding?"

His dimple disappeared as his smile fell. "You ran goddamn back alleys again, didn't you?"

She threw back, "Watch your mouth."

He pointed his index finger and shook it once in her direction. "Watch your ass before you get it shot off trying to play super hero."

"There are no capes involved."

"And no super powers either," he countered.

Sloan scoffed, mouth hanging wide. "I beg your pardon, but I've got mad skills and weapons. Who needs super powers?"

"You said you were done."

"I was."

"But?"

"I got antsy. There's nothing to do at the apartment but wait for the next call."

"You can always come hang out with me."

She wrinkled her nose. "Your mom's lucky I didn't punch her last time. I don't think I have the restraint to chance a second encounter."

"She was trying to be helpful."

"Hand grenades are helpful. She's intrusive and single minded."

"Tell me how you really feel," he said with a snort.

"I'm sorry, but you're her son. If she wants to play matchmaker with you, and you allow her, that's one thing. I'm off limits. A lifelong companion, I do not need. And if she thought that grab-ass with the greased-lightning hair was a catch, she's one terrible judge of character."

"She said you were cold as the Arctic shelf."

"Every once in a while, a blind man's bullet finds its target."

"Anyway," he said, throwing his palm in the air. "It's not like I live with her."

"She's at your place so much, I thought she lived with you."

He gave a dull, "Ha. Ha."

"If your mom isn't there, then it's the female hordes, clamoring for a turn to get in your pants. It's disgusting!"

The door opened, stalling his retort. A handful of their team members rushed in. *Finally.*

Ryan leaned close, eliminating eavesdroppers. "Stop looking for trouble, or I'll be forced to put on tights and be your side-kick."

"Grody," she whispered back.

"Stone cold killers don't use the word 'grody.'"

She shrugged. "They don't wear tights either."

"Seriously," he said, the laughter in his voice neutralizing the word. "We need to find you a new, more sedate hobby."

Commander Tucker breezed through the door, followed by a clump of late-comers. They all wore suits of the grey-scale variety, and most hated every second of it. Cover stories added security though, and a mass of lawyers couldn't show up to work in full-blown tactical gear without stirring suspicion. With a good color job, the boss could pass for one of her peers. In such peak physical condition and with decades of combat and covert ops experience, she'd bet money on him in almost any situation, against nearly any opponent. Plus, he had a perpetual steely calm to which she could relate. It also helped perpetuate his youthful visage. No worry lines. The only tell was his silver fox hair.

Ryan offered in a whisper, "Knitting?" As soon as the word was out of his mouth, he shook his head. "Ah, hell no. Forget it. You'd use the needles to castrate someone."

Tucker's dark eyes scanned the room as he walked toward the head of the table. Placing his laptop on the elevated surface, he typed in a short line of code and began without preamble.

"We have verified intelligence. Today, March fifth, at approximately ten hundred hours, an assassination attempt on the newly appointed Central African Republic President Yannick Toussaint Bakou will be made on US soil. It is our mission to prevent this attack."

The inane shuffling of papers ceased, as did the foot-tapping from the new guy at the opposite end of the table. Ryan retreated from her space and straightened in his chair, obviously realizing his next hobby idea had dropped a few rungs on the ladder of importance. Sloan glanced at the digital readout on the screen monitor. Six hours until the kill shot. Not much time.

Tucker clicked the laptop's touchpad and an image appeared on both screens.   "This is CAR's President," he said with a nod toward the picture. "Bakou is in Washington, D.C. attending the US-Africa Business Summit. He's scheduled to speak alongside three other dignitaries at a public event being held in Meridian Hill Park. Introductions begin at zero nine hundred hours with dignitaries taking the stage at zero nine twenty. Each foreign leader has been allotted twenty minutes talk time. Bakou is slated to speak second.

"Most of you know what's at stake here. For those of you that don't, I'll spell it out. After nearly five decades of civil war in the infant nation, Bakou is the Central African Republic's first genuinely elected democratic leader. Joachim Dolingba rigged the 2003 election, hijacking CAR's government for ten years of corrupt rule riddled with human rights violations. After leaving an honorable twenty-year military career, Bakou created stable economies in his and three surrounding villages through trade and education.

"Yannick Bakou must not die. Today, the stability of a nation and the lives of hundreds of thousands rest on us."

Air in the closed room thickened with the weight of duty. The collective inhale of its occupants was measured, purposeful. All accepted the incredible challenge.

"I speculate the assassin will take the shot toward the end of his speech. That leaves us less than six hours to find the sniper's nest." The commander's chin shot up. He scanned the room, locking eyes briefly with every person as he continued. "We're dealing with a logistical nightmare. Security is thin and the park is wide open. The shot could be taken from one of nearly a hundred buildings from twenty times as many windows. Also, the shot could be taken in cover at the park."

A few hushed curses colored the air.

Commander Tucker tapped the computer again, and the image on the monitors changed. "The hit has been ordered by arms dealer Devereaux Kendrick, known in many circles as 'The Devil.' This US citizen abandoned the country nearly forty years ago for London, where he married the now deceased aristocrat and multi-millionaire, Elizabeth McCord."

The *whoosh* of pumping blood roared in Sloan's ears as the man came into focus. Her thundering pulse drowned out Tucker's words. Words she needed to hear. She tried to calm the storm ripping through her chest. Breathe. In. Out. In. Out. Nothing happened. Lighting cracked behind her eyes. This was it, what she'd waited a lifetime for, and she was going to screw it up if she didn't focus.

Beneath the table, Ryan's shoe nudged hers. Instantly, the room snapped into sharp view. She ventured a glance at her partner, who showed no interest in anything except Tucker. *Good.* Only he had noticed her unrest. She raised her chin to Tucker who continued the briefing.

"In the late 80s, Kendrick moved to Senegal, Africa and grew his own guerrilla armies in Liberia and Sierra Leone with McCord's money. He ate up open territories and began funneling black market weapons to anyone with valuables to offer— diamonds, gold, women. The bastard even dealt in child slaves."

Sloan's stomach did a shimmy of the vomit variety. She breathed through slightly parted lips to counter the quake. Ryan slid her a piece of gum. She should love him, marry him, and have his gorgeous babies. He was her counterbalance. Her sanity.

"Like any good gang leader," Tucker said, "Kendrick is jumping in the new guy, sending him to do the dirty work of taking out the African president. He's grooming this man to be his successor, unless we stop him."

Again the picture changed, but this time the bottom dropped out of her stomach.

Chapter Four

The group assessed likely nest locations on intricate digital maps that gave elevations and measured distance-to-target at the touch of a button. The areas surrounding Meridian Hill Park were divided into quadrants, and then the team was split into four teams of two. One team in the park. Everyone else scouring structures.

No surprise, Ryan and Sloan received the sector of buildings with the highest shot origin probability. When it came to mission completion, they got the job done come hell, high water, bullet wounds, or sudden explosions. Heck, even a derailed train and embattled militia hadn't stopped them from achieving their objectives. Today Tucker looked to them for another miracle.

While Sloan cataloged every word swirling around her out of necessity, another part of her brain regurgitated and distilled the bullet of information she'd taken between the eyes. She scrutinized the image of Baine Kendrick that Tucker had placed on the screen. The Devil's son dwarfed the others around him, in both height and breadth. Even the Range Rover he hiked a leg into appeared smaller than she knew them to be. Suntanned skin peeked from a radiant white suit, which made the dark-brown crop of hair and scruff of a new beard look charcoal. Baine Kendrick was a grizzly, and nothing about him looked familiar, not the fierce expression on his face nor the fiery blue of his eyes.

It had been twenty-one years since Sloan had seen him. And every hope, every desperate prayer she'd ever had that the kind hearted boy she'd once known would find a way to escape his father's heinousness, died an abrupt death.

After dismissal, Sloan bolted from the tomb-like confines of the conference room, slipping past Commander Tucker as two other operatives snagged his attention. Steady legs ignored the quiver in her gut and carried her past the elevator and down the corridor to a solid-slab metal door fit for a world bank. One retina scan, passcode, and identification swipe later, the hunk receded into the wall long enough for her to pass. Four weapon-covered walls welcomed Sloan like a fetus to the womb. Breath came easier as the scent of gun oil filled her lungs. It came even easier still after she shed her suit jacket and button down in a fit of movement, leaving her in a white cotton tank. With a flick of the wrist the garments sailed through the air, landing in a heap at a bank of lockers, two sets of which bracketed a table in the center of the room. She stopped at the black-topped island, bracing strong hands on its edge. Legs braced apart and head hung between wiry shoulders, Sloan stared at the floor without seeing it.

Hope crossbred with loathing, despair, excitement, and agony. A mongrel of emotions ripped at her insides, sending tremors coursing through her body.

"What the fuck?"

As a rule Sloan didn't cuss, but desperate times and all.

If she allowed the torment inside her to continue, she'd spend the rest of her days a curled lump on the cold floor. Sloan hadn't allowed her emotions such control since she left Africa. Not since she was a child.

Memories flashed. Her father stood in the schoolhouse doorway, his tall, yet narrow, white American frame struggling to block the rebel soldier's view inside. His fluid Krio words begged the shorter black man who brandished an Uzi to leave in peace. "Only children. They are only children learning to read and write. They cause you no harm. Please."

The man nodded, the tiniest gesture of acquiescence. Sloan kissed her mother's coffee-colored arm in relief, though her grip, along with the ten other children who all clung to her, their teacher, did not lessen. Then outside a scream lit the morning afire. Gun shots followed. Rapid succession bursts sounded through the thin wall they huddled against. The soldier's face shifted, darkened in a way no Hollywood demon could ever rival, and he stepped toward the door. Her mother's cheek, wet with tears, brushed her forehead as she hugged her close and whispered in her ear. "I love you always, my Sia Kolat."

Remembrance burned a hole in her gut. Straightening, she forced the reel into the deepest crevasse of her mind. If she didn't pull it together, she'd die a victim of Devereaux Kendrick, as much as her parents had. He would win. And that she would never allow.

A scarce second after the door *swooshed* open again, a black duffel bag skidded across the table and stopped at her clenched fists. Ryan bumped his fist to her shoulder—their code for "Be strong." "Filler' up."

Half a minute behind him, teams filtered into the armory. The room livened. Lockers, slung wide, clanged like cymbals. Velcro shrieked as bulletproof vests were donned in an attempt to barricade life inside the wearer's chest. Bullshit banter, a coping mechanism for some, peppered the air.

Sloan unzipped the bag and the cool comfort of battle prep and procedure doused her nerves in ever-welcome ice. The rattling deep inside froze. The memories resettled under layers of permafrost, the safest place for them. With no thought, only highly trained muscle memory, she prepared for the battle ahead.

In the bag she carefully situated a pair of MP5 submachine guns, two M4 assault rifles, copious amounts of ammunition, a handful of stun grenades and small radius explosives. In the field it was always better to over prepare. She never again wanted to be stuck behind a couch, with bullets ripping holes in the upholstery beside her head, and think, *Gee, sure wish I'd packed that extra round.*

Dan, the foot tapper, laid his duffel out on the table next to her. When she glanced up, he flashed yellow smoker's teeth from behind a swart complexion. His head bobbed to a silent beat, making his dingy black hair flutter. With wide eyes, he said, "Twenty years or somethin' like that the CIA's been tryin' to nail this Devereaux guy. This is our chance. We take out his son, we get him."

"Capture. Not kill," Sloan said, emphasizing each word. "If he's dead, he can't talk."

"Right," he said, bobbing all the while. "It's just, that's a long time to be after somebody."

She accepted the bag's impressive weight and walked away. The ADHD nightmare had no concept of a long time. Ryan had already changed. Decked from neck to toe in black tactical gear, his towhead shined like a beacon. At her locker, one down from his, Sloan laid the bag down, plucked her discarded clothing from the floor, and thrust it inside the metal box.

"Thanks." Her word hardly carried in the bustling room.

"Ah, you're good," he said. Hiking a thumb, he added, "Better than twitchy over there."

"Not saying much."

His large fingers wrapped around her wrist. When he moved closer a shadow cast over her. The hustle behind was blocked from the gesture. Sloan's gaze locked with Ryan's and his face tightened, a line creasing his brow. "It's saying a lot. Not many know about your past, but I do."

Yep, he knew most of it. She'd spared him, and maybe herself, the truly gruesome details. He knew a lot about her childhood. This being the Base Branch, a few higher-ups knew, but Ryan was the only one she'd ever told. And she'd told him more than was known at the higher levels, which was why she knew what was coming.

His grip tightened.

Sloan schooled her face and regulated her breathing.

"Slo," he said, which was what he called her on the rare occasion he meant business. "Baine Kendrick?"

Though she'd expected it and heard it only minutes ago in the briefing, the name cut like a knife. Instead of doubling over in pain like her body pleaded, she jutted out her chin and quirked an eyebrow in question.

Ryan's blue eyes searched her face. "He's Devereaux's son. He's the assassin. Our target. He's also your friend. Can you complete this mission?

Can you capture him? Can you kill him, if it comes to that?"

Sloan rotated her wrist and gripped Ryan's thick forearm. "*Was.* Was a friend. And to the rest of it...yes."

Chapter Five

Sloan followed Ryan's double-timing boots down the abandoned building's stairwell. Three more flights to ground level. Her heart steamed like a locomotive, chugging inside her chest. They'd run nearly a marathon's worth of stairs and corridors in the last five hours. The only thing they were running now was out of time. Ryan battered the door with one shoulder and they left the neglected structure for a blacktopped alley.

They both squinted at the blinding sunlight. *Damn.* Sloan had watched the shadows grow through the early morning hours. The sun pitched long tar pits across their paths, but as the sun rose the dark spots shrank with each cleared building. Now, only a sliver of shade remained.

Sweat dripped from Ryan's chin, landing with a splat against the jet-black cotton tee that peeked out between the V of his loaded tactical vest. If his shirt was anything like Sloan's, it could be rung into a puddle. Droplets tickled as they snaked down between her breasts. Dewy perspiration matted the hair pulled into a low pony-tail at the base of her neck.

Ryan pulled the map from the cargo pocket of his fatigues and Sloan checked the time.

Into his comm, Ryan said, "Alpha team, reporting A7 clear."

"Oh nine thirty five with three left to search. We're not going to make it." The irritation of knowing they were nearly out of time slipped down the length of Sloan's spine, cooling her like a dip in an ice bath.

Her partner's jaw clenched. "Mother—"

Before he could finish the expletive, Sloan fist-bumped his deltoid and took off toward the next building. He followed suit, big boots thunking along.

"We've been looking from highest probability down, based on clinical numbers." Sloan stopped behind a service road dumpster. When Ryan did the same, she pointed to the three remaining structures. "What do you see?"

"More damned piles of brick."

"Noble," she warned.

"I know. I know," he said, as he raked a hand through his wet hair. A spray of sweat fanned the air. "It's all air and opportunity for this fuck to take the shot." He expanded his chest in a deep breath and let it out in a rush. "There are people coming and going at all three buildings. The first two, A8 and 9 on our grid, are twins. Same height and width. Window sizes are comparable in all three. Twins are the same height as the last building, A10."

Sloan saw it an instant before Ryan breathed, "Domed roofs. The twins are domed."

They took off together in a dead sprint. Ever the good boy, Ryan radioed, "Alpha team, requesting permission to break protocol. A8 and A9 are twin buildings measuring taller than A10, but have domed roofs. A10 has higher elevation making it the most likely shot origin of the three remaining."

Tucker's voice answered, "Are you two in agreement?"

When they rounded the corner and saw that the tree in front of the building had been recently cut for the construction of street lights and a bus stop, they both barked, "Yes, sir!"

"Permission granted. Proceed with caution."

Ryan replied, "Yes, sir."

They stuck close to the brick, trying to stay out of sight. Neither wanted the type of greeting forewarning brought. They kept the MP5's slung across their chest tucked under their wall-side arms and their badges dangling in plain view, to keep pedestrians from panicking. Maybe, because it was D.C. and it was only the two of them, they'd only garnered mild curiosity all morning. And even that had been from small, wide-eyed children.

No sooner had the thoughts run through her mind, than an old lady, complete with leashed grey poodle and poodle-poofed hair, shrieked as they entered the lobby of A10. She scooped the dog into her arms. Her floral print muumuu billowed around stark white calves and knee-highs crinkling at her ankles. Four other people in the lobby stilled, as though suddenly rooted in place. A mother clutched her young son to her chest, shielding him with a half turned back. Two large black men in business suits surveyed them, expressions wary.

Sure, the women's reactions were understandable given the way she and Ryan looked, bodies armored and armed for battle. The men's wary expressions would have been justifiable, if it were not for two things that calmed Sloan's strumming heart instantly.

One, this was a low rent building in a high rent district. The men wore designer shoes worth more than she made in two weeks, and she didn't make chump change. Two, Sloan knew how to read expressions. In her line of work expressions told more than words ever did. Translating them correctly often meant the difference between success and failure. Life or death. Their wariness didn't contain an ounce of fear, as it rightly should, given their situation.

The dog barked, and the men flinched, ever so lightly moving meaty hands toward guns concealed beneath pricey suits. Now that she looked, the impression of their machine guns was clear.

Ryan spoke, "Everybody, stay..."

He paused as Sloan flung thin blades through the air. They flashed in the fluorescent light then stabbed into the mens' bellies. Before the first dropped to the linoleum tile, Sloan closed the gap, pistol drawn. She relieved them of several weapons and their communication devices. Since neither would likely die from the wounds, she restrained the moaning man with zip ties.

After removing the women and child, Ryan restrained the unconscious one. When it was done, he spoke into his coms. "Confirming A10 as the location of shot origin. Just took out two of Kendrick's hostiles in the lobby. Requesting back up."

Tucker replied, "Affirmative, Alpha Team. Were shots fired?"

"Negative."

"Proceed. Dispatching all teams to your location. If possible, report as you advance."

"Affirmative, sir."

Sloan broke in. "Sir," Ryan's gaze shot to hers in question, but she continued, "requesting permission to split and search."

Ryan growled, "No."

She shook her head and whispered, "No time."

The commander replied, "Affirmative."

The golden boy cursed. She ignored him, turning her vicious expression on the man at her feet. "Where is he?"

The man whimpered and tried to hide his face in the floor. Sloan wrapped her slender fingers around the cool metal handle protruding from his gut. He jerked back against the wall. "No. Please." His Xhosa accent rounded the words. He looked to Ryan, eyes pleading. "No."

She pulled the knife from his flesh, and stifled his scream with her hand. The blade showed crimson in front of his sweat-slicked face. She held it there, letting him study it for a moment, his eyes as big as matching moons. "Where is he?"

Expelling a ragged breath, he said, "Roof."

Sloan pulled the knife from the other man's belly, wiped them both on her pants, and put them back in the sheaths as she moved toward the corridor. She handed Ryan one of the still-quiet coms she'd taken off the men and lightly punched his shoulder.

"You too," he said, before turning and heading up the east stairwell.

She sprinted up the west.

A few flights up, she spoke into the coms. "At least we know he's not on the roof."

"Yeah," Ryan said. "So where the hell is he?"

"Twelve or eleven. He needs the elevation to make the shot."

He used his authoritative voice, deep and oh-so-manly. "I've got twelve. You take eleven. Affirmative?"

"Negative. Whoever gets there first takes the top floor."

Ryan clipped out an agreement. Certainly, like her, he'd already ramped up his effort to reach twelve first. Neither wanted eleven, when it was possible, but highly unlikely, the shot would be taken from the lower level. It would make a tricky shot, near impossible, except for those highly-trained few who graduated from the likes of SOTIC.

Could Baine be that good?

Much remained a mystery about the man being groomed to take over a war profiteer's army. On the surface, he appeared to be an average guy. A lawyer with dual citizenship and a healthy bank account living in London and the States equal parts of the year. Nice, but nothing too catching to a layman's eye. But put on diving gear and plunge below the surface with a Base Branch expert and his records fuzzed around the teenage years and all but disappeared after the death of his mother. Untraceable travel. Little movement of personal funds. No love life to gossip about.

His cover was good and many layers deep. So deep, even The Base's analysts hadn't whittled it into a discernible creature.

Sloan had an advantage though. She knew Baine. Not what had become of him, but she knew the core of his being. She'd thought she'd known him enough to bet her life on the fact that he'd never become the soulless mirror of his father. As it turned out, she'd been wrong. So very wrong. Strategic bombings, assassinations, and choking other weapon runner's supply routes had been attributed to his hand. Those Sloan couldn't get worked up over. Bad guy deaths didn't count in her book. But killing peaceable leaders to maintain regional unrest and bump demand, she couldn't abide. This wasn't his first presidential assassination. There'd been rumor of two others.

He'd even headed a town raid—something she could never forgive.

Fate was an evil witch, turning her soul's savior into her target and sole link to destroying Devereaux Kendrick. She'd laugh at the irony, if she had time. Instead, she thought about the traits of the boy she'd known so long ago. Three words sprang to mind. Remarkable. Determined. Unpredictable. Those words slowed her jogging knees enough that when Ryan whispered over the coms, "At eleven now. I'm taking twelve," a thrill quieted all the ramblings in her brain.

"I'm on eleven. Moving in," she answered, knowing Baine was somewhere beyond the heavy white door with the crackled black numbers one-one.

Ryan answered, "On twelve. Moving in."

Her hand gripped the cool hard handle and the enemy's channel crackled to life. In a strained whisper, Sloan barked, "Hold."

"Holding."

A crinkle in the static ushered a deep baritone, "Check."

The element of surprise took a swan dive off the roof and landed with a splat on the sidewalk outside. *Damn.* She'd hoped the enemy line would stay quiet. Then she'd hoped the voice would give something away. A nest position would be nice. *Not that lucky. Ever.* Without knowing the correct response code, answering was as good as picking up the radio and saying, "*Hold still. I'm about to look up your skirt.*"

Her partner knew it too. He spoke into her ear. "Radio silent. Move."

"Affirmative." Sloan moved silently through the doorway. MP5 in hand, she took in the vacant hallway through its crosshairs. The fluorescent lighting above and rows of apartment doors nearly flush with the corridor's walls made her an easy target. So, she moved quickly, looking for signs of the man and, as he had an entourage, the men she hunted. Her ears pricked to every noise. Some she dismissed. Kids playing. A couple screwing. The pre-game show blaring. Silence behind a door two-thirds of the way down screamed for her attention like a naked ninety-year-old running to catch the Metrorail.

So much could be found in the silence.

She visually inspected the door. Nothing stood out. No marks for forced entry. No blood from an unfortunate tenant who happened to have the best view. And by her judgment, this apartment provided the easiest shot. The quiet was absolute. The dishwasher didn't hum, nor did any other appliance. With a mental fist to her shoulder and a settling breath, Sloan eased a steady hand to the knob. The door moved ever so slightly.

The thing wasn't latched. Having already tipped her hand for anyone watching, she flung it wide and inched back to the cover of the wall. *One. Two.* When the sounds of cocking weapons and firing bullets didn't fill the air, surprise pinched her brow. *Three.* She darted into the room ready to crouch behind the nearest piece of furniture, but the empty room made it both unnecessary and impossible. One cloth covered-table sat at the center. To the left an open closet door revealed the fall line of a homeless person. Nada. To the right a partitioned wall and scrunched curtain displayed a meager bathroom and shower that hid no goons. Two well-worn pans hung from silver hooks above an old stove that jetted out from the wall.

Warning tingled down her spine. Still, everything remained fixed as she cleared the room a second time. She eyed the apartment's door curiously. No one stormed through it. Then her gaze swung to the table. Its polished wooden legs peeked out from under a canvas painting cloth. Stepping toward it, Sloan gripped the edge and pulled. A suppressor and hand-painted forest-camo barrel of a sniper rifle peeked from beneath the fabric. Quickly she moved toward the window. A groove had been cut around the frame. Paint chips lay scattered on the floor and sill. Through the glass in the great distance a large white structure stood out from the green park grass.

The stage.

A glance at her watch revealed the time. Zero nine fifty five. She swallowed back the nerves that threatened bile into her throat. "Where are you?" Her words were no more than breath between parted lips. Sloan walked the few steps back to the table, yanked the sheet from it, and the gun stared back at her. As she moved to the shooter's spot, Sloan ran a hand down the scope. Bending at her middle, the podium came into sharp focus, as did the sweat-sprinkled head of Yannick Bakou. In the same instant the air in the room shifted.

Sloan whirled in time to see a wide chest barreling toward her. Her submachine gun came up an instant too late to be of use. She'd been hit by a truck once before, but its blow had been more glancing than this. Air fled her lungs as her core bore the brunt of this attack. Her bones went from solid to rubber. Her head snapped forward on impact and then cracked back onto the floor. Carpet be damned. Whatever was underneath was hard as rock.

She could only blink as more men rushed from the apartment across the hall. Three, plus the lug on top of her. Through the pain, she tried to kick free, but her legs and right arm were pinned. The midnight-black skin of a forearm levered from her chest to the lee of her chin, limiting her intake of air. Bad position. Bad timing. Bad all the way around.

Rather than fight, Sloan relaxed.

"That's right, bitch," the big man said with a thick African accent. "Submit."

Yeah, right.

Relaxed, her middle finger stretched enough to reach the blade in her sheath. Swiftly, she slid the blade out, fisted it, and rammed the metal between the man's ribs. His bellow vibrated her eardrum, but before she could push him off the muzzle of a pistol pressed into her temple.

His voice was deep. The one from the radio. The one from her memories, but different. So different. "Don't move."

She couldn't see Baine. The pressure of the gun held her head in place. Trapped between a thug and a bullet, she couldn't fight. She couldn't avenge her parents. Couldn't stop the bad guys. This was not the way things were supposed to end, but it didn't look like there was much hope for that now. Rage and loss filled her as it had in the days after the schoolhouse attacks, as it had before Baine had shown her hope in the life she had.

The man atop her wheezed as blood filled his lungs. "Shoot her," he gargled.

The barrel lifted from her skin and everything went dark.

Chapter Six

Blood and brain matter dripped down the walls. Pooled on the polyester carpet. "Son of a bitch," came a familiar voice. It pitched higher than she ever recalled it doing and took on a panicked quality. The room blurred in a swirl of whites and reds then went dark. The room quaked. A sharp pain reflexively tightened her jaw and brought forth a drunken, unwelcome consciousness.

Dead eyes stared back as Sloan opened her eyes again. A warm breeze stifled the air, but she breathed easier than before the earthquake. But then it happened again. The room shook, jarring her tender body. She wanted to curl into a ball. She wanted to sleep for a week. Fatigue weighted each limb. Even her fingers refused to move. Reality pricked the thick veil of fog as again the room convulsed, only it wasn't the room moving. Something moved her. Hands. Two hands explored her sternum. They trailed over her chest then up her neck.

The need to move, to defend herself, was so strong the haze lifted in an instant. Pain or not, Sloan turned her head to find her assailant. Instead she met the tightly drawn face of Ryan Noble.

"Slo?" The question in his tone told her she was in a world of trouble. *Oh God.* Everything came back in a whir. *Oh God.* Were her brains scattered across the floor like all the others? How could she see Ryan? Hear him? Feel the warmth of his touch? Was she paralyzed?

Panic had her scrambling. Dizziness hit the moment her head moved. Still she continued feebly, making little headway.

Ryan's hand shot out. "Whoa, take it easy."

She clamped onto his arm and clawed her way up off the blood soaked floor, and practically onto his back.

"Jesus," he said. "You must be okay, because you're stubborn as ever. Here, let me help." His other arm cradled her back and he pulled her to her knees.

Sloan slumped over him. Her face rested on the back of his neck. One arm looped over his shoulder and under his opposite pit. Her other arm draped his back and both her hands clutched his vest. One ragged sob escaped her lips before the question that wrought it from her did as well. "Are my brains on the floor?"

He hugged her tight. "No."

But his clipped tone told her there was more to the story. "Tell me," she demanded.

"You're covered in blood and it's fucking everywhere. I swear to God, I thought you were dead. I just... I...need to check you out. I need to make sure you're okay."

"Okay."

"You're gonna have to let me go, so I can do it."

"Okay," she said, but didn't move. Just clutched her only lifeline.

Ryan loosened his hold around her waist. "Let me take a look."

Reluctantly Sloan slid back to the floor. Sitting this time, she took in the aftermath of the room for the first real time. Four bodies littered the perimeter. All four were head shot. Their limbs lay in contorted positions about their middles. The guy who lay next to them was the one who tackled her. The one she killed.

The table sat empty to her right, gun missing. Baine was missing too. Several things didn't follow logic.

Surprise. Surprise.

All business, Ryan asked, "Where do you hurt?"

She winced when Ryan prodded her skull, but ignored his question for one of her own. "Did you...do this?"

"The men? No. I heard the sniper shot. Four pistol shots followed in rapid succession. When I got here—"

"Is Bakou dead?"

"Yes. Died after they put him in the ambulance on the way to the hospital. Which is where you're going. You've at least got a concussion, if not a fractured skull."

"It's not fractured," she dismissed, swatting his hand away. "Where's Baine? I know he was here. He held the pistol to my head. I thought..."

Ryan's fist bumped her shoulder. The featherlight gesture didn't jar. "You're okay. Thank holy hell." His jaw worked before he answered her question. "The gun and Kendrick were both gone when I arrived. The other units went after him, but turned up nothing. Fucker vanished."

"Why'd he kill his men?"

"He knew we were on him. Maybe he didn't want anyone getting caught and talking. Maybe they weren't his men."

"Meaning what?"

"Say he's tired of being the errand boy. Eliminating those loyal to Devereaux, especially when he has an excuse, could make a move against his father that much easier."

They were both quiet for a few seconds. Sirens wailed from far off, heading their way. His open palm grabbed her shoulder. "I'm sorry I wasn't here." Sloan shook her head. The action stabbed pain into her skull like tiny shards of glass being forced into the meat of her brain. "I'm sorry he got his shot, but mostly I'm sorry he got away and we lost the only link to Devereaux."

Sloan placed her palm on his shoulder. "I may have screwed the mission, but he didn't get away."

One of Ryan's brows arched in question.

She wiped a blood-covered hand down her pants then pulled a GPS locator from her pocket and offered it to him.

His brow rose higher—if that were possible, since his brow already practically grazed his hairline. "No way."

"I put a tracker on his gun before everything went upside-down. I knew something was off when I found the riffle and the room vacant."

"Nice work. He'll lead us straight to Devereaux, but we can't move on him until we have his black book in hand. We needed Baine to locate the book and get the codes."

"As luck would have it, I took out an insurance policy a few hours ago. It covers situations just like this. I know exactly how to get to Devereaux and his precious black book. And I know exactly how I'm going to kill him."

Chapter Seven

Baine cruised along the thin strip of asphalt with an arm draped over the wheel. The other propped on the window sill. He wiggled his fingers, flirting with the currents of sunbaked air sailing by. Only a handful of clouds dotted the sky alight with blinding rays and the clearest blue of his mother's eyes. The horizon called to him with its dusky mixture of waist high grasses and squatty trees hosting limbs that stretched wider than they were tall.

Zebra speckled the view like sheep did back home. More than once in his time in Africa he'd been stopped by a moving herd of the striped animals, wildebeests, and even elephants. The real treasure was catching a glimpse of a big cat. Something about their predatory and virile nature shot a thrill through his veins, just like it had when he was a kid. He grimaced. No lions or leopards today. But he was about to deal with something far more dangerous and far less beautiful.

The Land Rover dipped with the pitted dirt then evened as Baine steered the sleek black utility vehicle off the rutted road onto a smooth stone drive. Uniformly cropped grass hugged the edge of the private entrance and precisely circled the rows of lush Leadwoods that shaded the path from the harsh South African sun. Past the drive a manicured garden bloomed, lending a vibrant prism of colors to the near-blinding green of the lawn. Florets clustered around birds of paradise that strutted leaves of blue and orange along his way. Red flowers sprayed high from the ground like a fountain of spurting blood. A curving line of buds exploded along the border of the estate's perimeter wall. Thick, flowing vines distracted from the bastille impression the protective barrier might otherwise give. Perennials wound their way from the drive to the opulent estate, warmly welcoming guests.

Two guards packing fully automatic machine guns negated any warmth in appearance the parcel held. Not that he'd been fooled by appearances in a long time. Both ebony-faced men lowered their weapons that had been fully prepared to turn the fine machine he drove into nothing more than a sieve. One, Rute, Baine thought his name was, came to the driver's door.

"Apologies, sir. We did not know it was you," the man said, repeatedly raising his hands in peace.

Easing a forearm onto the black metal of the door, Baine's skin sizzled. He ignored it. He'd felt plenty worse over the years. The man took a noticeable step back as Baine tilted his head through the open window. Sweat slicked Rute's face. With a flick of his index finger, Baine gestured toward the other guard still blocking the thick metal gate behind the guard. "Mind telling him to move?"

Rute nodded, and flapped an eager hand at his comrade. "Yes, sir. Apologies again. Just when you left, you drove a different car." He paused for a moment, studying the vehicle. "Master Kendrick's men will be following shortly, sir?"

Baine leveled his gaze on the man's deep brown eyes. "No," he said simply, before straightening behind the wheel. Within a few heartbeats the gate opened and he continued up the pristine path to his father's estate.

Four whitewashed gables rose high into the clear blue sky. Their ornate curves hooked and dove in the air, punctuating the two-story Cape Dutch roofline. From the grand white wall the front entrance's rich bois de rose wood gleamed more robustly than mahogany. Baine maneuvered the car through the circular drive, past the four-car garage connected to the front of the house, and parked the SUV by the rear courtyard.

He'd delayed laying eyes on Devereaux or his lackey Kobi for forty-eight hours. The flight from a private D.C. runway to Kruger's Mpumalanga International Airport had proved an insufficient amount of time to deal with the shit bouncing around his skull. With only a two-hour drive to conclude his journey from Nelpruit to the isolated game lodge his father currently called home, nestled between Ulusaba Game Park and Blyde River Canyon, Baine went off grid. He snagged the cheapest hotel he could find in Hazyview, and enjoyed hot stale beer in the deepest hole-of-a bar he could find. He hadn't worked much out in his head, but it had been nice not being Baine Kendrick for a while.

Still, his nerves weren't ready to confront the men. Not without pulling his Reeder twins and blowing them straight to hell. The 1911 custom 10mms hung ready for action in the shoulder holster over his grey tee. A gift from a stateside friend, they hadn't let him down yet. But no matter how much his trigger fingers itched, he'd have to wait. Plans only worked when followed. And this plan had been years in the making. Baine refused to give the impulse life. His plan had far better aftermath.

He retrieved his bag and rifle case from the back and made his way past the scrawling gate toward the pool. With only one hour until drinks, then dinner and the confrontation sure to erupt when his father discovered half his men were dead, he opted for the back entrance to avoid inquiry. Not to mention the revulsion the sight of the man wrought inside him.

The intake of breath followed by a groaned sigh told him his fortune continued to run the hard line. Luckily, if there was anything lucky about catching his father with one of the maids, he'd already come and they were on the opposite side of the water from where Baine walked.

"Son," the man's voice was practically jovial. *And why shouldn't he be? He'd just gotten head.* Baine stopped, but didn't turn. He caught quite enough in his periphery, as Devereaux discarded the woman with a flick of his wrist. She scurried into the servants' entrance, one hand covering her mouth, the other shoving her breast back inside her shirt. His grip tightened on the straps of luggage he carried.

"I heard poor President Bakou died from injuries sustained in an assassination on American soil," he said with a hint of his Texas drawl.

Baine enjoyed his own British accent all the more because it differed from his father's. One more thing to thank his mum for. "I heard the news also."

A silk robe billowed as the man walked around the pool toward Baine. Thankfully, he'd knotted the front closed by the time they faced one another. His father was a big man. Thick and ruthless. With black hair and eyes and a soul to match. Baine looked down on him. Literally and figuratively.

The older Kendrick's too-white teeth flashed behind red lips. "Well now. I'd say that's cause for celebration." He turned his palms up, as if in offering. "We have a fresh batch of beauties due within the hour. A gift from Madam Walters for our successful contract. Now, go get a shower, and make yourself presentable. You look like a dust-covered mountain gorilla."

"You smell like one too," he added with a wave at his crinkled nose.

Certainly he did, since he'd driven through the bush in the heat of the day with all the windows down. Any excuse to shove off was ace. Baine stepped into the rear foyer and shut Devereaux out with a nudge of the door. A series of sobs echoed across the high ceiling, presumably belonging to the woman who'd retreated from the courtyard. He turned away from the noise, walked up the grand staircase, and to his room.

When most people entered their own personal space—a home, a bedroom, a thatched hut on the hard dirt—visage gave way to their true nature. For some, the distance between the two was no more than a face of make-up or a forgotten hand over the mouth when belching. For others, the space between was more like dead bodies in a corner. Baine's demeanor held firm as he stepped inside his suite, for his were not the only pair of eyes in the room. Three pairs, in fact, captured every move he made. One caught the bed. Another his desk. One more the balcony doors. The one in the bathroom he'd repeatedly accidentally splashed water on. *Oops.* There were ears too. Of course all of them were electronic and chapped his arse. But they were part of the game he fancied as much as his adversary.

Baine turned on a bedside lamp. Three ten-foot-high beige walls appeared from the darkness, supporting a thick pattern of woven, dark wood beams overhead. The fourth wall, just as tall, painted the most vivid shade of red possible, abutted the headboard to a mammoth bed, where he deposited his clothes bag. Rifle case in his grasp, Baine walked to the balcony doors opposite the bed and flung back heavy curtains. Brilliant light filled the room, giving it a tinge of warmth.

Beyond the glass over the hideous fence, the grass grew tall and wooly. It deviated in color from green to brown and shifted with the wind. Above it, a few scarce trees breached the horizon. Most barren arms of wood reached out for the sky. In the distance a herd of elephants ambled, no more than a series of wide dots. The sun leaned toward the limit of the magnificent view. The only real view from the compound. Africa in its unruly state.

He could watch it for hours, and had many times before. Sometimes the only thing that let him maintain his grasp on sanity was the view. And his view of the big picture. Reluctantly, he moved away. He ignored the desk at the far end of the room and marched for the bathroom. After a quick sweep with his homemade detector Baine felt certain no more bugs had been added while he'd been away. He stowed the gun in the massive safe hidden in the closet wall.

A shower being next on the list, Baine crossed from the closet to the vanity. His father wasn't right about much, but the gorilla comment had been rather accurate. A thin layer of dust coated his face and arms. Dark stubble shadowed his chin further. The *sod-off* glare he presented added to the effect. Before he began the long process of disrobing, he twisted on the faucet. Warm water rushed out and he washed the grime off his hands. In the basin, brown marred the pristine white. Surprisingly, it wasn't red. It should have been. There was so much blood on his hands.

While he undressed and arranged his weapons within easy reach of the shower door, Baine thought about the cock-up in Washington, D.C. And wondered, not for the first time, how in the bloody fuck they'd found out about the hit. His fists clenched, bunching the grey shirt in his hand. The obvious loose wire in the circuit of information for Kendrick business was the one with loose legs, of course. But before leaving the capital, he'd paid her a visit.

"Surprise," he'd said when Madame Walters stepped from her shower. She hadn't started like most women, or men for that matter, would when attacked from the rear while wearing only water droplets. Considering what she did for a living, the woman was probably used to it. Probably one of those who liked to get banged that way. Rough and tumble. Even in a chokehold, slammed against the cold white marble by a man twice her size, she didn't so much as whimper. Though, she stiffened like a day-old corpse when he positioned the point of his ka-bar against the flesh of her belly.

"Who did you tell about the arrangement? Know, if I don't believe your answer, you won't live to hear your scream." His words were only a whisper, but he watched her reflection turn ghostly white.

Since reaching adulthood Baine hadn't met anyone who could successfully lie to him. Tracy Walters' wide-but-steady eyes and forthright expression had convinced him, she hadn't told a soul.

Kobi Ross looked to be the next most likely suspect. Sure in his place as Devereaux's underling, he'd place a high-stakes bet by tipping off the authorities in an operation the senior Kendrick had a piss load of money riding on. But the pay off—Baine in jail, or better yet, dead, and him the only option to take over the business— could have been a risk worth taking.

The bugs were Kobi's doing. A pitiful attempt to get the goods on Baine, and prove himself more valuable to his boss than the man's own son. Baine would dig quietly to verify, but it seemed likely. Every beady-eyed stare the slick-haired twitch-nose gave him was a *piss off and die*, if he'd ever seen one.

When the hot water hit his skin all thought turned to her. Gooseflesh raised every hair on his body. His dick raised too. Damn the thing. Never in his life had he faltered from a kill decision. He made a judgment and it stood. The four men he'd ended with no more than a twitch of his index finger. They were loose ends that needed tying.

He lathered the rag to a sheen of frothy bubbles and started with his face. His lats were tight from shimmying down the side of the apartment building in his scramble to get away. Had his rifle case not had a shoulder strap, he would have had to leave it, and that would have been worse than parting with any woman. No sooner had the thought run through his mind, than he knew it was no longer true.

The water beat his back as he scrubbed the cloth over his abdomen. Her face flickered in his mind. Irises like amber jewels, encircled by pure white. Cheeks made for smiling after a good toss in the sack. Thick supple lips, the red of garden buds, for sucking him hard and swallowing him deep.

A feral growl rumbled in the glassed space as the suds slicked his raging erection. Blast that mouth of hers, and her for being there at all. For now she was inside his head, making him lose the death-grip he'd always had on his control.

His hips rocked into his hand and there was nothing he could do to stop the intense pleasure, since he could only experience her in this safe way, in this fantasy. She was alive. He could have killed her. Loose ends and all, but there would have been no way he could have had her like this, if she were dead. He leaned over, bracing his left hand on the wall. He lowered to his forearm as the pressure inside pulled him down. The force of his release tensed every muscle in his body. A roar of frustration and visceral satisfaction threatened to break free from deep within, but he clenched his teeth against it.

More wrung out than when he entered, Baine exited the shower to dress for dinner, the dressing-down, and parade of whores awaiting him—all of which held zero interest for him.

Chapter Eight

They were ushered into a living room like cattle about to become slabs of beef. The muscular butler, who looked more like an assassin than a purveyor of tea and crumpets, said in a luxuriant British accent, "Master Devereaux and the other gentlemen will join you shortly. Please, be at ease in the parlor."

Two of the three high-class escorts eyed the handsome man in black and white as though he were the first course in a bevy of cock they planned to devour that evening. He winked a green eye at them, which was playful and quite out of character from the stern, all-business man Sloan had covertly studied since he'd picked them up at the airport in Nelspruit. Up until now he'd played the perfect manservant. Instinct told her it was an act. Several times she'd caught him stiffening the ease and efficiency naturally allied with his movements. Maybe he was one of those bodyguard servants, but the cool calculation in his behavior whispered trouble. She'd have to keep an eye on him.

As if sensing her attention, Lawrence slanted his gaze in her direction, but didn't turn. Interesting. He bowed at the waist. "If that will be all, ladies, I'll have your bags brought up to your rooms. You've been shown your rooms, but Master Devereaux asks that you not wander about unescorted, unless you would like to make use of the pool and patio."

Yep, she'd caught the emphasis the first time. *In the parlor.* Then he left the four of them in the decadent room. They stood in a row before a towering fireplace and three sofas that cost more than her car. What looked to be an original Monet, the face of a young man blotted in acrylic, hung on a wall book-ended by floor-to-ceiling French doors which led out to a lovely side garden.

The same two who'd blatantly lusted over the butler spun around, drinking in the opulence of the space. More like gulped, since their mouths hung open. The third escort, Lana, stepped forward to address them all. Sloan made four in this party of pussy.

In a surprisingly stern voice, given the slightness of her build, Lana said, "Ladies! You are not sidewalk hookers. We are dignified. Educated. Worldly. High-class companions. You would do well to remember that. Master Devereaux deserves the very best we have to offer. So, class it up or you'll be dismissed. For God's sake, he was the help. Gorgeous, but not our concern."

Their eyes narrowed, but their shoulders straightened and their hands folded neatly in front of them. "Now then," Lana continued with a quarter turn toward Sloan. "I've worked with Cynthia before," she said, gesturing to the blond. "And Nena worked with Madame Walters, personally. But I don't know anything about you, other than Madame highly recommended you.

"You're striking enough," she said, her thin brow severely arched. "But I like to know who I'm dealing with, especially in a crucial job like this. Tell me, Sloan, who have you worked for?"

She hadn't done this kind of work, ever. Sloan hadn't even done this kind of play in years and years. Even then it had been more of an experiment. The kind of work she did do, however, would make the regal woman with the low-slung bun and stunning blue dress faint.

"I can't divulge that kind of information."

"Good girl," Lana said, but her words were drowned out by the sudden roar in Sloan's ear.

The doors opened and in walked The Devil.

For a thousandth of a second everything froze and she was five again. Small. Powerless. Terrified of the man looming before her. His dark eyes condemned and large frame threatened.

Her heart thundered inside her chest, sending shocks of lightning scorching through her limbs. The entourage that followed blurred in a sea of unadulterated rage that erupted so ferociously it overrode every life-preserving tendency she'd honed over the last twenty-six years of her existence. Every bit of glacial ice liquefied in her chest as it burst with molten fury.

No options presented themselves. Only one action could douse the boiling hatred steaming the blood in her veins. Sloan scanned the buffet against the wall nearest her for a weapon. Not that her hands wouldn't do the job just fine, but to get to Devereaux she'd have to go through two linebacker types. She'd have to move fast, but she could slit their throats before the men knew what was happening. There was no way she'd make it out alive. There were two guys behind her life's target. Plus a handful of armed guards throughout the grounds. And Baine was here somewhere.

She was ready for death. His. Hers. Sloan sidestepped toward the antique wood. With a discrete slide of her hand, the cool metal of the butter knife nestled into her palm. She inhaled one last time.

A voice in her ear stopped her dead.

"Here, miss. Let me get that for you." Lawrence's warm fingers encircled her wrist and squeezed. The move shocked her back to sanity. The red faded from her eyes, and her muscles uncoiled. She'd nearly thrown away years of work and potentially hundreds of thousands of lives over her hatred for this one man. "Would you like jam or butter on your biscuit?" he asked, taking the knife from her loosened grip.

What?

"Jam. Thank you," she replied in a hoarse whisper. Her pulse continued to thunder, but the winds of common sense moved the black clouds a safe distance away.

"My pleasure. I wouldn't want you to hurt yourself."

Sloan slanted a look at him, but he ignored her, going about his duties. Slathering jelly. Pouring tea. Adding milk and sugar. When he turned, his expression was butler-blank. Did he know what she'd intended to do, or did he just think she was incapable?

His neatly coiffed hair, clean-shaven jaw, sharp suit, and manner said innocuous, but the breadth of his shoulders, power in his grip, perception in action, and depth of his eyes screamed trouble.

"Here you are, miss," he said, ushering her toward the gold settee. Once seated, he placed the food on the small table near her knee, stood, and addressed the room. "Could I offer anyone else tea or a biscuit?"

Before long, Devereaux and Lana snuggled on the divan across from her, ignoring the appetizers the butler laid out. Behind her Cynthia batted lashes with a bodyguard while another smoothed his hand down her back. She arched into him, and smiled over her shoulder.

Sloan sensed eyes on her before she saw him. Kobi Ross, Devereaux's second in command for the better part of a decade, advanced on her like predator to prey. If he only knew how reversed their roles were.

Now that she'd reined her emotions and focused on the importance of the job, Sloan morphed from killer to Mr. Ross's entertainment for the night. She smiled coyly as he approached, looking at him through a fan of lashes. The only thing harder than acting pleased by his attention had been pulling back from the brink earlier. And she had a feeling in the knotted pit of her stomach that things would only get more difficult over the next few days.

Kobi took her hand in his clammy grasp. "Good Lord, you fell from the heavens."

Yep, right into hell.

He raised her hand, his head lowered, and cold lips smeared a kiss on her skin. This close, the aroma of hairspray and gel stung her nostrils. She giggled when she wanted to gag.

"You smell divine. Like chocolate and a dream."

Sloan didn't laugh much, but the absurdity of his comment had her biting back a deep chuckle. What a sleaze. Men didn't talk like this. Not any men she'd ever been around. And she smelled like soap. Really nice soap, but soap none the less. Why chocolate? Because of the color of her skin, probably. Her earlier inner tantrum had flushed her creamy, light-brown skin to a deeper tone.

"You should taste me," she purred.

Kobi Ross puddled into her hand. A stupid look of lust washed over his sharp features. The lines around his mouth lengthened as it fell open and his tongue lolled out like a dog. His pupils dilated and his brows shot up. As much as she hated it, this man was the most logical place to start looking for information about the black book. Well, Baine was, but she didn't want to wander into that mine field. Not ever, if she could help it. Not that she'd seen him since, well, they were kids. She'd only felt the barrel of his gun in D.C.—and the butt, apparently.

After hours of research and lobbying with Commander Tucker and Ryan for her plan, they'd come no closer to answering the burning questions about why he'd killed his father's men, and why he hadn't killed her. If it had been him at all.

Maybe Baine was a *good* bad guy who didn't kill women or children, if he could help it. Not outright anyway. The work he did with his father killed them, regardless. So, he was a bad *bad* guy. Period.

The big hand that had been on her arm crept over her shoulder and along the nape of her neck. Gently, Kobi shifted her long hair to the opposite side. Without visibly tensing or losing the pleasant twist of her cheek, Sloan steeled herself for the touch to come. The cushion dipped as he eased closer.

"I'd love to taste you, but just a nibble now. You're my dessert."

Warm, moist breath tickled the sensitive skin below her ear. The door behind them opened and closed, and then Devereaux's booming voice stalled Kobi's advance. "Ha! My son's finally arrived. Let's eat."

The man too near her huffed

A large shadow cast over them, and a voice filled the air. "I can't believe you're not happy to see me."

Sloan dared not move. But she couldn't stop the hairs on the back of her neck from prickling. If he'd spoken to her, the death reprieve he'd given a few short days ago would be shorter than she'd hoped.

"You've interrupted an important tasting," Kobi answered.

"She'll wait," Baine said in his husky voice. "I'm starved."

Lawrence nodded to Devereaux and opened a door. "This way, please."

The group transitioned into the dining room. Somehow she got sandwiched between Kobi and Baine, who she'd yet to look at directly. Head down, she walked, or rather was corralled, toward a center seat at a long dining table. It could easily sit three times as many guests than were present and was decorated with creamy linens and vases of splashy green flowers. To her right Baine sat, his gaze also straight ahead. To her left Kobi crowded. Across from her, Devereaux took a seat and coaxed his escort onto his lap. She was spared his gaze as his mouth lingered on the woman's porcelain flesh. All around, tension rippled through the air like a heat wave in the Sahara.

Coming in late, the other two escorts and bodyguards made their way to the table arm-in-arm. Devereaux spoke up, "I'm sure, after his days away, my son would enjoy some company."

Both women's gazes shot up, searching the room. When they found him, both smiled easily. Only Nena, the bobbed-cut redhead, was able to wiggle out of the men's grasp. Triumphantly, she sashayed around the table. In a throaty voice she said, "I apologize. I didn't know your son was joining us. It would be my pleasure to give him some..." she lingered for a moment, before adding, "...company."

He stood, pulled out Nena's chair, and the woman exaggerated her movements, poking her round ass at him before sitting. Sloan hadn't liked the other woman before. Now she grouped her in with the bodyguards and butler as expendable. With the ring of a bell, tray upon tray of food arrived on servant's hands. They distributed plates piled with slabs of meat, bowls of stew, and an array of sauces and jellies that imitated the colors of the rainbow. Without fanfare the men began filling their plates.

Beside her Baine's suit-covered arm didn't move. His hand, nearly as large as the dinner plate, rested on the tablecloth only a foot from her. It looked nothing like the small grit-and-grime covered hand of the kid that used to play with her behind the woodshed of his father's old estate. His fingernails were cropped short and free from dirt. Two prominent veins curved from wrist to knuckles just under the tanned skin, which boasted a light sprinkling of dark hair. Looking at this man's hand, her insides quivered once. It was no more than a phone would vibrate when receiving a text, and she had no idea how to interpret the message her body sent. She knew enough to be completely befuddled by it though. Concern knit her brow until Kobi's hand on the fabric of her mid-thigh stole her attention. Mindlessly, he strummed his fingers over the ruched material of her cocktail dress as he ate with his other.

Sloan tuned out the infuriating sound, and struggled to tune out the little shakes of awareness Baine's nearness stirred. She pushed the food around her plate like any good waif would, and tried to keep the sneer off her face when glancing at the horrid man across the table. All of a sudden, Devereaux lifted his head from Lana's neck and turned his gaze to Baine.

"Where the fuck are Ty and my team? They should be here to celebrate. And why the hell didn't Walters send more of these lovely creatures? I'm sure these ladies are talented beyond belief, but there are four of them and ten of us. Not exactly fair odds."

The breath stalled in her lungs. She'd known this would be a volatile situation, but she'd expected this explosion to take place behind closed doors. Not here in front of the paid entertainment— which went to show how expendable they were as commodities.

Baine raised his chin from where he'd been studying his plate, and looked Devereaux head on. "They're dead, and I told Walters to cut the order in half."

"What do you mean, they're dead?" The older man's cheeks reddened.

"Never coming back," Baine replied coolly.

Kobi stood, knocking into her chair, which screeched over the wooden floor. She breathed sharply in response to the jolt, ready for anything. "What the fuck did you do?" he demanded. Spittle flew from his mouth, and from this angle she noticed his crooked teeth.

Devereaux shook his head. "I'll handle this, thank you."

Kobi quieted, but remained standing, leaning over her. Devereaux's jaw clenched and brow scrunched, and for the first time she noticed how much the man had aged. Wrinkles of time creased his forehead. Brown eyes lit with anger sunk into the framework of his face. The darkness of his hair lightened with grey, not only at the hairline, but sporadically over his head. For more than twenty years the image seared into her brain, the one that haunted her daylight and dreaming hours, had stayed the same, a stagnant sneer of youthful ambition and malevolence.

Through gritted teeth the old man asked, "What happened?" After a breath, he added, "I want details. Don't make me find them on my own."

Chapter Nine

Baine chuckled, and the acrid sound burned Sloan's ears. His laughter, healing in the past, now frightened with its hollow peals. His profile dominated her periphery. Dark, rumpled hair barely touched the slope of his forehead, which peaked gently at thick brows. Below them long lashes protected eyes she'd yet to regard. A prominent nose gave way to thick lips invented for loving and a wide, sturdy jaw made for boxing.

His humorless laugh died abruptly. "You requested a hit on a nation's president on American soil, in its capital. You want a hit in a first world nation, you deal with first world problems. Heightened security. No access. A population with a bloody load of time on their hands to poke their noses where they don't belong. Then you insist on sending a mob of knuckle-dragging fools with me. The situation was fucked from the outset."

A small part of Sloan had held out hope that Baine hadn't been there, since no one actually saw him in D.C. Well, that plane just got blown out of the air. A thousand questions shot across Sloan's mind in an instant. None had answers. Each question spawned only new questions. The most critical one at the moment—would he recognize her from the bloodbath in Washington? Thank holy hell she hadn't made eye contact with him. But realistically, how long could she avoid his gaze?

"Details," Devereaux bit out.

"Ty got into it with an old lady outside the apartment. He stepped on her poodle's foot. She went nuts. Close to shot time a couple of cops knocked on the door. Instead of dealing with the situation quietly, Ty opens up on them through the door. I took the shot early while shit went sideways behind me. The cops got a few lucky shots. Killed two of your guys. I killed the rest and got the fuck out."

The other women in the room blanched. One gasped. Sloan rejoiced at their reactions. They camouflaged her shocked expression, because she couldn't comprehend why he'd just lied. Maybe, if he hadn't admitted killing any of his father's men, she could understand him creating the fictitious scenario. Why bother, if he was going to admit to killing them anyway? To add more questions to the infinite list, why did he save her? If he recognized her from D.C., would he reveal her identity? Would he remember her from childhood?

She waited for someone to jump up and down, pointing and screaming, "Liar! Liar!" No one moved for an eternity, and Sloan realized she was the only one who knew he'd lied about how the D.C. massacre went down. Sure, parts were true. He'd probably seen the old lady with a poodle. He'd shot his father's men, only more than he'd let on. The best lies were re-sculpted truths. Another question struck Sloan. Could she use this knowledge to her advantage?

Kobi broke the silence. "Why'd you kill them?"

But Devereaux answered. "So he could get away, and they couldn't talk." The man bobbed his head. "I'm not happy you cut my home force by a third, but I'm pleased you limited my exposure, and returned, of course.

"I don't need to remind you both," he said zeroing in on Baine then Kobi, "how important it is that things run smoothly from here on. Everything rides on the completion of this deal."

Lana swallowed hard, and feigned a smile when Devereaux rubbed his thumb over her jaw. "Enough business for one night."

As Devereaux said, it was so. Drinks flowed and spirits rose. As the meal advanced Sloan saw why Lana commanded the big bucks. Shortly after the confrontation she molded herself to The Devil. Whispering in his ear and petting him up, Lana took the rage right out of the bull while keeping her surroundings in check with casual, but calculated, slanting glances. *Smart lady. Too smart.* Yet another person she'd have to keep on her radar, plus the little morsel about the all-important deal. As if her darn radar wasn't blipping out already.

Backup hadn't been an option on this mission. Hell, it had taken every bit of juice the pictures of ball-gadded Senator Byron Graham had to get her in the fold of fanny Madam Walters shipped to Devereaux. Having Ryan play her handmaid and flaming makeup artist would have been priceless in both humor and support. As it stood now, her closest allies hid and waited for her signal nearly thirty minutes away on the best of timetables. She pictured her friend and the rest of the four-man team pacing, cussing, and playing poker to pass the time. Four days on her end was fast work. On theirs it was an eternity in purgatory.

Sloan shifted her legs toward Kobi in an effort to shield her face from Baine's view, not to block out Nena's lips on his neck or her hand on his knee, advancing with each hollow laugh she gave. Kobi's gaze bore a hole into his plate instead of her breasts for a change. The wiry man stabbed the meat from some animal, eland or springbok, and carved it with jerky movements. Each bite he washed down with a small glass of clear liquid, and then he waived his hand in the air.

A server stationed on the wall behind them stepped forward, poured Kobi another shot of Stoli, then retreated only to return a few moments later. With the money they worked with she'd have thought the ambitious man would've basked in the bills that weren't his own by tossing back Belvedere. She scanned the room. Chivas Regal. Remi Martin. Imperial. He chose to drink bottom shelf liquor while the top shelf labels were available. Interesting. Of equal interest was the rate with which he consumed the alcohol. She'd counted six shots in as many minutes.

Having the man snockered worked to her advantage. Having him passed out at the dining room table screwed her more than any of the men in the room planned to. Most of them anyway. Baine hadn't so much as glanced in her direction. A gift, and somehow a curse.

Sloan leaned toward Kobi, making certain the heart of her bare breasts greeted him along with her words. "I hope you save room for dessert," she cooed to the man who had peasant tastes and severe impulse control issues.

As if just remembering she existed, Kobi's head swung around. Swamp-brown eyes surveyed her, not head to toe, but mouth to boobs, then back to boobs.

"How in the hell could I forget about you?" he mumbled, almost to himself. His gaze rose from her chest, and their clarity surprised Sloan. Apparently, this man had loads of practice tossing em' back. "You're the best part of the meal. In fact, I've suddenly lost my appetite for the main course altogether." His hand snaked possessively under the hem of her dress, and rubbed the top of her thigh. He closed the gap between them in a rush. Sloan lost what little appetite she had as his lips neared hers.

"A toast," she giggled, turning her face and retrieving her glass of wine just in time.

His brow knit together, but he flicked his hand at the server and returned her smile. "If we toast together, we drink together."

"As you wish."

"Another glass," he demanded to the young man in black and white.

Kobi slid her the small glass, sloshing its contents. "What'd you wanna toast?"

Playfully, Sloan wrapped her forearm around his. "To wild nights."

The sinister laugh said he agreed, a little too much.

The liquid cooled its way down Sloan's esophagus and plummeted into the hollow of her gut. When Kobi gestured for more drinks, Sloan snagged the roll off her dinner plate.

He thrust the shot at her. "To wild days."

After four more rounds, Sloan could take no more toasts to wild anythings. Liquor in her enemy was her ally. Liquor in her was her enemy's win, and therefore unacceptable. So, she changed tactics.

Pulling his head toward her with a firm grip on his tie, she pled into his ear. "Take me to your room." A nip of his lobe drove the message home, and elicited a moan from his throat.

Kobi stood on sea legs, and took her hand in his. "Follow me."

Sloan ignored the wobble in her own legs. Instead, she focused on the thick back in front of her and the path he took. Out of the dining room through a lavish vestibule. He ignored a curving staircase in favor of the hallway on his left. Down the other hallway were the working girls' rooms. Five doors lined the new corridor—three single doors on the left and one set of double doors on the right. He turned into the room on the right, confirming her suspicion that Baine's and Devereaux's rooms were on the second floor, along with The Devil's office.

He flicked on a light and two lamps sparked on either side of a queen sized bed. The room was nice, but no more so than the one she occupied down the way. Before taking in all the details she required, Kobi's weight pushed her against the now closed bedroom door. Sloan relaxed her muscles, which screamed for the freedom to unleash hell on the slimeball. In this inner struggle the liquor actually worked in her favor, taking the edge off her razor sharp reflexes. His hands breeched the privacy of her skirt and kneaded the flesh of her butt. She closed her eyes and breathed through the scorn his touch created. When those cold lips plundered the curve of her breasts, Sloan thought about the lovely cry they would surrender just before she broke his neck.

Muscles loose, Sloan held her inner self in a tight ball, allowing only the facade of playgirl to permeate. Until his mouth climbed her neck and moved toward her own.

"You must excuse me for a moment," Sloan begged, slipping her hands up his chest and pressing him back slightly. The motion disconnected his lips from her skin, settling her tilting stomach in the slightest way. He seemed dazed, pupils wide as they struggled to center her. She used his state and the momentum she'd built to slip from between him and the wall.

"No," fled his lips in an unyielding tone, but it was his biting grip on her wrist that stopped her cold.

Sloan turned, eyes apologetic. "I just need to get ready for you."

"You look ready enough. I know I'm ready," he added with a nod toward his pathetic excuse for a dick.

"I'll be one minute," she said, but his grip held. Time to switch tactics again. "I drank too much at dinner, and I know it's a little crass, but I really need to use the restroom before we get started."

The blood flow returned to her arm as his fingers loosened then released her. She smiled. "Fix yourself a drink. I promise to make it worth the wait."

"I know you will," he replied, tone tipping toward harsh.

Once behind the bathroom door, Sloan locked it, turned on the sink to full flow, and threw herself at the toilet. A mixture of bread, bile, and liquor fell into the bowl thanks to a well-placed middle finger and the thought of Kobi's mouth on her skin. No way in hell could she let the alcohol cloud her judgment or dull her reactions. Sloan flushed away the mess, rinsed with mouthwash, and blotted the make-up under her lashes.

With seconds to spare she considered her reflection. Her hair remained impeccably styled in a low ponytail that cascaded down her back in uniform ringlets. Amber eyes as clear as the Baltic gem. None of the drama within showed on the cool exterior. A lifetime of training did that trick. Blotting the bold lip-stain she applied, Sloan smiled, and opened the bathroom door to deal with Kobi Ross and find a clue to the whereabouts of Devereaux Kendrick's black book.

The best laid schemes.

Chapter Ten

"Wow! This place is amazing."

The young woman drooping off Baine's arm tilted her head in an awkward angle to take in his suite. He was amazed the words came out in any discernible form, since she stood with one foot dangling over the cliff of pissed drunk. One gust and she'd be legless.

"Can I get you a drink?"

"Yes. Please," she nearly hollered into his ear. As acting crutch, Baine helped her over to the bed with only a slight weave and wobble in between. The duvet's fabric snapped, echoing in the big room, and puffed up around the redhead as she sank back onto the covering.

"You're amazing too," she said, raising one brow. Her hands fumbled around the top of her short dress, pulling here and tugging there. She looked like a pretty cat stuck in a sock. The thought made the corner of his mouth quirk up as he turned. He didn't like cats, but boy, were they amusing for a minute.

Baine made his way to the bank of floor-to-ceiling shelves where a decanter of single malt scotch sat. Glasses clanked as he arranged two and poured in the dark liquid. With his back to Kobi's camera, Baine added three drops of clear liquid to one. By the time he returned to the bed, the cat was out of the bag, or dress, as it were. She lay starkers across the mattress, chin propped in one hand.

"You don't waste time."

"Not tonight," she said, curling her index finger at him. "Most of the time this job is work. But every once in a while it's pure pleasure."

On a different night, he might have entertained her. Occasionally, he eked a modicum of satisfaction from the stale entanglements. Most times, he left the bought women to the others. When his father made a point of giving him a girl, he dealt with them.

"Then," he said, moving to the bedside and handing her a drink, "we drink to pleasure."

"To pleasure," she agreed before tipping up the glass.

After she emptied it, Baine took the glass and returned it to the shelf. He flipped the power to the antique turntable on, and lowered the tonearm onto the record. Pablo de Sarasate's artful violin filled the room with haunting beauty. Sarasate was fine. Nowhere near his favorite pub band, or better yet, silence. But the music served two purposes. Annoy the bloody hell out of Kobi and keep him from hearing any other noises.

Baine returned to the bed. Red's head had slipped from its perch and nestled into the comforter. She smiled up at him under heavily lidded eyes and tried to sit up. He leaned over, flipped the switch, and the room plunged into darkness. After pulling the covers back and arranging the pillows, Baine lifted the small woman and rearranged her neatly on the bed, then pulled the duvet over her naked body. A small sigh breached her lips as she snuggled into the sheets.

"Sleep well," he said.

The first inconvenience dealt with, Baine's curiosity and irritation ripped from their neat restraints. His fists clenched as he moved silently from the room. In the bathroom he locked the door and placed a folded towel at the threshold to block any light from the cameras. He slapped the closet light on, then shrugged out of his jacket and tie and slung them at the hamper. Both articles of clothing smacked the wall before plopping to the floor.

"Par for the course," he grumbled.

Back at the safe, he punched in the code and retrieved a thin black laptop and started it up.

Kobi thought himself Devereaux's watchdog, constantly nipping at Baine's heels and barking in his ear. Like a dog with a bone, Kobi had curled his lips and raised his hackles the moment Baine had shown an interest in his father's dealings nearly two years ago. It either showed the man's desperation to stay in Devereaux's good graces or spot on instincts that Baine was a bad jack, or both. Regardless of the reason, Kobi had screwed up his plans for the last time.

Baine sat on an armchair in the massive walk-in, typed his way through several security measures, then clicked on the video icon. Kobi had bugged Baine's room, but obviously, from the hours of footage Baine had viewed, never thought his own haven could be bugged. Baine just hoped the fucker had been stupid enough to leak the information about the assassination from his room. In which case, Baine would have the proof on file, pass it along to his father, and wave good-bye to one of the two things standing in the way of finally taking his father out.

A levity he hadn't felt in a couple of decades made his deep inhale a bit easier. The pinwheel on the screen whirled as he waited for the video feed to load. After a spell the console came to life, unfolding the dated log of days past on the left of the screen, offering menu options across the top, and in the center a reel of the current stream. Baine hunched toward the computer trying to figure out exactly what transpired in Kobi's rooms at this very moment. He gripped the base of the display with both hands, tilted it back to remove any possible glare, and moved the computer closer still.

"Bloody bang."

Baine watched the woman who'd been at the end of his barrel scant days ago step from Ross's bathroom all legs and tits in a tiny dress. She looked nothing like the hard-hitting agent he'd hammered over the head in that vacant flat, but it was her. No doubt. Her features, though in costume, were too strikingly unique.

Barmy.

How could he be so unaware, so incompetent, not to notice her at dinner? For fuck's sake, she'd been sitting right next to him, but he'd automatically discounted her as the hired help. A rookie cock-up for sure. One that could ruin everything he desired and worked damn hard to get. One that could get him killed.

Kobi straightened from the bedside table where he'd been hunched and rubbed the white of cocaine off his nose with the cuff of his jacket. *Old habits.* He beckoned her with his other hand. "I have something better than a drink."

With a hip-rocking gate, she met him at the bedside. The chav gave a bobbing nod and crooked smile as though he were Casanova himself, and not a total douche. She peered over his shoulder at the offering.

"Oh," she said, pulling her hand to her bosom. Lashes batting, she added, "I've never done that before."

Kobi laughed. "A virgin. I'm surprised, with your line of work and all."

The woman's laugh held no amusement, and veiled another emotion that flickered in her eyes. Hatred. Anger. Disgust. Baine didn't know, but was certain one or all applied. But Kobi missed it, busy ogling her chest.

"Could you show me how," she asked.

He snorted two lines in tutorial, then stumbled forward, missing her hand completely when trying to hand her the fancy straw.

"Are you okay?"

She offered her hand and he levered his way up her body to stand straight.

"I'm... I... I'm so good," he slurred, nuzzling his head into the crook of her neck.

Baine removed his hands from the computer, afraid he'd snap it with his grip. He crossed his arms over his chest, but his hands balled into fists anyway. How had she gotten here? She couldn't have followed him. He'd backtracked and circled so many times leaving the scene it had been a damn miracle he'd found his way back to the airport at all. Plus, he'd knocked her solid. There would have been no way she could have followed. Hell, the fact that she wasn't still in a bed resting spoke to the kind of person she was—tenacious as sin—and he didn't like it one bit.

After a brief embrace, Kobi stumbled left before slumping to the ground in a useless pile. The vixen kicked off her heels, adjusted the top of the dress to cover the crests of her breasts, then squatted down to Kobi. She hooked her arms under the bracket of his armpits and wrestled his weight onto the bed. Once on the comforter, she stripped his suit, tie, shirt, and shoes off and unbuckled his belt. Nose crinkled, she averted her eyes, pulled back his trousers and fished out the guy's dick.

"What the hell," Baine whispered to no one.

The appendage sagged pathetically over the edge of his underclothes, garnering a quirk of her eyebrow. "Heh." She tossed pillows from the bed and rumpled the sheets, then splashed some vodka on the bed before overturning the bottle on the nightstand. Finally, she slanted the lampshade and stepped back, wiping her brow with the back of her hand. She turned away, but paused, then wiggled a black thong down her legs and left it puddled on the floor.

Baine ignored his dick as it stirred at the sight. And refused to let his mind wander up her muscled thighs to her sweet apex.

Can't go there, McCord.

When she prowled the room looking under every cushion, opening every drawer, and quietly tapping the walls and floors, Baine knew exactly what she was looking for. His blood boiled. No way in hell was she getting her hands on his father's black book. It was his by blood right or by blood, whichever came first.

She wouldn't find anything because he'd already been through that room on three separate occasions looking for leads to the book. And she wouldn't get an opportunity to look anyplace else. He should've killed her the other day and saved himself a world of trouble.

Chapter Eleven

The shakes woke Kobi. Sadly, there was no earthquake or hot humping female to blame them on. Need burned from the inside out. Just one hit to tide him over. Take the edge off. A swipe of his hand over his forehead confirmed he was melting, as sweat ran down his arm and dotted the sheets. His skin lied with its chill.

Oh, it hadn't been this bad in a while. Not since the day Baine popped up, out of nowhere, and showed interest in his father's business then refused to leave.

The big broody fucker.

The fuzziness of Kobi's mind and ache of his body stopped that train of thought with another tremor. He needed another line. A short one to ease the burn. He crawled to the edge of the bed and pulled the silver tray to his face. The inhale burned his nose, but in the best fucking way. Almost instantly, the shivers stopped and the fire in his head smoldered. He flopped onto his back and blinked several times before his eyes adjusted to the blinding sunlight streaming in the window and the ceiling came into focus. His tongue stroked along the points of his teeth. The film it found there forced him to move.

He needed a drink and a shower. Maybe another little hit. He'd been good for a while now, holding things together for the boss. He eyed the powder, and his heartbeat sped in response. Now wasn't the time to screw up. No way was he going back to slum life. Devereaux plucked him from the streets and gave him everything he'd ever desired. He owed it to the man to protect him, even from his own son.

Kobi levered up on an elbow to find his Jimmy hanging out and his room, or at least the bed area, destroyed. He palmed his still sleeping dick and searched his brain for any memories of the festivities that had caused the mess. None came to life. No, that wasn't true. He remembered snorting. Always did. And he remembered a fucking goddess. Trouble was, he couldn't recall her naked and on him like he usually did, no matter his altered state.

When he stood a cold wet puddle greeted his left foot.

"Son of a bitch."

He hobbled to a brown and white patterned rug and wiped the liquid onto the coarse material. From the state of his bed it appeared he'd had a hell of a good time. It pissed him off he couldn't remember any of it.

Time to get dressed, find that cunt, and make some new memories.

Chapter Twelve

Stroke. Stroke. Breathe. Stroke. Stroke. Breathe. Sloan's sun flushed skin prickled quickly in the cool water. For the next twenty minutes, she focused on the rhythm. She released every concern from her mind and swam. No, in hooker mode her legs couldn't kick as furiously as she wanted nor arms stroke as hard, but her muscles still sang. The effort gave her brain a welcomed respite from the restless night.

Covert work had always been Sloan's forte. Morphing into someone else. Hiding who she was. What she'd endured. But this assignment held in the balance every desire she'd clung to since the day she'd quit mourning her parents and started fighting, everything she'd thought beyond her grasp after so long struggling to make it a reality. This assignment had also tapped a well of emotion she'd thought long ago drained.

"Nice stroke."

His voice destroyed her solitude. The dark timbre resonated down Sloan's spine like a cellist's bow being dragged across the C string. A fresh wave of gooseflesh crested over her. She curled the water's surface and turned toward Baine. Words froze in her throat. Thick and unruly dark hair cropped neatly around his ears, but dipped and swayed wildly at his forehead. The perfect handle for screwing. *Jezuz.* If that one wasn't enticing enough, the swells and dips of his traps, shoulders, and biceps provided a feast of options to grip while riding the sculpted V of his hips. Everywhere she looked his swarthy skin wrapped taut—over a defined eight pack, thick and sturdy legs, corded forearms. The short crinkles of brown hair that peppered across his chest and peeked out from the waist of his swim trunks sizzled her brain.

"Thank you." Sloan aimed for courteous and non-solicitous, tamping down the resentment, warring curiosity, and wicked lust he stirred inside her with every bit of self-control she possessed.

The bespoke suit he'd worn so well the night before had been traded for charcoal swim trunks and a towel slung over one shoulder. He moved toward her with grace that belied his bulk, before dropping his towel on the chaise next to hers. Of all the chairs and loungers in the place, he'd chosen the only occupied lounger on the entire patio. The act, though in all likelihood innocent, rang in Sloan's ears like a war cry. A deliberate move in a complicated game of chess. Having just finished her laps, his timing was too perfect to be coincidence.

Baine turned and settled his gaze on her. Sloan searched for any sign of recognition in the sky blue orbs, in the tautness of his square jaw, or the furrow of his brow, and found none. *Good.* If he recognized her, the mission would be ruined. Not that she'd live to see the fallout. It was good that his eyes hadn't alighted with remembrance, but heedless of the boon, emptiness pitted her belly.

Every battle honed instinct screamed for Sloan to retreat. In submission, she pushed off the bottom and glided to the stone outcropping only a few feet away from the enigma that was Baine Kendrick. She should hate him on sight. Anger roiled just under the surface, but the sudden and undeniable physical awareness of him played bumper-cars with the ire and her brain.

"It's all yours," she said, levering herself out of the water. Thousands of droplets rained off her body, and Baine's intent study likely cataloged each. Like a damn schoolgirl, her cheeks heated.

"That's good," he said. A smile pulled at one corner of his mouth. Then he added, "I think you would put me to shame in a proper race."

Sloan shook her head, unable to speak. The twinge of memory of two forgotten children racing over the green grass was too sweet and painful to rouse.

He held out a towel, and she forced her feet to close the distance. Proximity sent a jolt of electricity coursing through her, similar to the energy that surged before a fight, but different. She swallowed hard, struggling to ignore the nuance, which made her hyper aware she wore only strategically placed strips of spandex. When her fingers closed around the terry cloth, Lana and Cynthia ambled through the doorway onto the patio. Their conversation quieted once they saw her and Baine. The women waved.

"Good morning, ladies."

They beamed at him as they walked by, then settled on side-by-side lounges at the opposite end of the row. Sloan nodded and soaked up the excess moisture from her hair and body in preparation for her escape. She secured the towel around her body with a tuck of its tail at the top of her breast, and gave him the best smile she could muster.

"Enjoy the—"

"Lotion me," he asked. Though his tone made it sound like more like a command.

Sloan turned a palm up. "I'm sorry, I don't have any." She motioned toward the other women. "They might have some, and I'm sure they'd happily help."

"And you wouldn't," he countered.

While she sputtered, something she didn't recall ever having done in her life, he reached across her to a side table and plucked a tube from a decorative bowl. His body came so close to hers the heat he radiated seeped into her marrow. As he retreated, the dusting of dark hair on his chest tickled her arm.

"Here," he said, slapping the lotion into her hand.

He sat on the end of the chaise, elbows on his knees. Hunching didn't diminish his presence in the least. In fact, it drew Sloan's attention to the sloping topography of his chest and the spread of his shoulders, which dwarfed the chair under him. When she didn't move he tilted his chin up and directed her behind him with a thick arm.

She circled him in a wide arc, but surrendered, tucking behind him on the hard wood. Clinically, like she treated a field wound, Sloan uncapped the sunscreen, deposited a dollop on her palm and began rubbing it onto his back. From his nape she worked her way out over his shoulders, denying the tingle the friction created below her waist. Until he leaned into her touch.

Her belly skittered, then churned at the absurdity. Of all the horrible things she'd done in the name of greater good, this topped them all. Because a small twisted part of her enjoyed the closeness to Baine. There were layers of deception, anger, and betrayal between them, but hope hid underneath like a tiny, dingy marble under a landfill of trash. And wasn't it ironic that he'd been the one to instill that hope inside her.

She'd been a terrified girl in a haunted house. Alone in the universe. Her loved ones' dead bodies ripped from her clenched fingers. Trapped as a slave. Utterly hopeless.

Then one day a boy, bigger and older than she by a few years, she'd guessed, had wandered into the basement where she'd been washing linens and asked her to play. When she'd declined, he'd put the bag of marbles in his pocket and silently stepped up to the basin, grabbed a napkin, and scrubbed the cloth against the washboard. For one week he showed up, helped her with her chores, then went about his business. The next week they'd hurried through the chores, and then actually played. He taught her how to shoot marbles, and had even given her one the last time she'd seen him.

But they weren't kids any longer. And there was no hope for what he'd become.

Sloan snapped the cap closed. "All done."

Before she could stand, he spun to face her. One brow furrowed. "How is it a woman like you ends up in a situation like this?"

"A woman like me?"

"You could choose another line of work. Toned as you are, you could be a fitness instructor."

"Sometimes we choose our fate," she said. "Other times it's chosen for us."

The cleft between his dark brows deepened and his jaw clenched then released. "And sometimes it's what we make it."

Sloan eased back, suddenly aware that his face was less than a foot from her own. Quietly, against all of her better judgment, she asked, "Is that what you're doing, making your fate?"

His lips parted, but no words came. She recognized motion by the door, but when she saw Kobi with his arm draped over Nena, dismissed it as a threat. Anticipation jingled her nerves as she waited for his response. She didn't know what she expected from him. He didn't owe her, nor the hooker she played, any explanation. But damn that hope.

Abruptly, her head was jerked left and cold lips like those of a dead fish sealed over her own. Sloan clutched fistfuls of the towel, fighting the instinct to pummel the man's gut. His tongue dampened the edge of her mouth.

"Sod off, Ross," Baine swore.

The words were quiet, but held a threat that caught the man's notice. He broke away from her lips. It was all she could do to keep from scrubbing her mouth with the back of her hand.

"I had her first," Kobi Ross boasted. "And we have some unfinished business." Hiking a thumb toward the other escort, he added, "I won't leave you empty handed."

The redhead winked at Baine, and reached for his arm. "Let's go have some fun."

"No. She's mine," Baine said, his voice flat and his intense glare never leaving Kobi.

Sloan's stupid heart jumped at his words.

In defiance, Kobi's hand bit into Sloan's chin and he wrenched it up. Before Sloan had a chance to remind herself not to react, Baine's arm shot out. A choking sound gurgled in Kobi's throat as Baine's hand encircled the column of the man's neck. Kobi's eyes widened. His hands flew to Baine's wrist. He struggled to wrench the hand away. The heels of his shoes heaved against the ground and his body bucked.

"If you want to continue breathing, I suggest you take the redhead and be on your merry way." With that Baine released his grip.

Kobi stumbled back, heaving in air. Nena placed a steadying hand on his shoulder and he slapped it away. The look on his face oscillated between embarrassment and pure hatred as he stomped past them, the other quirk-browed women, and then through the back gate.

Baine grabbed her hand and pulled Sloan off the lounger, not giving her time to collect her covering as it loosened in the upheaval. He moved with authority. Chin up. Shoulders back. He aimed for the manor, drawing her behind him. The towel fell, entwined her legs and pitched her off balance. Still, he refused to slow. To keep from meeting the stone pavers with her face, Sloan yielded her grip on the fabric.

Through the threshold of the rear entrance, he spun on her. His wide chest crowded her in, until her back met the cold wall. Sloan had no idea what to say or do. So, she kept her mouth shut. Had the whole scene been a tiny turf war between the two men? It was the most logical explanation. But Baine regarded her now with nearly as much hostility as he'd forced upon Kobi. His dark expression made the young girl inside her vanish and the warrior surge forward, smacking a fist to her armored chest.

But, just as swiftly, her inner warrior stumbled.

The palm of his hand glided over the slope of her chin, warming the abused skin. His thumb scrubbed over her lips. Once. Twice. The rough pad of his finger stung her sensitive flesh again. Then he inclined his head. Baine's face hovered so close to hers stubble rasped her cheek. Sloan breathed him in on a gasp. Her head spun from the redolence.

He stilled for a moment, save for his breathing, which seemed almost pained, the inhale and exhale ragged. His hand slid up the nape of her neck. His fingers wove in her hair and tugged. Unwilling to fight him, her chin raised to meet his gaze, which honed in on her mouth.

His lips covered hers. The pressure of him was unrelenting. He pulled her in to the kiss with his hand and pinned her to the wall with his body. Warmth engulfed her. From the tips of her lips to the soles of her feet, the chill she'd harbored earlier scorched in Baine's onslaught. This was no embrace. It was an out and out attack on the tiny space inside her mind where things made sense. Where everything was good versus bad. Black and white. In this space she was a tool for justice and Baine was part and parcel with the enemy. No matter their youthful friendship. No matter how good his mouth tasted.

And Lord, if sin had a taste she'd found it.

His thick lips parted then bracketed her lower lip. Balmy wetness soothed her sensitive skin, but enlivened a nature she had no idea existed inside her. A need so carnal and base screamed to life. Unbidden, Sloan's hands groped Baine's hot, hard lats. To her shame, she did not push him away, but held him in place while her body arched against his.

Her lips muffled his curse an instant before his other hand smoothed over the length of her neck. Where his grip on Kobi had meant to harm the other man, it only tormented Sloan, hovering just above her heaving breasts. Her whole body tingled with awareness, but not in the usual way. This had nothing to do with tactics and everything to do with yearning.

A moan of anguish or desire—of which, she couldn't be entirely sure—breeched her lips. His other hand, which had been still at his side, ran up her thigh. The roughness of his palm heated her from the inside out. Baine's fingers bit into the bare bottom revealed by the bathing suit. In response her body quickened, nipples tightening, core clenching.

"Ahem. Might I offer you some towels? You look a bit wet."

Again Baine cursed. This time, however, the words came through loud and clear. He growled it out as he broke the kiss. With one hand he held her to the wall while he created a gap between them. The sudden withdrawal served the same purpose as a bucket of ice water. In less than a second the world around her refocused.

Behind Baine, Lawrence, the butler, stood, a pile of towels balanced neatly in his hand. The set of his mouth almost disguised his mirth, but the sparkle in his blue eyes gave him away. Once again, Sloan was intrigued by Lawrence's stealth and uncanny timing, but before she could attempt to figure the man out, Baine turned on him.

He snatched a towel from the pile. "That'll be all."

"Are you sure I can't interest either of you in a drink?"

"Yes." Baine's tone bordered on harsh, but he seemed to rein it in when he turned back toward her.

Lawrence bowed his head then retreated down the hallway as quietly as he'd arrived. As much as Sloan wanted to study the servant, Baine's brilliant eyes owned her attention. They didn't flit about her face, but bore into her eyes. Searching. She trembled under the scrutiny. Actually freaking trembled like a rabbit staring past the wolf's teeth down his throat. His size didn't intimidate her. Though in the few times she'd seen him all grown up, he'd used it for that distinct purpose. His searching eyes scared her because they saw too much. Elicited too much.

He leaned in and draped the terrycloth sheet around her. His breath was hot on her ear when he whispered, "You're so much more than a dime trick whore. See you tonight."

While her breathing stilled in her chest he turned and walked away.

Chapter Thirteen

She didn't have the time or inclination to be angry or embarrassed while the drama unfolded in the hallway. But she had the rest of the damn day to go over it time and again in her head. Now as she evened her lipstick for the evening's festivities it was no more than a jumbled heap of ten different kinds of crap.

You're so much more than a dime trick whore.

The words played over in her mind for the thousandth time. And again she tried to discern their meaning. He hadn't come during the afternoon to try his hand at killing her as she'd half expected. But he'd said he'd see her tonight. So, maybe he'd try this evening. A small part of her held out hope the words hadn't been a threat at all, but praise for the caliber of woman she was.

Yeah right. Hope didn't live long in the pit of Sloan's soul.

Hope hadn't gotten her many places in life. After her parents' murder and her enslavement at the Kendrick Estate in Lungi, Baine's friendship had given her hope. She clung to it after Devereaux sent him away. When she'd been shipped across an ocean in a metal container with a loaf of bread and a jug of water, hope saw her through the terrifying week of night. Hope bloomed anew when she met the beautiful American couple to whom she'd been given.

But more than anything she remembered the day her hope died.

Sloan's instincts and training were all she had. Instinct said Baine knew what she was and planned to stop her. Then again, her instincts, or more accurately, her body, had betrayed her once already today.

Her hand trembled as she guided the cascade of diamonds to the hole in her lobe. Instead of cursing the weakness, she ignored it. Pheromones were to blame.

In high school while all the other kids were busy underage drinking and having backseat sex, she focused on academic excellence, archery, debate, and becoming proficient in eight languages. Got into Princeton and worked day and night to get the Bureau's or Agency's attention. There was no room for friends or relationships of any kind.

As graduation neared it became apparent that she was socially awkward and asexual at best. Since the CIA liked their agents well adjusted— she'd had no clue to the existence of the Base Branch—she made it her goal to adapt. Like a checklist, experiment, or mission, she had sex with people. She found men more easily manipulated than women, but not for the obvious sexist reasons. Women were more self-conscious, and therefore wary of compliments and seduction. Hell, she even had a "relationship" for nearly a year with a man she felt little for, just to see if she could.

So, this jitterbug in her stomach was inconvenient, considering her track record, but nothing more. If his smell got to her, she'd hold her damn breath.

A knock sounded at the door and dread filled her belly. She wouldn't allow him to kill her, but she wouldn't relish taking his life either. Dressed and ready for the festivities, Sloan grabbed the sparkly clutch with a knife hidden in the frame, straightened her shoulders, and headed for the door.

"What the hell was all the chaos you caused at the pool," Lana asked as she stormed the room. "We are paid to entertain. Not stir up trouble." Her form fitting dress accentuated every curve as she turned on Sloan, palms up in question.

At least it wasn't Baine. "They have some rivalry going. I was just in the wrong place at the—"

"Save it," she cut in. "Devereaux heard all about it and wasn't pleased. You need to diffuse the situation. If anything happens at dinner, you'll be sent away."

The porcelain palms dropped to her sides and her brow knit together. She added, "And I'm not certain it'll be in one pretty piece. So..."

"I've got it. Make nice."

Lana released the breath she'd been holding. "Good." Her stilettos tapped as her rear swung in time to the movement. At the doorway she turned. "Don't be late."

The moment Sloan crossed the threshold into the sitting room all eyes were on her. Not in the, "Wow, she looks so good," way, but in the, "Oh, she just stumbled on the high wire," way. Lana perched on the edge of a settee next to Devereaux, legs crossed, leaning toward him, but her eyes sparkled with interest in Sloan's direction. She, and the other ladies in the room, awaited her fall.

The Devil, busy tapping the display of his phone, paid her no attention. So, Sloan smiled sweetly and nodded to Lana like a good little escort.

The damn butler stood next to the dining room door all prim and proper, waiting to be called upon.

Yeah right.

Kobi had yet to arrive, but her real problem leaned against the frame of the French doors studying her.

Sloan knew how to take a hit. It was second nature for her to roll a shoulder, step back, block, weave, or absorb the force and use the momentum to throw her attacker off balance. Yet, there was nothing she could do to stave off the impact of Baine's steady gaze. He looked at her and saw...everything. Like every secret she harbored, every hope and fear, were unveiled for his eyes alone.

She huffed out a breath at the idiocy of the notion, but still struggled to discredit it. Especially when he beckoned her with the slightest nod of his head. As she steadied her quivering nerves with bold steps in his direction, she examined him, looking for any signs of weapons or weakness.

His most prominent weapons called her attention first. Hooded by dark lashes, Baine's blue eyes glinted in the final shreds of daylight. A fine suit matching the color of his dark hair covered his body and nearly hid the butts of two handguns nestled below his shoulders. Thighs about the diameter of her waist fit easily in his slacks and revealed no trace of a holster. Not that she discounted the probability he had one or two somewhere on his lower half. The scruff on his chin had turned into the makings of a close-cropped beard, and she discounted its significance...right up until she was forced to swallow the saliva that had pooled in her mouth.

The man was a weapon. Finely honed with little to no weakness about him. Not a lawyer. Not a friend.

"You look stunning," he said when the toes of her heels were only a few feet away from his surely custom dress shoes.

"You don't look stunned to me," she replied, searching his face for any reaction.

The corner of his mouth quirked. "Good. I can't give you any advantage over me."

"Why not?"

He scanned the room before returning to her, then said in a quiet rumble, "When I answer, keep in mind where we are."

Confusion furrowed her brow. Caution told her to back away. Curiosity kept her in place. "Okay?"

He waved the butler over and placed his empty glass on the tray he carried. "Scotch. Straight."

Lawrence nodded. "Anything for you, miss?"

Sloan cleared her throat before she was able to speak, suspense and irritation having tightened it. "No, thank you."

The butler winked at her playfully before turning away from them.

Baine ripped her gaze from the butler's back by settling his hands on either side of her neck. Heat radiated from his big palms to the pads of each finger and sent what should have been a warning alert, but instead launched a pang of desire to her belly. He gathered her hair in his hands. The weight of it lifted from her chest and back for a moment before he settled it, running his hands down the back of her neck and spine to her tail bone. The motion pulled her to him. Her head automatically snuggled into the hollow of his neck, as he cupped her ass and pulled her closer still.

A hint of cologne and sex shot up her nose. Like the cocaine she'd been offered the previous night, his scent was a drug she'd best let alone. She exhaled him slowly, trying not to savor him or dread the room's plain air she tilted up to inhale. Before she had a moment to lament, his teeth nipped a trail up her neck.

When he reached her lobe his lips enveloped it, diamond and all. She bit down on a moan. He removed the grip she hadn't realized she had on his coat and kept her hands burrowed in his, not giving an inch of space between them.

"I wouldn't have expected such an honest reaction from an undercover Branch Agent."

As every muscle in Sloan's body went taut, Baine's grip tightened on her hands. Not painfully so. Just enough to pull her back from the edge of sanity. Back from pulling her knife and going to work on everyone in the room she could get to before she got blown to bits.

"Relax," he whispered. "I don't want to fight you. I watched you take out Bull in D.C. and I know how handy you are with a knife."

His lips grazed her cheek, and then he was there, resting his forehead on hers. Those deep blue eyes exploring hers.

"So," he added, "do us both a favor and keep that purse tucked under your arm."

Bastard.

He released her hands and straightened, her gaze now level with his throat. Sloan stood stunned like a piece of petrified wood. How in the fuck did he know she was a Branch Agent? Even Branch Agents didn't know all of the other Branch Agents.

She wasn't one for profanities, but if ever a situation called for one or a hundred...

Fuck. Fuck. Fuck.

His lips spread into a thin smile and he leaned closer. "It takes brass balls to stand there after that kind of blow. I'm impressed."

She smiled back, mirthlessly. "Don't be. It doesn't take balls when you're a person with nothing to lose."

Baine's brow pinched and his smile faded. "That's unfortunate, because I need you to have a bit of self-preservation, if we're going to make it through this week."

Sloan ran her hand up his tie, ignoring the hard topography of his chest. At his collar she looped in three fingers and pulled. To anyone else it would look like an embrace. Her other hand snaked up his throat, ready to strike him hard and fast in the esophagus. Big or small, people went down when they couldn't breathe.

In turn he wrapped his arms around her waist and pulled her close. "Are you going to hurt me?"

"Maybe," she growled into his ear. "Why didn't you kill me in D.C. and why am I still alive?"

"I hate to see such a nice rack go to waste?"

"Try again," she threatened, adding pressure with both her hands.

"All right." His head turned and his lips captured hers.

She didn't fight him. There was no use, in a room full of people who expected her to do exactly what she was doing—seducing Baine Kendrick. Being seduced by him wasn't in either of her job descriptions. But damn, if his lips weren't the hottest things she'd ever felt. They melted her resolve into a puddle and had her hands breaking rank. Her fingers left the stubble of his neck and delved into his hair. She clutched the softness, holding him to her.

His tongue caressed her top lip and without hesitation she opened and allowed him in. Their tongues collided in battle. One overpowering the other again and again until they both panted for air.

He turned his head gently, breaking the kiss. "How was that?"

"Just playing a role, Kendrick."

"Ah, you keep on telling yourself that, lovely. Maybe you'll believe it, but I wouldn't count on it. And how about you stick to Baine, when you call my name?"

"You still haven't answered my question," she said against his pulse, which wasn't the only one in the room galloping.

"Would you look at that," he said in feigned disappointment. "No time to chat. Dinner is served."

Chapter Fourteen

Every time his son walked into the room, pride swelled Devereaux's chest. Not that his fit torso needed any help standing out. Mid-fifties and he bagged babes less than half his age. Without paying for it. Still, he'd created a work of art from thin air, starting by sharing his impeccable genes and ending with the way he had carved out his son's ruthless nature.

He rubbed his hand over the lump at his heart.

It had been touch and go for a while. A long while. Baine was such a damn nice kid. It took years of paring to find his selfish core. Maturity helped. The testosterone, sheer size, and power sharpened his patsy edges. He'd thought that losing his mother would have helped remove the final vestiges of protectiveness. He'd been so fucking wrong. It almost cost him everything.

With no heir to pass his power and fortune, what good was having it? Kobi had been eager to take Baine's spot. The sewer rat was kidding himself if he thought for a minute Devereaux would leave his empire in his addicted hands. He'd snort through it in a month. *Never.* The loyal dog had a place at the table. Just not at the head.

His boy finally came around, as he'd felt certain he would. Power. Money. Pussy. Gets a man every time.

Little by little, Devereaux fed his son all three. And now, Baine was the man to take the helm. He'd proven it by taking out Bakou, and even his own men. Brutality harnessed power, and his son learned from the best.

He'd answered the who. The only question left was the when. When would he give the day-to-day dealings over? Devereaux tapped the date on his calendar. Not the date he would cede control. The date he'd gain control of five territories at once. By the end of the week he'd double his wealth and cement his place as the number one arms trafficker of all time.

Again his hand found his heart.

"Dinner is served." The butler's call pulled him out of his thoughts and into the present. Which was a pretty damn good place to be with a hot tongue on his neck and an eager hand crawling up his thigh.

Devereaux put his phone in his pocket and turned to his latest lady. He'd already found her hot in all the right places, except one. This lady was hot for a husband. A rich one. Disappointment would come knocking on her door pretty damn soon. He'd already been saddled once out of necessity, and when the necessity died, so did his one and only wife.

"You can finish me off after dinner," he said.

She smiled. "My pleasure."

No, it'd be his.

He left the couch and the escort followed. For the first time he noticed his son tangled like a fuck-pretzel with the troublemaker. How the hell could he have missed that kind of display? Shit, he got wood just looking at them all but devouring each other.

Devereaux waited until they disentangled and walked his way.

"Son," he greeted.

"Father." He nodded.

"And who do we have here?" he asked, offering his hand.

Her smile, hesitant and coy, captivated him. "My name is Sloan, Mr. Kendrick. Nice to meet you."

He cupped her small hand in his and brought it to his lips. Lord, she was smooth as silk. "I hear you've stirred quite the ruckus between my son and Mr. Ross."

Her eyes dropped. "It was never my intent—"

"Yes. Yes. I'm sure. Those two are merely sublimating. They fight over you because I won't allow them to fight over me."

Again she gave him that smile.

"But," he added, looking at the siren and his son in turn, "don't cause trouble where there's already plenty."

"Yes, sir," she complied.

"I'll screw who I choose, when I choose," Baine said unapologetically. "That dog of yours can look elsewhere."

"I see you're not getting soft on me, Son, which is all I hoped to assure myself of with this little tribunal. Can't have you developing protective feelings for the hired help."

"Feelings," the man snorted. "Don't confuse them with fucking. Besides, you beat them out of me long ago, Father."

"One can never be too sure. Speaking of trouble, where is ole' Mr. Ross?" he asked the room. "He can't miss dinner. We have much to discuss."

"I'll get him," one of his men said.

After the salads were taken away, Kobi Ross weaved his way into the dinning room and onto the chair across from him and next to Baine.

Devereaux addressed the latecomer. "I see you've already partaken of the spirits this evening."

"Surry bosss, it won't happen again," he slurred.

"If it does, I'll take you out back and shoot you myself."

His hands gripped the wooden table and the whites of his eyes grew. The conversations around the table stopped.

"I see I have your attention." Devereaux smiled. "This is a critical time in our negotiations. We have important things to discuss, but I can see tonight is lost. I need everyone at the top of their game. Understood?"

"Yes, sir. I'm sorry, sir. It won't happen again." Ross bowed his head.

Conversation carried on after a quiet minute.

Devereaux dug out his phone. His finger tapped harder on the date. His pulse raced like it only did when success was imminent. Fucking didn't hold a candle to this kind of rush. Nothing did. A smile crept onto his face. If only his father were here. God, how he'd love to rub his nose in it. The sorry S.O.B. Hell, he'd like to show his mother what a real man looked like—unafraid of success and the undesirable things you had to do to get it. Able to fend off the temptations of artificial uppers and the fake thrills of the gaming scene.

He patted his hand reassuringly over his heart.

Chapter Fifteen

Sloan sat so rigidly in the chair next to him, he could have used her as a human flagpole. An image of her naked body draped in Union Jack flashed in his mind. The red cross of Saint George covering her breasts and baring her... *Saint Mary, Mother of God!*

What in the blue bloody balls was wrong with him? She'd walked into the room and turned him into a horny teenager, all semblance of higher cognitive function out the door.

Baine laid the fork on the edge of his plate and leaned toward Sloan. When he felt the warmth radiating off her skin, he breathed, "Act like I just said the most indecent thing you've ever heard and you like it."

On command she leaned back, meeting his gaze head-on with wide eyes and her lower lip caught between her teeth. She poked him in the ribs hard enough to break one, and somehow she made it look playful. Baine sucked in a breath and grit his teeth to mask the pain that radiated through his middle. The cunning woman curved her sultry lips, batting her thick lashes like an innocent.

Once the pain subsided he moved in again. Maybe this time she'd administer a lethal blow, making all his worries disappear. He braced and whispered while he nipped her jaw. "Make it look like you want to screw my cock so hard you'll break it, so we can get out of here."

Her sharp draw of air wasn't feigned, neither was the blush on her cheek. The thought of a hooker blushing shook his shoulders with humor.

"What's so funny, Son?"

"Just enjoying the entertainment," he drawled.

"A toast," his father said. "To success, family, friends, and gorgeous women."

"Hear, hear," Baine agreed, but only to the first and last. *His* success and the remarkable woman to his left.

After Sloan returned her champagne to the table, she seized his hand from his lap. A mischievous expression played over her lovely face as she interlocked their fingers and brought them to her mouth. Slick warmth enveloped his middle finger. Desire so hot and heavy it made movement impossible, except for the slightest rise and fall of his chest, rushed over his body. Her tongue cradled his sizzling nerve endings. Those pouty lips clamped down in a perfect O, then dragged from knuckle to tip.

With little care of anything else in the world, much less the room, he grabbed her arm, pulled her up from the table and out of the room. Unlike the last time he'd hauled her like a cave man, she followed with eager steps barely missing his heels. If only she knew what he had in mind called for little talk and a whole lot of action...he wondered, would she come as willingly? Because, if he had anything to do with it, she'd be coming soon.

They practically flew through the foyer and up the stairs, footfalls striking as rapidly as the beat of a Massai drum. Baine's heart drummed

much the same. At the top of the stairs, Sloan
pinned him to the wall. He should have reigned her
hands or, at the very least, prepared to block an
attack. Hard to do when he operated on primal
instinct, filling his palms with her exquisite
backside and pulling her against him.

"Tell me why you haven't killed me already,
and," she added when their bodies met, "why your
hands are always on my bottom?"

"Well," he said, nuzzling her neck, "they
haven't found a better place to be, but with you this
close, I'm sure that won't be a problem."

She punched him in the gut with as much
force as a man three times her size. He would have
groaned or congratulated her on a straight-up sock,
if he could breathe. All he managed was staying
upright.

"Start answering my questions or this is
going to get ugly fast."

"You're supposed to be a hooker, remember?
You might try acting hookerly," he gasped.

Her eyes, tiny shimmering suns, darkened
like an eclipse as her brow knitted.

"Fine," he said, "but we can't talk in my room
until I turn on the music."

He motioned her ahead.

"You first."

A snort of laughter broke the tension. "You
always this suspicious?"

She returned it. Her nose wrinkled. "Usually,
far more cautious."

"I'm not surprised," he said as they fell in
step together.

At his bedroom door he paused and flashed
her a wicked smile, just because he knew it'd irk
her. "There are three cameras with audio in the
room."

"Sick bastard."

"Yep, Kobi sure is. So, make it look real, escort."

Her mouth fell open and he flung the door wide to escape her wrath.

Like a professional, she fell into the role. Eyelashes batting and hips swaying, rocking the shit out of his world, Sloan entered the room.

He locked the door and passed her, heading straight for the music, but she caught his arm.

"Not. So. Fast," she drew out in a voice made for perfume ads or dirty call lines. But her biting grip sent the real message. *Not so obvious, dumb ass.*

"We do have all night," he said, matching her languorous tone.

"Scotch. Straight."

Something about the way she demanded his drink of choice wormed its way under his skin and awful close to his heart. Then again, there wasn't much about the woman that didn't get under his skin...in the most terrifying way.

He poured one drink and slammed it back before flipping on the haunting violin and fixing another. When he turned she was there, probably making sure he hadn't spiked her drink. *Smart.* She drank it as he had, with a toss of her head, and then placed it on the nearest shelf.

Fingers fisted in his lapel, she pulled him down and held him a scant inch away. For a moment they breathed the same air. Though he longed to ravage her mouth, he savored her, mapping the features of her magnificent face—the natural arch of her brow, eyes large enough to lose himself inside. The round tip of her cute nose and the sharp V of her jaw. The dark cream of her skin he could never tire of tasting.

Hoarsely she pressed, "Why? And I swear, if you don't answer, you'll regret it."

Yep, balls. Big brass ones. She didn't care that he looked down a good foot into her eyes, that he doubled her in weight and tripled her breadth. Her fierce gaze told him as much.

"We want the same thing, where my father's concerned."

Her top lip trembled, almost imperceptibly. "I doubt it."

Baine smoothed his hands around her slight waist. "We can help each other."

"Are you going to hold him down while I disembowel him on the grasses of the Highveld and watch as the animals have at him? Are you going to listen to his screams? Smile when he begs for death?"

"No."

"That's what I thought."

He pulled her to him. "And neither are you."

"Am I not?"

"It wouldn't make you any better than he is."

She shook her head.

"You're better than him."

Her head continued to shake. "You don't know anything about me."

Lord, he longed to tell her how wrong she was. To tell her everything, but so much hinged on his mission's success. He couldn't blow it over feelings. Over history. So, he hedged.

"I know him. I know how to hurt him far worse than any blood sport you could dream up."

"I'm very creative," she taunted.

"So am I."

Baine unfastened the hook at her neck and tugged the zipper down to the base of her spine. Sloan stood motionless, except for her breathing and searching gaze. As he continued, he gauged her reaction for the slightest clue that she wanted him to stop. Her hold on him remained steadfast. The rise and fall of her chest increased when he hitched the hem of her dress an inch, then another, until the curve of her bottom peeked out.

Like before, he filled his hands with her ass, and then lifted her up to eye level. And he waited. Prayed and waited.

Finally, she moved.

All semblance of thought evaporated. Only the feel of her was left. The scent, the need also remained. Their noses bumped before her lips crushed his. Hot and wet. And again, her response was more ardent than he could have imagined.

The fabric of his jacket creaked as the seams strained under her intense grip. It bit into the back of his neck and he smiled as their lips battled.

"I won't drop you. Promise."

"A promise from a killer? I think I'll hold on."

Her words bit more than the fabric, and they shouldn't have. Even as she kissed her way down his throat, anger, frustration, and longing fueled his retort. "Are *you* not one too?"

She pushed out of his arms in a flash and he let her go, immediately hating the chasm he'd created between them. But he was a fool not to realize it'd been there all along. Craving something didn't make it so. It only emphasized the futility in wanting it so damn much.

Moisture gathered in her eyes, but nothing fell. Sloan's jaw clenched, but she didn't yell or flee. Only stood looking disheveled, and hurt, maybe.

Her voice cracked on the first words. "I am what your father made me."

Fuck her all the way to hell and back. Baine's eyes burned and his gut rocked unsteadily. He laughed to keep from crying. "I am what my father made me, but I am not what you..."

He stopped for a minute. Unable to breathe, he ripped the suffocating jacket off and tossed it on the bed. His fingers pinched the muscle of his waist. That grip was the only thing holding him together. The only thing keeping him from exploding with truth. Which would help neither of them, and put Sloan in further jeopardy.

His eyes closed on her confused expression and on the rage building inside. As much as she hated his father, he hated the man more, and himself a little for the familial blood flowing through his veins.

Her palm cupped his cheek. A sign of what? He didn't know and didn't open his eyes to find out. Sloan was a professional killer. She could rid him of his weapons and shoot him dead in less than a second. If she killed him, his fight would be over. His worries. His anger. He didn't want to die, but he chose to put his life in her hands. To trust her as he hoped she would trust him.

That was his last thought before she yanked the tie free from his neck. In a breath his torment morphed into lust. His eyes flew open to Sloan's slender hands working his holster over his shoulders. She placed it on the bed with his jacket and returned to unfasten the buttons of his shirt. That combined with the sheer look of erotic excitement smoldering in her gaze set him off. He grabbed her thighs and levered her off the floor. Unquestioning, her legs wrapped around his middle while she continued to work on the buttons. Her warm weight settled around him and his cock surged back to life, constricting against the front of his slacks and nudging the V of her legs.

With three ground-eating strides Baine reached the balcony doors and threw them open.

"Plan on tossing me over?" she asked with a smile.

He bit her shoulder and she moaned. The sound rolled down his spine, landing heavily in his balls.

"I plan on fucking you senseless, without an audience."

"So, logically, you head for the nearest terrace," she said, sarcasm thick in her voice.

Despite himself and every obstacle they faced, Baine laughed. "The cameras face away from the house. Guards won't start patrol for another hour. And everybody's at dinner.

"Besides," he added with a nod toward the potted shrubs, "there's foliage."

"Then you won't mind this?" Her eyes sparkled with mischief a second before she tore the remainder of his shirt apart. Tinny sounds *pinged* off the concrete and *tinged* off the glass.

"God, no," he breathed. "Not at all."

She peeled the fabric over his shoulders and bared his chest. Her palms frantically roamed his exposed skin.

"I like your impatience," he said as he pinned her body to the house with his own.

Sloan's fingers entwined in his hair then heaved his head toward hers. His fingers left the nestle of her neck, and when they were eye level, she drew him to her mouth. It was less of a kiss and more of a mauling. Their lips shoved together, wedged in between each other.

Baine seized her bottom lip, sucked it into his mouth, then drew it out between his teeth. Her hips bucked and she arched. The motion sent shock waves through his dick as she rocked on its tip.

Velvety cleavage spilled out of her dress as she pressed against him. And suddenly, he was as impatient as she.

He pushed the green dress over her hips. His reward was two overflowing handfuls of smooth skin. It molded in his palms as he squeezed. While one hand ran up her sleekly muscled thigh, the other sought warmer, wetter flesh. His fingers dipped into the valley of her silky cheeks and found a swath of lace. She groaned into his mouth as he followed the fabric around, pressing firmly over her most sensitive nooks and crannies. When he found the lace at her core soaked through, it was his turn to groan.

"You're so fit and goddamn ready. Tell me you're ready," he begged.

She nodded as she kissed a trail from the curve of his mouth to the slightly ticklish skin below his ear.

"No. I need to hear you say it."

She tracked her way back until the moonlight gleamed in her eyes. "I'm ready."

With both hands he ripped the delicate barrier from her body. The pads of his fingers slipped between her folds. She arched again and he attacked her exposed neck, nibbling and inhaling her unique scent. Verbena and scotch. He found her clit and gently stroked the slick ridge. It grew larger and firmer from his attention and her breathing became shallow.

Baine found her mouth and slowly inserted his tongue as he mimicked the same motion with his finger, burying it inside her. God was she ready. Hot and smooth and tight.

"I thought you'd be bigger," she panted.

Laughter shook him and she licked the bend of his smile. He abhorred leaving her core, but if

ever there was a time to prove your manhood, this
was it. A belt buckle, button, and zipper later,
gravity and his erection nearly did the job for him.
The broad head of his penis buffeted her slick
feminine opening.

With little thought or finesse, Baine pushed.
She keened and her hold tightened on his hair as
velvety heat surrounded the entire length of his
cock. Her swollen lips clasped its base, sending
bolts of ecstasy straight to his balls, numbing his
brain. He pulled completely out then thrust home
again, reaching the wall of her cervix.

Sloan dug her heels into his butt and began
rolling her hips in time with his pounding. Hell,
that's what it was. Unabashed. Uninhibited.
Animalistic blows between bodies. Never before had
he been this barbaric, this mindless with lust.
Unchecked for care or concern about his sheer size
compared to a woman's.

But she made no move to stop him. In fact,
she skewered his lats with her fingers, biting into
his skin through his damn shirt. She pulled him
into her as fiercely as he pushed. She bucked and
moaned.

"That's more like it," she breathed.

Her words spurred him on. He braced his feet
farther apart and supported Sloan's weight with his
arms on her thighs and his hands cupping her lush
ass. Repeatedly, he raised her high then eased her
down his shaft.

Baine could tell she was close. Her body was
one hundred percent wet and willing. She panted
and purred, and nearly strangled him with her tight
channel and her roving hands. But something
about the way her brows knitted tight told him her
mind was getting in the way. Her eyes had been
closed for too long.

"Sloan, open your eyes. Look at me. Look at us. How well we fit. How needy we are for this."

She bit her lower lip, but looked down where their bodies joined. Her breath rushed over his chest, sultry and warm. Their gazes met, her brow smooth. Red flushed her cheeks as she wrapped her hands around his neck and rolled her hips. Those dark creamy breasts spilled over the top of the dress again as she arched and vibrated in his arms. Her head turned toward the night sky.

"Oh yes," she shouted.

Her inner muscles shackled his dick deep inside her body. His balls weighed a thousand pounds before she squeezed the most painfully amazing orgasm from them. The pressure raced up his cock and exploded into her womb. His eyes closed against the exquisite ache. Every muscle in his body contracted as he came. Hard. So hard his knees buckled as the last of his ejaculation spilled into her.

Slowly he sank to the floor, supporting them both on his knees and the balls of his feet with the last vestiges of his strength. Sloan lay draped over him. Her head rested on his shoulder while her arms dangled over his back. The closeness surprised and sated him. He hadn't expected her to be so passionate, open, and engaged. Especially considering who she was, who his father was, and who she thought him to be.

A ruthless killer.

Maybe she wasn't far off the mark. Because, when he needed to be, he was exactly that.

He shoved the mental monopoly to the side and focused on the strumming heart, not inside, but against his chest. It hummed like the flaps of a hummingbird's wings. Baine turned his face toward hers and savored the warmth of her flushed cheek on his. His hand smoothed the ebony hair over her head then lifted the damp strands off her back. As though the grasslands were in tune with their consumed state, a gentle wind skipped across their skin and rustled errant wisps of her hair.

The breeze must have revived Sloan. She peeled herself off his chest then stared down at their still connected bodies. Her eyes widened as they met his gaze. Her jaw jetted out slightly.

Totally spent, Baine braced, the best he could, for the storm.

Chapter Sixteen

Sloan had never been a fool, until she fooled herself.

She hadn't lied to Ryan when he'd asked if she could kill Baine. She had and would never lie to him, but apparently she didn't hold the same scruples about lying to herself. *Mother fucker.* She could no more kill him than she could put a barrel in her mouth and pull the trigger. She could no more turn him away than she could refuse water after spending two days jogging across the desert. And both went against every scrap of intel, training, and intelligence she possessed.

He was the enemy. No matter how much sorrow his eyes held. His touch stirred the need within her soul. Despite years of longing for something more than hate to fill her heart, she found herself longing for the security Baine had once given her.

What had she done?

Betrayed her country. And worse, betrayed herself.

Disgust roiled in her belly. A cold sweat broke out on her upper lip. She pushed Baine's chest, but his arms held her firm. Again, she pressed.

"Please, don't do this," he begged.

The pleading in his voice squeezed the welling tears from her eyes. She fastened them shut against the torrent of emotion. Her head shook back and forth, as if her brain couldn't comprehend the sentiment.

In response to her jostling, he stood. The movement caused the length of him to shift inside her and she was struck with grief. Their bodies tangled together created the most beautiful thing she'd ever seen or experienced in her entire life. And they could never be.

"Stay," he whispered. His hand cupped her cheek, stilling her outburst. The pad of his thumb swiped at the wetness on her face.

"Let me go," she demanded.

"I can't. I should, but I can't."

The tenderness in his voice and actions unhinged her. It pushed her too near the edge of hope, and her cynical core revolted. Anger met and surpassed misery. The need to be free of his embrace vibrated through her body.

Sloan's fists beat his chest. She kicked and tried to lever herself off him, but Baine held tight. Her eyes flew open and she seared him with a hostile gaze. "Let me go," she demanded again.

"Sloan, please let me—"

She stopped him with an uppercut to the jaw.

He didn't stagger, but she'd stunned him enough to slip from his arms and place several feet between them.

"Damn," he said, shaking his head to clear the fuzz.

While she adjusted and zipped up the dress the best she could, Baine righted his pants and waggled his mandible. Sloan grabbed her shoes from where they'd fallen and stepped around him into the doorway.

His words stopped her.

"I heard the crash. There was no warning. No squeal of brakes. Not the small silence before impact. You know the one where everyone holds their breath, hoping not to hear the impending collision? It was just this awful screech of crunching metal. I knew without a doubt my mother was dead."

When she turned back toward him, Baine shifted and looked down at his hands as he scrubbed them together, obviously uncomfortable. He'd fastened one of the remaining buttons on his shirt, but the tails hung open. He looked younger and somehow smaller, maybe. No, not smaller. Hard for a man who stood four or five inches over six feet and weighed about two of her to appear small...but vulnerable, maybe? The adjective seemed out of place on such a man, and, Lord help her, endearing.

"All the reports said she had a massive stroke, causing her to lose control of the car, and she died from injuries sustained when she struck the building." He smiled and Sloan saw roots of deep sadness in the glint of his eyes and the wrinkle of his brow. "But," he continued, "a head-on impact doesn't leave a circular entrance wound on one side of a person's skull and blow the other side completely away."

"He ordered the hit," Sloan stated more than asked.

Baine's gaze met hers for the first time since she fled his arms. "She was leaving him. We both were. Not that I'd ever really been with him. I spent most of my youth at boarding schools in London, I had thought, because both my parents didn't give a shit about me. Turned out, it was my mother's way of protecting me."

A silent minute passed then Baine stepped forward and pinned her with his blazing no-nonsense gaze. "I will strip my father of everything he holds dear. His wealth. His business. His power. And his legacy. I'll make him go on living in the dirtiest back hole prison with nothing, hurting him more than any physical pain or death could."

He closed the gap between them. His scent polluted her air. Sloan bit her cheek against the piercingly decadent aroma. His warm fingers on her chin turned her face up to his.

"You can help me, Sloan, or you can get the hell out of here. Out of this house and this continent. Do you understand?"

Her fists balled at her sides.

"You want to hit me again, don't you?" he asked. The barest hint of a smile played over his swollen red lips.

Damn him and his smile because the expression infuriated and softened her at the same time. "I want to knock the smugness right off your face."

"That's my girl," he nodded.

"I'm no—"

"Figure of speech," he cut in, holding up a palm. "What's it going to be?"

She swatted his hand from her face. "There's no way in heaven or hell I'm leaving."

"I know," he responded with a purse of his lips. "So, you're going to help me?"

"Depends."

"On what?"

"Whether you have a solid plan or not."

He took a step back and raked a hand through his already rumpled hair and down his face. The scratch of his whiskers sounded like the ripping of Velcro. Her face and neck burned where the hair had buffed her skin.

Baine grabbed her hand and, once again, dragged her behind him. He towed her so often she felt like she owed him money for the service. Tired of being jerked around, Sloan put on the brakes.

He kept tugging, but placated her in soothing tones. "Can't really talk out here and I have some things to show you."

"Okay, but you know I can manage walking *all by myself.*" Her voice went soft and sweet on the last few words.

He freed her hand and continued walking. "Smart ass."

"You seem to bring out the best in me."

Inside the bathroom he closed and locked the door then made his way to a closet. Sloan hung close to the door ready to make her escape at any moment. The bathroom was large, but sharing the space with Baine made her twitch. Claustrophobia was a weakness she didn't possess, but perhaps people could develop it. She'd heard it could be triggered by a traumatic event. And fucking like animals with the enemy certainly qualified as traumatic, dramatic, and too amazing to wrap her mind around.

"Come." He urged her forward with an impatient hand when she didn't move. "Jesus, I'm not going to bite."

"You already did." She pointed to the faint outline of teeth on her shoulder.

"And you survived."

Would she? She wasn't so sure the events of the night wouldn't lead to the infection of a metaphorical organ she rarely used, and a slow painful death. Damn her heart.

She huffed out a breath, squared her shoulders, and walked into the closet. He'd had plenty of opportunity to kill her and he hadn't. So, for the time being she trusted him not to hurt her. But after she'd served her purpose, who knew?

Baine turned his back to her and shoved some pricey clothes down the rack. He removed a panel and depressed a series of numbers on the keypad on the wall.

"You need a better safe. Give me a minute and a half and the right tools. I'd have you cleaned out."

He slanted a look at her over his shoulder. "I was hoping you'd say that. See, to debilitate my father's empire we must access his safe. In it he holds bank records, his dealings with every buyer and seller, and a list of government leaders on his payroll—all in one book."

Out of the depths Baine extracted a folder and handed it to her. It held three pages—a sketched layout of the house, top and bottom floors, a layout of an office, and a photo of a safe, complete with make and model written in the margin.

"The plan is simple. Tomorrow after dinner, I distract Kobi and my father while you excuse yourself, break into the office, crack the safe, and swipe the book. We meet in your room after, confirm we have the intel to bring him down. Then we do just that."

"If you have all this information, why haven't you already gone after the book?"

Shit, if she'd had this intel, Devereaux Kendrick would've been worm food two days ago.

Baine shook his head. "Don't get all blustery on me. Devereaux never entered his safe or even revealed its location to me until the day I shipped out to D.C. While away I confirmed the make, model, and specs of the damn vault, and it's nearly impossible to get into without the code. Which I have been trying to find since I got back."

"That puppy's about as tight as they come." Sloan didn't even know if she could crack it, but she'd try her damnedest. "What about cameras?"

"He's a paranoid bastard. So none in the office, out of fear someone in security would use them to compromise him. Only has them in the hallway and they sweep. If you're as good as you think you are, they shouldn't be a problem."

"Fine. But you're suggesting we do this—just you and me," Sloan asked, trying to keep the *are you nuts* out of her tone.

His lips spread in a wide grin that made her swallow hard. "Pretty much."

The twinkle in his eye told Sloan he left out some details. Thinning the particulars in a situation like this was a good way to get their butts shot off. She shoved the folder at him. "What?"

He hiked a brow. "What?"

"Deception doesn't become you."

Quiet for a while, Baine seemed to mull that over then cleared his throat. "You're the first one to say so."

She shrugged one shoulder, but didn't let his comment derail her. "What aren't you telling me?"

His hands nestled into his pockets. "Too perceptive for my own good or am I really that transparent?"

"Who knows. Now give," she demanded.

"All I'll say is I have an ace up my sleeve."

That damn butler. It had to be. But she didn't reveal any hint she knew what he talked about. "Well, with twelve to two odds, we'll need all the help we can get."

His smile fell and the azure of his eyes darkened as his jaw strained. "We have to be on the same page. I know you're capable, but I don't want you killed cleaning up my mess."

"Devereaux Kendrick is a lot of peoples' mess. And don't *you* worry about *me*."

Baine set the folder on a mahogany dresser then placed his hand lightly on her shoulder. Eyes haunted and expression troubled, he said, "I can't stop myself from caring about you."

The best laid schemes
Of mice and men go often awry

Chapter Seventeen

Sloan fled as though he'd pulled a knife and promised to spill her guts onto her stilettos. He called out to her, his deep voice rumbling in the granite and stone confines as she fumbled with the lock and doorknob. She didn't look back. A backward glance would reveal the hurt in his eyes. She'd glimpsed a hint of it as she pulled away.

Her legs carried her quickly through the bedroom. Mindful of the cameras, she didn't run, but the urge reared its head when she passed the balcony where they'd taken each other so completely. The doors still hung open and her panties lay in a ruined heap on the masonry floor. Sloan's heart dropped into the pit of her stomach and bile sloshed up her throat, threatening to escape. Gaze locked on the door, she marched on, swallowing the sickness back.

She refused to slow until she exited the room and made it down the service stairs. Glancing left and right, Sloan surveyed her surroundings, not wanting to be caught off guard by anyone else this evening, but all was quiet, almost eerily so. Or maybe that was only her twisted perception.

Once inside her bedroom Sloan slid down the door. The heel of her palms ground into her forehead as she tried to block the last two hours from her mind. It didn't work. The quivers in her belly eased, but a soul-deep sadness eked in.

Sloan bit down hard against a sob. Her chest heaved with arid huffs. The metallic tang of blood tickled the end of her tongue, but she ignored it, caught in a hollow hell of her own making.

The last time she'd cried like this, she lay in a huddled   ball on the dirt floor of the servant's hut with twelve other children the day after she watched her parents' executions. At the time, she'd thought she would never stop crying. And now she felt the same way. Tears rained down her face, spattering on her chest. Her hand clamped over her mouth and her body shook with raw emotion. Then that stupid question began as a chant in her mind.

Why? Why? Why?

Logically she knew it was the single greatest waste of time to ask the inescapable query. *Why*, didn't matter. Nothing would be solved by answering the *why.* Any of them. Why didn't her parents take her to the States when unrest erupted in their backyard? Why hadn't someone stopped Kendrick before he ordered her town massacred? Why had she believed in hope, when all life proved on a daily basis was treachery and despair?

Then suddenly the question changed.

What?

What hurt worse, that she could no longer trust herself, or that Baine had stirred that damn useless notion of hope with his declaration? Whether his words were honest or not, the effect had been the same. And the emptiness that was her life seared her broken heart. She pressed her hand against the ache.

If she died tomorrow, she could think of only one person who'd cry for her. Only one. And even Ryan would buck up given a little time. They were partners and pals when on mission, watching each other's six and blabbing to pass the time, but in D.C. they led separate lives. He had friends, family, and plenty of late night entertainment. She had the job, her training, revenge, and nothing else. Sure, he'd invited her into his world time and again, but that son-of-a-bitch called *fear* always drew her back. Kept her huddled in her shell like a turtle. Fear of opening herself to anyone, depending on someone then losing them, having them reject her, or worse, be ripped away, imprisoned her.

Owen and Barbra Harris might shed a superficial tear or two. For the cameras. For those around them. Not for her. The couple held such promise for a terrorized little girl. With sweet smiles they'd welcomed her into their immaculate home. They'd given her a soft bed to sleep on, clean clothes to wear, and she got to shower daily. She still remembered Barbra's care and concern for her. The way she'd combed her hair each morning and night. How she'd tucked her in and left the bathroom light on so she wouldn't fear the dark. Her voice had been a soothing, even cadence when she read Sloan three books each night before bed.

The hope Baine's friendship had ignited burned bright in her chest in the Harris home, until two little lines on a stick snuffed it out. They were having a baby. Sloan rejoiced over the notion of becoming a big sister. She looked forward to protecting and nurturing a life, and even having someone look up to her. But instead of being included in the tiny miracle, they cast her aside. The little African orphan.

She should have been grateful. She had the best tutors and handmaids money could buy. By age eight she spoke half as many languages. She expanded that knowledge base when she attended the best boarding school in all of North America and then graduated from Yale. Most of Devereaux's child slaves were sold into the sex trade and became pawns for dirty old men. Sloan was never violated. She never longed for any material thing, but she'd have given them all up, she'd have slept on the dirt every night, for a hug or the soothing lull of a bedtime story.

Anger dissipated the sadness. There was only one reason Sloan's life was as desolate as the Arctic shelf. There was one reason she was often compared to that cold isolated place. And she was about to decimate him once and for all.

Resolve shot through her veins like adrenaline and she pushed off the floor. Baine's scent hung on her, a decadent ensemble too rich for her current state. That, plus the sticky between her legs and the overpriced undercover, and under-covered, outfit had Sloan restless for a shower and her sweats. More rational now, she didn't freak about some seminal fluid. She took the strongest pill on the market and had been given two rounds of anti-STD drugs before leaving the States, which for women in her line of work was standard operating procedure. Never knew what you'd be forced—or willing—to do to complete a mission. It wasn't a perk, but reality. And reality was a heartless bitch.

Chapter Eighteen

Sloan's finger tapped Morse code in super speed on the bedside table. Soon the incessant sound annoyed her so much she thought about her own digits. Instead she jumped up and paced the line again. Bathroom door to window and back. Determined to steer clear of Baine today, she'd holed up in the room for the last eight hours, ordering in breakfast and lunch trays. Now she had energy to burn. The thought of leaving the house and going to Kruger National Park for a run had lodged itself in her brain two hours earlier. It wasn't like she had work to do. She couldn't contact her people to confirm Baine's story. All she had was a beacon to call in the cavalry laying low several clicks north, and it wasn't time for that, yet.

The last drop of her patience hit the floor with a thud. She'd changed into running gear an hour ago. Who was she kidding? She needed out. An ounce of peace before the coming war. Sloan eased out the door and down the hall.

"Where are you going?" Lana asked, meeting Sloan head on at the rear foyer.

Sloan relaxed her stance and inclined her head toward the woman. "For a run," she said with a smile. "Have to keep at it or these curves will take over. Want to come?"

Lana wrinkled her nose. "I do yoga. Running is too high impact. It'll give you varicose veins, you know."

"No way?" Yeah, she'd take spider veins over a bullet in the butt any day.

"You need to keep an eye out for those," she said, shaking a finger at Sloan.

"I will."

Sloan ducked into the garage not wanting to chance the higher traffic areas of the house. All three doors were up and she bounced twice on the bottom step before pushing off on the balls of her feet at an easy jog.

She saw Kobi step out from behind a Hummer only a half-second before she plowed into him.

His arms came around her greedy and tight. "Whoa, where you runnin' off to so fast? We have some unfinished business."

She played stupid. "I'm so sorry. I didn't see you there. I was just headed out for a run."

"Well, there's been a change of plans." His uneven teeth practically waved at her from behind his spread lips.

God, she wanted to kick the crap out of him. It'd be easy. And fun. But she couldn't blow her cover over this slimebag. She'd have to find another way out because she'd kill him and hide his body before she'd sleep with him.

She'd slept with a man once for the job, and it wasn't Baine. As much as she wanted to say it'd been for the mission, the fact was she'd slept with Baine for herself and no one else. In the light of day she could admit it. The mental exhaustion of trying to deny it had gained her a restless night's sleep.

Kobi leaned in, flicking his tongue over her earlobe. Instead of sugarplums, images of his bloody nose and broken teeth danced in her head.

"I remember bringing you to my room the other night, but I don't remember your sweet, hot pussy."

Sloan tried not to vomit, or laugh in his face. "You were pretty wasted, but we had a hell of a time."

His hands bit into her arms as he turned her around and shoved her against the trunk of some extravagant car. "It's time I get a taste of what I missed."

Since most guys couldn't get it up when pissed, Sloan swallowed the rage threatening to erupt from her chest and changed tactics. "Maybe tonight. I'm still pretty sore from last night. Baine's cock is huge and he's a very energetic lover."

Kobi's voice dropped a notch from whiny and annoyed to comically deep. "You're a whore. You can't deny me."

His hands fumbled around the waistband of her athletic shorts. "Aww, I didn't mean to hurt your feelings."

Smack! His palm slapped across her face. Satisfaction and stinging fire diffused in Sloan's mind.

He hit pretty well *for a bitch,* but before she could tell him so, a roar quaked the garage. The impact of bodies followed and Kobi's grip was ripped from her. His body soared through the air and landed with a crash. His steroid-enhanced upper half smashed into the garage door tracks securely fastened into the participant wall while his chicken legs skid out into the sunlight.

Baine stood behind her, his chest heaving. "You wanna hit somebody? I'm right here. First shot's free. Fuck, I'll give you five. All I need is one."

Kobi scrambled off the concrete and swatted at the grit on the leg of his khakis. He snarled at the smudge of dirt marring his painted-on muscle tee. When his gaze bounced back and forth between her and Baine his face knotted tighter.

Sloan's protector stepped forward, absorbing all of Kobi's scowl. "Only chavs and pussies beat up women. So, come on. Prove yourself a man."

A growl rumbled from Kobi's throat as he rushed Baine, fists clenched to white knuckles. His right connected with Baine's chin. The crack of bone meeting bone split her ears. Baine's face kicked to the side, showing Sloan the barest hint of his scruffy jawline.

"One," Baine said.

The second hit landed in Baine's gut, hunching him, and called the slightest *umph* from his closed lips. Kobi laughed, sailing another gut punch as Baine straightened. Then another to the head.

Sloan's hand ached to join in and her lips twitched to demand a stop to this madness, but she stayed put. No good would come from interfering.

Before Kobi's knuckles had even left Baine's forehead on his final punch, Baine rammed an upper cut into Kobi's jaw. Teeth jarred teeth and his head flew backward. Kobi stumbled to the side then wobbled a few feet on jelly legs before meeting the grass in an unconscious heap.

"Ponce," Baine spat. Then he turned to Sloan. Fury squinted his bloody brow. "Are you all right?"

"I'm fine. He hits like a preschooler," she said, taking a deliberate step back and bumping into the car. "I didn't need you to rescue me."

Baine patted the cut above his jaw with the inside hem of his shirt. "I'd say primary schooler when he's really pissed."

For a moment the carved muscle of his abdomen, bronze of his smooth skin, and V of his happy trail mesmerized her. Sloan's mouth dried and her palms sweat. When he caught her staring, warmth flooded her cheeks.

"Did it ever occur to you," he whispered, "that *I* needed to rescue *you?*"

Sloan's breath paused. She didn't answer. Slowly she stepped around him and turned out into the day.

"Where are you going?"

"For a run."

He trailed her for the first three miles or so, hanging back about twenty yards. Not hiding and also not pushing. Baine maintained the comfortable distance and pace until Sloan stopped.

The mass of carved rock piqued her curiosity. In the shape of an angel, wings spread and face turned toward the sky, it stood beside the small dirt foot trail among the thigh-high grass. Sloan ran her finger over the rough tip of the wing.

Baine joined her in front of the statue. They shared a reverent moment in peace before she walked on.

When he sidled up to her, she asked, "Why is there a statue in the middle of the grassland?"

"A man from a local village was mauled here by a leopard nearly two years ago, just before I arrived at the compound. His family placed the statue as a memorial." He waited a beat. Then added, "This really isn't the safest place to run."

"It's safer than being locked in that house full of lions."

"You have a point."

Together they took off toward a tiny rock outcropping in the distance. No words were exchanged. They simply ran. But this time Baine stayed close, only a few feet back.

As each footfall brought them closer to the mass of bedrock surrounded by earth and springy brown grass, the hunk of rock seemingly grew. Sloan pushed her muscles, increasing the pace to a dead sprint. She wanted to leave it all behind for a minute. All the pain. All the fear. And just be.

The warm breeze kissed her cheeks and cooled the droplets of sweat beaded on her skin. Her quads simmered with the fire of her effort. A smile spread as she reached the base and leapt onto the cracked monolith. With careful footholds and finger placements, Sloan scaled the swell without hesitation. As if sensing her need for peace, Baine stayed below. At the top she stood only twenty feet from the ground, but in her heart she was one hundred feet tall. Nothing hurt and everything came into crystalline focus.

A large breeding herd of Cape buffalo dotted the horizon with black. The earth's light brunette hair stood on end as far as Sloan's eyes could see. A few fat-trunked baobab trees and rangy bushes speckled in between. Sloan kicked her chin up and stretched her fingers to the sky, letting the sun heat her skin. Life-giving breaths heaved in and out of her chest. Calm settled over her. She sank in pure gratitude and pulled her knees into her, hugging them lightly while she watched the simplicity of nature.

After what seemed like ten minutes, but was probably more like thirty or forty, Baine eased down behind her, putting his back to hers.

"Lean on me," he offered quietly.

She sank back into him and he pressed a fraction of his weight into her. Surprisingly so, the contact grounded her further in the serenity.

Together they breathed in the untainted air and watched the herd move lazily across the land. They'd been quiet for so long his voice made her heart jump.

"I used to play under a tree like that," he said, raising his arm to a stand of three scraggy, leafless barks, "with my best friend, for hours and hours at a time. The thing was base for tag, a fort, a castle, the bad guy we slew."

Sloan smiled even as tears fell hot on her cheeks.

He continued. "Every time I see a tree like that I smile and wonder where in the world she is? How she's doing? If I'll ever see her again?"

Baine coughed and his voice wavered. "It was nearly twenty-two years ago. That's stupid right, to think about someone from your youth when you've both probably changed so much?"

She pulled in a ragged breath. "No. Not if they made you happy. Not if the memory of them still does."

Sloan laid her hand over Baine's where it rested on the limestone next to her and weaved her finger between his. She longed to tell him that little girl was hidden somewhere inside her, still hoping to see his bright smile and kind eyes. But the wall around her heart wouldn't allow it.

"Yeah," he said in an almost wistful tone.

He held tight to her hand, caressing the side of her hand with his thumb.

As the sun kicked toward the horizon Baine stood and pulled her up. His lips brushed over her forehead quickly then he stepped back. "We need to get back. The big cats like to hunt at dusk. And tonight, so do we."

Chapter Nineteen

"What in the holy fuck happened to you?"
Devereaux bellowed.

Every head in the dining room snapped to attention, eyes a little wide as they searched out the cause of their master's displeasure. Sloan watched too as Baine walked to the table where she'd been seated for nearly ten minutes. The ease with which his hips rolled and his shoulders swaggered gave no hint of the beating he'd endured earlier. His face, however, told another story. It appeared camouflaged in lop-sided tactical paint. Black bruises underlined his left eye and peeked out from under his hair on the right side of his forehead. The cut, having scabbed over, blended with his eyebrow pretty well. The marks had darkened significantly since he left her at the door to her room nearly three hours earlier.

"I tripped and fell. Isn't that what Mom used to say?" Baine answered.

The razor's edge of his voice and the words they conveyed whittled at Sloan's heart some more. Whether consciously or not, Baine had been carving himself a home in her chest all afternoon. All her life, really. But today the whittling ramped up. He'd protected her, even when she didn't need protecting. Though he had the ability to tip her on her ear, like he'd done last night, he also had the ability to ground her. He gave her a sense of long sought peace and quieted her demons.

Now, if they could just vanquish their snarling creator. "Don't get smart with me, boy. Your mother earned every punishment she received."

Sloan's left hand clenched so tightly in her lap her close-cropped fingernails cut into her palm. She waited for Baine's to do the same, but none of his rage showed as he eased into the high back chair next to her. He dragged the napkin off the gold-rimmed plate and smoothed it onto his lap. Calm and collected. Yet, his gaze remained fixed on his father.

"As did I?" Baine asked the callous man.

"Someone had to rid you of your fanciful notions. Aren't you glad I did? Look at the fine man you've become." Devereaux leaned forward, squinted then added, "Minus the wreck of your face."

"Damn," Baine said with an *aw-shucks* snap of his fingers. "There goes my modeling career."

Devereaux scoffed. "Whoever beat you should have done a better job."

"You can give him some pointers. Learn from the best, they say," Baine shrugged.

"Enough," Devereaux said. The plates and silverware bounced in front of him as his fist gave his order exclamation. His gaze shot straight to Sloan. She did her best to breathe and smile. "Though I have an idea about what went on in my own home. Tell me now, what happened."

As they'd planned, Baine didn't acknowledge her, even with Devereaux's wicked gaze cursing her for living. He signaled Lawrence with a nod. "The usual." As the *more-than-a-butler* butler bowed and turned, giving her his signature wink, Baine smiled.

"I stepped on your dog's tail. So, I let him take a swing."

"Or three," Devereaux said. His head shook as he spoke. "I'm tired of playing referee to an adolescent game of ass chasing. We have far more important things to deal with."

"I realize that, Father, which is why Kobi and I are square. Aren't we?" Baine asked the man in question as he entered the room. "There are no hard feelings, are there?"

Kobi's gaze bounced back and forth between Baine, Sloan, and Devereaux, ignoring the other five people in the room. Finally his roving eyes settled on his boss. The pitiful man's jaw puffed like it'd been stuffed with cotton. It muffled his words, but no more so than his drinking had the previous night.

"No, sir. We're just ready to make this deal happen for you, Mr. Kendrick. And I want to say how sorry I am for the other night. I don't know what got into me, but I can guarantee it won't happen again. I'm about business."

As Kobi nuzzled up to Devereaux's plump butt cheeks, Baine slipped his hand up her thigh, straight to her core, where he slipped his finger into the lace of her panties. The boldness and shock of his action, especially since they'd talked about being hands off as to not draw attention to her or get anything started with Kobi, released the first wave of adrenaline from the gates. It galloped like a 'roided gelding from her crotch and plowed smack into her heart, causing it to ripple from the impact.

Just as quickly, his hand retreated to the scotch glass without the least wiggle on her clit or nod of acknowledgement. Curiosity and frustration rolled through her until she shifted in her seat and felt it. Something was in the crotch of her panties. Small and thin, but definitely a foreign object.

Man, she'd passed information a whole number of ways, but this one took the cake.

The men had lapsed into serious discussion about a shipment of weapons due to drop soon. Sloan would kill to know the when, where, what, and how of the deal. It sounded huge, and if a shipment like that succeeded, a whole lot of people would suffer. But this was her cue to move. She'd have to trust Baine to relay the details or find them out for herself when she got the damn black book.

Anticipation tickled her fingers as she rose from the table. Talk about wish fulfillment. She was about to accomplish a goal she'd worked toward for twenty-plus years.

"Can I help you, miss?" Lawrence asked. His formidable bulk towered over her.

"Sure. Point me in the direction of the nearest ladies room," she said.

"Through the double doors, down the corridor, first door on the left," he said with a smile. "Hurry back."

"Absolutely," she nodded.

Down the hallway Sloan had to yank the reins in on herself a few times like a jockey holding back his eager horse. Her legs itched to run and her heart beat fast enough to supply oxygenated blood for the action. *Poom. Poom. Poom. Poom.*

She strolled into the bathroom, taking note of the cameras positioned at each end of the course with a casual glance. On the other side of the door Sloan kicked off her heels and stuffed them behind a potted plant. She removed the knife from her purse frame and slid it into the leather already strapped to her thigh then fished a tiny piece of paper out of her underpants.

A twelve-digit code spoiled the otherwise blank white parchment. Sloan vibrated with excitement. It started deep in her chest and radiated out to her fingertips. *How in the world had he gotten the code?* With zero time to ponder the question, she memorized the series, ripped it into bits, and washed it down the sink. She scooted the last piece down the drain then continued preparing.

Out of the clutch's belly she pulled a small hook pick and shoved it into the front of her dress. She abandoned the electronic panel she would have used to crack the safe. The thing was too big to fit in her cleavage and since she had the code, she'd just as soon have her hands free to move. The radio jammer came last. She flipped it on, just in case things went sideways, secured it inside the bag, and shoved it out of sight with her shoes. All the while she'd been counting the camera sweeping sequence in her head on ten second intervals. So far she'd only lapsed two rounds.

At *seven* she placed her ear on the door, straining to hear any sounds beyond. *Nine.* Sloan held her breath and cracked the door, scanning the parts she could see. All clear. On *ten* she bolted midway up the corridor. Crossed to Devereaux's door. *One. Two. Three.* After a well-placed pick the lock gave and Sloan swooped into the office, closing the door and locking it behind her.

After hours of studying the layout in her mind she moved surely through the room. Passing between two wingback chairs and a massive antique desk, she reached the exquisite painting at the end of the room. A woman with a flowing golden mane leaned her palms on a railing. The elegant gown and ethereal setting of lush green trees and bright red flowers did nothing to hide the sadness in her tight smile and dull eyes. She assumed the woman was Baine's late mother, Elizabeth McCord.

Sloan tested the frame, running a hand along the edges. With a firm tug the right side swung wide. The safe lay behind it nestled into the wall. The proverbial pot-o-gold. It didn't glitter. The gunmetal-grey soaked up the light, but the computerized keypad and screen sure sparkled. Her fingers glided over the keys, striking off the memorized numbers in a steady rhythm.

She would have sworn the world stopped spinning for a suspended moment in time as the screen went black while analyzing the data. Her entire body stilled in a second of wild certainty.

The screen flashed the words *Incorrect Passcode.*

Chapter Twenty

"If you needed a patsy, Kobi would've been ideal. But I guess you found a better one. Taking down a Branch Agent will make Papa proud and give you a fall guy, or girl, as the case may be.

"I can't believe I trusted you. You have more secrets than the CIA. You're obviously no lawyer. I mean, what lawyer can fight like a pro, shoot like a trained sniper, and kill without remorse," Sloan bit.

Baine eased the bathroom door closed and raised his hand in surrender. "I have never and will never betray you."

He took a hesitant step forward. Sloan's hand tightened on the custom 9mm she'd found in his safe. The twenty-eight-round clip the monster held would be enough to take out everyone in the house. Wisely, Baine stopped advancing and even stepped back where he'd been.

"I couldn't stop a herd of women from leaving the dining room on their sacred bathroom ritual without being suspect. Since you had the code I expected you'd have already retrieved the book and been back in the bathroom. I figured you'd have been rushed to get back to rights, but I knew you'd manage.

"Now, put the bloody gun down and let's authenticate the book, so we can get changed and move before Devereaux notices it's missing."

She may as well have handed him the gun and let him drill one shot in the center of her chest. His deception hit her square between the eyes like a sledgehammer's blow. The choice to trust Baine ripped her psyche to shreds. The choice to love Baine decimated her heart like the coastal lands in a typhoon's path. Though really, her feelings for him hadn't been a choice, but a reaction she'd been helpless to stop, like the winds and roaring waters.

"It was always about the book for you, wasn't it?" Sloan didn't know why she asked. She didn't expect anything from him but death. Whether slow and painful or fast and unnoticed.

His eyes narrowed and his fists clenched. "Damn it, Sloan. It is only about the book for me as much at it is for you. If we don't take this book from my father, he'll use it to kill more people and claim more territories."

"You only want to take his place. That's why you made certain I wasn't in the room when you discussed the next shipment. It's why you gave me the wrong code." Her voice pitched as she spoke and she was helpless to hold back the volume or her cursed tears.

Baine's eyes widened. "What do you mean, *wrong code*?" He stepped forward then, seemingly oblivious to the weapon she had trained on his heart. "Did you get the book?"

"No," she hollered, "because I trusted you. I left my tools and you sent those whores to the bathroom so I wouldn't have time to get it."

His chest rose and fell rapidly, but he didn't attack. Baine stood there looking at her, his jaw slack like he didn't know what to say. His lips closed and his features softened.

Baine dropped to his knee before her. His brilliant blue gaze never left her face as he grabbed his holstered pistols between two fingers and laid them at her feet. "Sia Kolat Johnson, first-born daughter of Sylva Kolat and Daniel Johnson, first friend and only love of mine...I have never, and will never, betray you."

Sloan hadn't heard her given name since the day her parents were taken from her. In the protection of her father's arms, he hid her face from the unmentionable things the soldiers did to her mother. But he couldn't block her mother's screams. So, rocking Sloan gently against his chest, her dad whispered the mantra over and again: "Sia Kolat Johnson, you are loved. You are loved. You are loved."

The weight of the memory and the weight of Baine's words brought her to her knees. The pistol slid from her hand. "You knew. This whole time, you knew," she marveled, her voice as thin as a reed.

Baine collected her in his arms and held tight. His warmth encompassed her and his lips brushed her forehead and hair.

"When we met as children, I had no idea what my father did. I knew what he did to me and my mother, but I had no clue about the atrocities he'd committed. I wish I had known. I wish I'd cared to know where his wealth came from, but I was away at school. I only saw him on holidays and then I spent my time avoiding him.

"I fantasized later about what I would have done, if I'd known what he did to your family. I was only eight and couldn't have done anything to help you. Hell, I couldn't even help myself when he got angry. And your parents were already dead, but if I could have saved you, I would have."

His hands smoothed over her arms and back as he continued, the words tumbling from his lips.

They hurt and soothed at the same time. Emotions whirled. Tears crashed onto her cheek.

"It wasn't until college that I began digging. I questioned my mom and she always cautioned me to let it go, that it wasn't safe. But I pushed relentlessly. Finally, she told me out of fear I would do something to catch my father's notice.

"There were no words to describe the hate I had for the blood flowing through my veins.

"My mother hated my father and planned to leave only a year after they were married. She found out she was pregnant shortly after, but kept it a secret. Devereaux Kendrick has many on his payroll. The doctor she saw happened to be one of them. My father told her if she attempted to keep any other secrets from him, he would cut the baby from her belly, and if she tried to leave him, he would kill everyone she'd ever held dear. So, she stayed. I still can't agree with her actions, but I wasn't in her shoes either.

Baine's chest heaved against her cheek.

"I demanded we find proof and go to the government. She was terrified of my father, of what he'd do to us for betraying him. But she agreed. And then he killed her."

Sloan twisted in Baine's arms and wrapped her own around his torso. She hugged him to her, longing to give him some of the comfort he gave. There were still so many things she didn't understand about Baine Kendrick. So many questions to be answered. Sloan's gut told her this man was good, despite everything he'd been through, despite the tainted blood that gave him life. In spite of every shred of intel she had on him. And her heart agreed completely. Her head, for once, gave itself over to the other ruling governs of her body.

Baine's knuckle tipped her chin up and she drank in his face. The harshness of this formidable man softened and Sloan caught not a glimpse of the caring boy she'd once known, but of the loving man he'd become. His eyes shimmered like a clear lake with unshed tears. The constant rigidity of his jaw hung slack as he stared at her with an expression close to...wonder, maybe.

Sloan closed the small distance between them and fused her mouth to his. Baine gave himself completely, letting her own him. Her lips pushed against his, molding their pliant silk to her own. Slowly, she nibbled his bottom lip and eased her tongue inside his mouth. Warmth enveloped her seeking tongue. Swiping and tasting, over and over she caressed him while his strong arms held her to him.

His words danced in her head. Perfect sentiments in an imperfect world. Her heart floated on hope she'd banished long ago. For if this man could love her, if he could be a shadow of the compassionate kid she'd known, then she would do anything to help him remove his father from power and even more to try and keep him in her life. Self-protection and caution be damned.

Cool air drifted over Sloan's wet lips as Baine pulled back, bracing both strong palms against her shoulders. His eyes were fiery blue and more intense than she'd ever seen, and for this man, this force of nature, that was saying something.

"I planted a camera in his office before I left for D.C. The code I gave you was the code he used yesterday. He must have rolling codes, which means he has a device feeding him the sequence. We have to find it. We have to find the code and get that damn book."

Baine's right hand moved to cradle the nape of her neck. He smothered kisses over her cheek and the bridge of her nose.

"We will take everything from my father for what he did to your family, my mother, and the thousands of others he's hurt. Your attempt on the safe will show on his report. But remember," he cupped her face and held it, making laser-straight eye contact. "You're mine. You belong to me and I belong to you. Above all, I will protect you."

Chapter Twenty-one

"They're spending a fuck load of time in that goddamned bathroom," Kobi spat.

The lion didn't respond. Only crouched on his bedroom floor, fanged grin gleaming as always. He'd like to shoot and stuff the creature again for its mocking expression.

Kobi stalked back to the computer screen, irritated with himself for bitching at a cured corpse, instead of marching down to Baine's room and making a fresh pair. He plopped down in the computer chair. His eyes crossed and blurred as he struggled to bring the black and white footage into focus.

The vodka he'd iced an hour ago tasted like water as he pounded it down his dry throat. He stunk too. Not just of metaphorical desperation— the whiff of B.O. he'd gotten with the liquor was enough to cause himself whiplash.

"Fuck it. Nothin' to see anyhow."

When he stood the chair scraped the floor, echoing a vile screech throughout the room. With a solid kick the polished wood skipped twice then slammed down. A satisfied grin spread his lips, until he turned back to close the laptop screen.

Kobi's jaw might have hit the keyboard for the shock of the scene unfolding before him.

Baine Kendrick, rough and tumble ladies' man, carried the hooker to the bed and laid her down as if she were a piece of fuckin' china, not a high dollar piece of ass. He eased her shoes off and instead of spreading her legs wide and ramming his dick home, kissed and caressed his way up her body.

Who the hell was this guy, Don Juan DeMarco? And what made him so special? To a whore? To the boss? Why him? Why not me?

Rage left simmering for far too long bubbled over. Kobi hefted the computer in his hand and hurled it across the room. It hit the floor with an anticlimactic thud, which only heightened his anger. On his way to the shower, Kobi planted a boot through the shattered screen.

"Just you wait, asshole. Just you fucking wait and see."

Chapter Twenty-two

Sloan had never given much thought to the concept of love, having had it in her life only a short while. It seemed more a dream than a feeling or memory. Over the years she'd clung to those precious moments to save the fleeting whips from the erosion of time. Still, practical things consumed her mind. First, life's essentials. Food. Water. Shelter. Then later, education. Revenge.

Love wasn't her salvation. Watching, eyes wide, as it had been ripped away, love morphed into her own broiling hell. The comforting punishment of physical training soothed her body, not gentle hands. Cold gunmetal in her palm calmed her nerves, not pillow talk. Logistics and tactics lulled her to sleep at night, not the arms of a lover.

But, once again the topography of her world had changed in a heartbeat. The beliefs that had gotten her through the void, independence and distance, sailed out the window in a hale gust of Baine's declaration.

"The cameras," Sloan whispered. Not that she believed for one moment her weary warrior had forgotten them, but perhaps he wasn't thinking about all of the possible ramifications.

Baine nibbled her ear and kissed the line of her jaw until his gaze evened with hers. His smile warmed her belly. In a rough, quiet voice, he said,

"I disconnected the audio. But fuck Kobi. Sloan, I can't properly make love to you on a bathroom floor, and that's what I need to do. Right now. If he wants to watch, let him."

His lips brushed hers. Only a graze, before his bristly cheek lay over her heart where the low-cut dress dipped, revealing loads of cleavage and yards of skin. He stilled, for a moment, except for his hands, which eased up the coverlet and smoothed over her palms. Their fingers interlocked, but the pressure didn't pin her to the bed. This wasn't a show of dominance, but of affection.

He connected them. Not in sex, but in love.

The perfection of his gesture formed a lump in her throat.

Baine raised his head, his smile gone. His expression, one she'd never seen, sent bursts of love shooting from her heart like a damn meteor shower.

"I'm about to love you so purely and completely, Kobi's eyes will burn and all your unanswered questions won't matter. You'll know the type of man I truly am, not by the intel or the assassinations, but by the way I love you."

Her heart expanded like a red giant, consuming the love Baine offered.

He buried his face in her palms, his breaths drifting through her fingers. Sloan didn't have the slightest clue how to compress into words the whitewater of emotions coursing through her body. So, she hugged his face with her hands, trying to reciprocate some of his tenderness. The bristles of his chin prickled as he placed his hands over hers and squeezed.

Full lips kissed away the tingle. Baine worked his way down the sensitive skin of one arm, sending little comets sparking through her veins.

She giggled and threw her free hand over her mouth to quiet the noise.

"Pure magic. That sound. Good Lord," he mumbled, still mapping the landscape of her surprisingly ticklish bicep, and coaxing another laugh from her throat.

"Ah, now I know your secret," he whispered.

"I have no secrets from you because apparently, you see right through me."

Baine shook his head while nipping her collarbone. "No, love. But give me time and I'll learn your many expressions."

God help her. She couldn't see past this day, this moment, this man, but the thought of him wanting her on the other side of this mess they waded in sent a thrill spinning through her belly and ramming headlong into her heart.

With Baine's reverent touch seducing her skin and his gaze adoring her form, she felt love as she never had before.

She ached with it.

Baine's fingers smoothed over her brow. "I've seen your sorrow, even though you try your damnedest to mask it. I saw wonderment out on the Highveld today," he stroked her cheek while he continued, "and when Kobi hit the ground, smug satisfaction. I'll admit, it made my chest puff out."

"It's a damn fine chest," she admitted. Just the thought drew her hands to it, the steely bulk immovable under her sure fondling. His tiny nipples beaded beneath his shirt as she played. The buttons came next. One after another Sloan worked his torso free and was rewarded with a view of his tanned, taut skin and carved muscle. She even glimpsed the swart hair that dusted the perfect V of his abs below his belly button and disappeared at the top of his pants.

"Look hungry all you want. I won't rush this."

Sloan rubbed her legs together in glorious frustration.

The corner of his mouth formed a crescent. "Patience, love."

"I thought you liked my impatience." Her hand fell over the edge of his oblique and rushed toward his belt buckle, eager to release his cock and get him inside her, to ease the angst building between her legs.

Baine took her hand in his and placed it over the hard column of his penis, his pants creating an irritating barrier. "I more than like it, but I'm doing my best to love you right." He dragged her hand away, collected her other in his grasp and raised them over her head, holding them to the bed as he loomed over her. "Now, where was I?"

His feather-light touch grazed her jaw and she arched into him. "I've figured out mad. Most people clench their teeth, but when you're angry, you poke out your jaw and cock your head ever so slightly. Then your eyes turn molten. I swear, they could burn me alive, if I got too close."

He kissed her lids before moving to the bridge of her nose and working his way over her lips and down the centerline of her neck. "I should fear that look. Any wise man would. It just makes me hard.

"In the foyer by the pool, when you turned it on me the first time, it took everything I had not to take you right there, not to wrap your legs around me, move that strip of cloth covering your exquisite ass and thrust into your pussy.

"And yesterday there was no holding back. No stopping myself when you came to me. I couldn't slow down. Couldn't take my time. My control broke and I had to have you."

A ragged breath escaped Sloan's lips. Her belly shivered as his words sparked vivid pictures of the scene he described and fanned the flame burning deep in her core. "I didn't mind."

His brows drew together. "My sore jaw would say otherwise."

"I... It's always been black and white for me. Good guys. Bad guys. And I've always been on the right side of the line. You were grey. Still are, no matter what my gut tells me...or the way you treat me. My mind just..."

Baine's grip tightened on her hands and he attacked her mouth. His lips slid over hers. He tugged her lips through his and rasped her with his teeth. Slick warmth coated her mouth and her sex. She groaned, Baine's mouth swallowing the sound as he pillaged.

Too soon he eased back, breathing hard, eyes storm-dark and filled with wanting. His head hung between his massive shoulders. The white button-down gaped at the top revealing the contour on his sturdy back. After one long exhale, Baine lifted his head and turned those amazing blues on her.

"In your situation I wouldn't trust me either. I won't put you in danger just to ease your mind about me. There are things you can't know. But know this...just like you, I learned that line at a young age, and just like you, I have always been and will always be on the right side of it."

That was all she needed for the last vestiges of doubt to evaporate. Stupid or not. Reckless or not. She believed him.

With every fiber of her shattered heart, she loved him.

"I trust you," she said.

Apparently, that was all he'd needed. Like a veil being lifted, the hint of concern at his brow and the tightness in his jaw vanished. He appeared younger and hungrier, if that was possible.

His head lowered to the swell of her breast. He cupped one with his free hand and pressed, the crest of it brimming the strapless top of the shimmering black gown. Hot, languid kisses smattered her chest. One rough yank bared her nipples to the pleasure of his tongue. The receptive light brown skin of her areola flushed a rosy hue as Baine dragged each in turn through his white teeth then flicked her pebbled tips with wet strokes, coaxing them to stiff peaks.

Sloan's back arched, urging his ministrations. She longed to spread her legs for him, to wrap herself around him and never let go, but his weight held her in place. Ever the agile soldier, she braced her back on the bed and thrust her hips forward, using her body as a weapon to get what she needed.

Even through slacks and the fabric of her dress, the broad head of his penis gave an electric shock on contact that made her eyes roll back in utter bliss. She rolled and rocked his hard length against her swelling lips and the hood of her clit.

A primal groan rumbled in Baine's throat. His hand left her breasts and clamped onto her ass, pumping her into him with greater force than she could manage on her own. Back and forth, he rolled his hips in rhythmic time, his shaft strumming her toward the edge. Her heart galloped over it as her breaths came in shallow pants until it stopped altogether, relishing the free-fall of orgasm.

When she finally exhaled, Baine eased back. "Sweet Jesus, you almost made me shoot off in my pants. Like a damn teenager. Your breathing...gets me. But maybe that'll hold you for a minute and you'll quit rushin' me."

Sloan couldn't stop her smile, his admissions and playful side getting the best of her.

"I was about to release your hands, but that look says you can't be trusted."

She winked. "Maybe I can. Maybe I can't. No risk, no reward."

He winked in return and a slight dimple formed at the corner of his crooked smile. "I'll just have to keep you busy."

He released her hands and straddled her body, slowly drawing down the zipper along her side then working the garment off.

Moving to stand at her feet, Baine shook his head. "A masterpiece such as I've never seen," he whispered.

The adoration in his expression made her melted-marshmallow gooey on the inside. She was no marshmallow, but something about this man transformed her.

With agile hands, Baine stripped his rumpled shirt, toed his shoes off, then shucked his pants and black boxer briefs in one swift motion. What a wonder to behold. She wasn't complaining, since she'd been cheated the other night by their impatience. The man who stood before her was a beast, in the most beautiful interpretation of the word. Thick muscles lay beneath his hulking frame. There was nothing angular about him, every surface curved by his cursed DNA and hard work.

His hands led the way, burning a trail up her legs. He held her thighs and spread them, gazing unabashedly at her femininity. That jaw, always so tight, hung loose, and he pulled his lower lip into his mouth, scraping it with his teeth. The bed dipped under his weight as he eased onto the bed, nudging her legs farther apart with his shoulders.

Baine's gaze held hers for a moment before his head dipped and his velvety tongue met her slick, smooth labia. His scruff abraded her puckered rim while he explored her lips, delving in, skipping across, lapping up. When he sucked her clitoris into his mouth Sloan gripped the sheets, looking for something to hold her on the bed while the tumult of sensations threatened to bow her off it.

He latched onto her clit, laving it with his tongue while he eased a finger, no, two into her wetness. Baine massaged her deep, his fingers curling and flexing. Like a damn dog, she panted as the world shrank even further. Only the sensations left. Only the ecstasy. When he levered her butt with his other hand, gaining better access, Sloan rocked her hips, shamelessly fucking his face. Baine groaned in response. His grip moved to her hips and his fingers bit into her skin as he pulled her hips to his mouth with punishing strength. When one of his fingers strummed across her anus, she screamed her release into the air.

His tongue rode out each spasm, lapping at her tender flesh and wringing every drop of pleasure she had to give. Utterly spent, her body went limp, except for her chest, which heaved in oxygen.

Contentment washed over her in a wave as Baine's arm encircled her middle and tucked her protectively into the lee of his chest. Though his still-hardened penis nestled against her cheeks, he gave her time to recover, brushing his fingers through her hair.

When his fingers migrated to her breasts, desire roared to life inside her belly as though it had never been appeased. Sloan ground her ass over his erection.

"Not gonna complain about my little fingers again?"

"Never," she breathed.

A laugh shook Baine's body as well as the entire bed. "Good."

"But," she added, "I am interested in your longer and much thicker appendage."

The words had hardly left Sloan's mouth before she was turned onto her belly. Baine's arm secured across her chest and his hand gripped her shoulder while the other stretched up her arm and entwined her fingers. The wide head of his dick slid easily between her closed legs in the mixture of saliva and her juices they'd created. It buffeted her opening, but didn't enter quickly.

Gradually, inch by provoking inch, he pressed into her. The heat of his heavy thighs finally rested on her bottom as his cock pierced her core. He stilled and touched his forehead to the side of her head. "You do the damnedest things to my control."

The compliment of his meaning made every feminine cell in her body sing. "I'd be right there with you, if you're going to come like a minute man."

He groaned. "Oh, you will come with me."

Yes, she would.

Baine hadn't moved since he'd burrowed into her pussy. Still her core pulsed, milking his shaft, revving her engine that threatened to roar over the finish line before the race had gotten good and started. Hell, one glance over her shoulder at his muscles all drawn tight in pleasure spiked her needle hard.

His forearm tightened around her, anchoring her for a slow withdrawal then his driving thrust. Sloan met the impact with an arching lunge of her own. Slapping flesh echoed in the large room. It mingled with lust-labored breaths. A cry of rapture.

The pace rose. Each erratic heartbeat brought another shockwave of pleasure as Baine's cock tantalized her G spot. Each forceful impetus scraped her already sensitive nipples and engorged clit against the harshly woven bedding.

Sloan clamped down on Baine's hand and rocked her hips. "Don't stop. Oh God, don't stop."

He nipped her ear. "Only when you make me."

"Never."

"Fu...cking works for me."

The growling groan of his voice sent Sloan reeling. Her wet walls convulsed, frantically hugging and releasing Baine's thick erection. A long, strangled moan signaled her nearing orgasm.

When the rolling pleasure ebbed, Baine pulled back and rolled her to face him. "I want to see you," he said before spreading and entering her once again. He dropped to his elbows, snuggling their sweat steamed chests together, and his hands smoothed through her hair, nestling against her temples. After three glorious rocks inside her body his jaw tightened. His eyes closed and his head rolled back. Muscles danced under his skin as his entire body tensed and curved.

He didn't make a sound, but Sloan saw the triumph in his face a second before he collapsed atop her.

The best laid schemes
Of mice and men go often awry.
And leave us nothing but grief and pain.

Chapter Twenty-three

There was no better gift in the world than the one Sloan had just given him. Power and money meant nothing. Her trust, her heart—they enriched him. Filled the blistered, gaping wounds he hadn't even realized he had. Made him more than his father's son. A genetic defect. More than a trained killer.

Baine rolled off Sloan. Abhorred as he was to leave her tight body, he didn't want to kill her with his bulk. Hell, after two minutes without oxygen a person could end up with brain damage, and it'd been about that since the most intense orgasm of his life had nearly taken his. The errant shooting star still skewed his vision as he cracked a lid to watch Sloan's reaction when he pulled her against his chest and pillowed her head on his shoulder.

Her almond eyes widened and her hands fumbled from her hair to her heart where they clung together. Then, in a flash, the uncertainty vanished. If he hadn't been looking he'd have missed it altogether. She snuggled into him and entwined her legs with his. Possessiveness and Neanderthal delight swelled his testicles.

He flipped the overhead light off then hugged her body close. Another thing she'd given him. Sure, he'd had her in the carnal sense before. But tonight, she'd surrendered her body to him, to pleasure and love with no doubts, restrictions, or qualifications.

In turn he'd given his as he'd never relinquished it before.

And now that they were bound to each other, he had to protect her gifts. Trust. Heart. Body. Easier thought than done in the precarious situation they could both easily drown in.

Baine smoothed a hand over Sloan's tousled hair, down her taut back and muscular thigh. He'd always been a man for soft curves and a little extra cushion, but his raging hormones and the prize in his arms had swiveled his head. Both of them. The woman was no slouch. Just like his, her body was a precision instrument, crafted to go where no one else could, do what few could, and kill with ease. A double win for Baine. With her, he could lose control. Something he'd never allowed himself. When lust flipped the switch on his brain, he didn't fear breaking her. Plus, she could handle herself in life and death situations with wicked grace. Which is exactly where the fuck they were.

"I should go. You don't seem like the type to let the ladies sleep over, and we don't want anyone to think this is anything special. Not that it is. Or. Not that you think—"

"You are very special." He wagged a finger between them. "This is very special. And on occasion the ladies have stayed over."

She drew away from him ever so slightly—like his words had hurt her. He couldn't help but smile. "Easy there. They only stayed over because they were too doped to leave. And before you ask, no, I didn't take advantage of them." Laughter shook him, not for the first time in her presence. Yet another thing, an amazing thing, she did to him.

"What?" she asked, jabbing a finger into his side for emphasis.

"We're more alike than you realize, love. That stunt you pulled with Kobi? It's my trick for dealing with Devereaux's whores." His laughter moved down deep in his belly. "Except, I don't trash the room or mess with their junk."

He got a light fist for that one.

"You watched," she squealed in a whisper. "Why am I at all surprised?"

Baine caught her hand in his and drew it to his chest. "Hey, turnabout is fair play. Kobi bugged my room first and you stole my moves. Had to hold it over your head because you may have executed it better than me.

"Now get comfortable. You're not going anywhere."

Before long her breathing evened as she drifted off, her delicate fingers wrapped around his hand. After her limbs sagged, he waited ten minutes then carefully eased from the bed and enveloped her in the blanket from the foot of the bed. He retrieved the holster he'd hung on the desk chair earlier and left one pistol on the nightstand for Sloan. The other he kept lightly in his grasp.

In the inky darkness Baine made his way back to the bathroom, his balls swinging freely. He scooped up the monster of a gun his grandfather, Desmond McCord, had commissioned for him after his mother's murder. Too damn bad the old man hadn't lived to see its completion. The torment of his only child's murder had ushered him into an early grave, taking the best example he'd had of a gentleman, leaving Baine without any family.

But he wasn't alone. Not like Sloan had been for all these years.

He had his surrogate family. Easton Wells, his grandfather's butler and Baine's lawlessly adopted father, kept him towing the line. When he stumbled on the line he could always count on his sister, Magdalena, Easton's daughter, to pick him back up, kiss his cheek, and shove him on. And when he crossed it he could always count on Law to kick his arse straight.

It made the corner of his mouth knot, thinking about everyone in the manor calling his rough-and-tumble friend by his given name, Lawrence, something he hated almost as much as Baine hated being called Kendrick. Well, maybe not that much. Still, they had no way of knowing they demanded tea and tarts from a man who could kill them with one bare hand while never jostling the spread on his tray. The sly son of a bitch wasn't blood. Thank God for that. He was, however, the only thing that had kept him from an all-out rampage in the fallout of learning of his father's treachery.

Better than family, Law was a colleague, housemate, and friend. Fate brought them together in college. Two hungry dogs competing for the top rank at Cambridge. Too damn bad they got beat out by a pompous-ass tenth-generation law grad.

Baine shoved those thoughts aside as he stepped inside the closet that he'd grown to think of as the Batcave, only not nearly as cool. No, he couldn't break into Devereaux's office. The man was at this very moment sipping brandy in his study, probably pondering the massiveness of his power and fortune as was his evening ritual. He could, however, break into his computer.

In less than ten minutes Baine had changed the log alert's time of failed attempt to properly frame Kobi, seeing as he and Kobi were the most

likely suspects and Baine had an alibi. Hell, he
even had proof by way of Kobi's video tapes.

Lightness wiggled about his chest as he
pulled his alibi into his arms where she belonged.

She scooted into him. "Wow, your skin is
chilled," she murmured.

"Yeah, sorry. I had some stuff to take care of."

She didn't ask what he'd been up to which
spoke volumes about how much she trusted him.
Sloan slipped her hand down his stomach and
wrapped her hot little hand around his growing
cock.

"I know just how to warm you."

Chapter Twenty-four

Devereaux sipped the last of the gold liquid down and placed the empty glass on the table between him and the massive portrait of his bitch of a wife. "Not so pretty now, are you, darling?" He didn't know why, but a large part of him reveled in this daily liturgy. Hateful worship of the woman who gave him the tiny foothold he'd needed to ascend the pyramid of power, who'd later tried her damnedest to toss him from its summit.

The delight came in knowing she'd failed. In knowing no one could topple him after this transaction. He smiled as he thumbed open the cigar box, cut and puffed the Gurkha to life.

"Now to work, darling. The money won't make itself. Though in your case it did. I work hard for what I want. What I deserve."

At his desk, literally fit for a king, King Edward VII to be precise, Devereaux opened the black laptop, swirled the touch pad, then froze. Every muscle in his thick body flexed at the alert that flashed red across the screen.

Devereaux loved women. He glorified them with his cock. Any time. Anywhere. But he'd never allowed himself to get enthralled with one. Fuck, one was hardly enough to sate his appetite. Not even his sweet Elizabeth. The disloyal wench.

The first year of their marriage had been, well, a sham. He'd wined and dined her, treated her like a Disney princess, until the pre-nup met its expiration date and her money became his. *Happy anniversary, sweetheart.*

He bet she'd rued the day she signed up for foreign studies, bringing her into his grasp. At the time he'd been the son of a wealthily oil tycoon. Only he knew his father had pissed away the family fortune at the tracks while his mother whored it away, buying houses and cars for her young lovers.

It'd been up to him to make his way in the world.

Africa seemed the perfect place to set up shop. With the unstable governments, corruption, and insatiable demand for weapons, all he'd needed was capital.

Thanks, sweetie.

She'd hated him, no doubt. But his son and her fear had kept her in check. He'd taken her inheritance and business boomed. Sure his hands were dirty, but that was in his blood. He only molded his pitiful DNA to suit his needs.

And now pussy made one of his guys do something stupid. He highly doubted any cunt was that good. Then again...

Perhaps he'd see for himself.

Chapter Twenty-five

I know where he keeps the codes! Sloan bolted up in bed at the startling realization. The rich sunlight pouring from the French doors temporarily blinded her sleep-hazy eyes.

"What's the matter?" Baine's voice rumbled beside her, bringing into focus the second and third revelations in under a second. *I slept. I slept with Baine all night. Well, almost all night.*

She squinted and blinked the indulgent room into view, settling first on the ornately carved wood ceiling then the thick draperies clothing the large panes of translucent glass. Waking up in an unusual place was unsteadying enough. Add to it a bedfellow and the stunning realization that she held the answer to all their troubles, and her typically agile mind addled.

Baine's soft touch beckoned her to face him. Loving reassurance floated in his brilliant blue gaze. Instantly the tightness in her chest eased and every doubt receded from her brain. *This was it. Love and long sought vengeance.*

He smiled and chucked her chin. "You scared the shit out of me."

No lie. The Glock in his hand said as much. Baine released a long breath then returned the firearm to the nightstand, placing it barrel-to-barrel to its mate. Easier to reach the grips, just in case.

She smiled at their like-mindedness and tackled him, catching him about as unaware as she'd ever have opportunity to.

A deep rumble filled the room as his arms enveloped her and he rolled. In a slick move he lay atop her. The covers entwined among their legs. His mussed hair and short beard gave him the look of a mountain man, not the refined Englishman he'd passed for last night. And oh the gods, that body of his. She worked around fit men every day. Fit for action. Carved by discipline. Finely honed. Just like Baine. But only *his* face, *his* love, *his* body made her drip with desire.

"You went from holy shit to light as a feather in two seconds. What's up?" His full lips pursed as he tried to work out the angles.

Ready to scream it from the rooftops and at the same time terrified at the ramification three simple words could have, Sloan's heart flip-flopped in her chest. So, she went with safe...safer...which would surely get a similar reaction. "I know where Devereaux keeps the codes."

Baine straightened his arms and loomed over her, eyes clouding. "So, you didn't really trust me." His words were soft. His features angry.

"What?" Of all the things for him to say to that, questioning her trust in him wouldn't have made her list. He turned away from her, swinging his feet to the floor. The muscles in his back flexed as he made a move to leave the bed over a big, huge misunderstanding. "Wait," she commanded. "You don't understand. I haven't been holding out on you.

"Look at me," she pleaded.

After an excruciating pause, he turned. Pain drew his face. And that was his own damn fault. Sloan left her elbows and perched on her knees in the middle of the bed, ready to have an eye-to-eye conversation, as Ryan called it.

"You want me to trust you. And *I do*. Yes, it was hard fought, but under these circumstances you can't blame me. Caution is only natural in people who've dealt with the kind of shit we've endured. But you're going to have to trust me.

"This is a two-way street, Londoner. I don't know where it's going and my hands tremble at the thought of finding out. I've been on my own for a very long time. For a girl who doesn't scare easily, traveling this road without you is far more frightening. So, like you asked me last night, do you trust me?"

His full lips pressed into a thin line. His chest rose and fell several times. Sloan's pulse roared in her ears as she waited, like it only did when she was helpless to stop something horrible from happening. The longer he stayed silent the thicker her dread became.

Finally he spoke. "Only now can I realize how truly difficult I made things for you. You're right. Trust doesn't come easily for either of us. And I have way more facts to base my decision on than you do." He hooked her hand from her thigh and brought it to his lips. "I trust you. I'm sorry. I...it just hurt, when I thought you'd lied last night."

Sloan cradled his cheek in her palm. "We're waltzing in the dark. There's bound to be potholes and pitfalls we don't see."

"But I have night vision goggles."

She giggled despite the ebbing tension in the room. "Not for this you don't."

"Yep, totally out of my element with you." He pulled her into his arms. "But I'm a quick study."

His strong fingers caressed her back, raising gooseflesh all over her skin, until those fingers dipped at the crease of her bottom. "Hold still. This won't hurt a bit."

She bucked and wiggled in his arms. "As much as I'd love to get lost in the ways of your fine fingers, aren't you forgetting something—like the key to our retribution?"

"No," he groaned against the crook of her neck. "I can multi-task."

"This is serious, Baine."

"So am I. I'm going to torture the information out of you."

Sloan's rebuttal fell into the back of her throat on a long moan as Baine gathered her hot juices on his finger and spread it from her puckered bottom over her throbbing lips to her clit. Talk about zero-to-sixty in two-point-four seconds. She knew a car could do it. She just didn't know *she* could, until now.

Her nipples flushed brown to hued red and pebbled. The image combined with Baine's hungry gaze on her and his fingers stroking deep inside her core caught her breath. She arched into his chest and her legs fell open, granting him unlimited access. He used it to circle her clit with a steady beat and perfect pressure. Literally, she couldn't have done it better herself. She came panting against his neck and riding his hand through the last waves of pleasure.

She collapsed back onto his arm. "See, I don't talk. Not a word."

"No words, just fucking hot moans. Damn." His head shook and he placed a chaste kiss on her lips, but she caught him before he could retreat.

Sloan slipped her tongue into his mouth, swirling and taunting his. She planted a hand on his solid chest and pushed him down to the bed. He watched her crawl up his body as he lay back on the bed, arms outstretched. "I am a woman. And *we can* actually multi-task. It's just too bad I can't talk with my mouth full."

"Too damn bad," he agreed.

With no waiting or finesse, Sloan guided Baine's already stiff cock to her wet core and impaled herself on the smooth instrument of pleasure. They both drew in sharply, thinning the oxygen inside the four walls. On an exhale, she relaxed and worked her hips in small undulating circles, bracing her hands on his torso for anchor.

"I'm very observant, Englishman. I noticed the bulge grow in your swim trunks when I lotioned you by the pool. I recognized Lawrence as more than a butler on day one." For that one, Baine jerked his hips, ramming the head of his penis deep into her belly. She moaned as again pressure built at her core.

"Mmm. Don't worry, he's damn good. No one would notice the microscopic details, except me. And judging by the grip you have on my ass, I'd say you're about to blow."

His laugh was hoarse. "You don't need to be real perceptive to tell that, but I'm holding. Plan on taking you with me when I go."

Baine's arms snaked up to her breasts and he flicked her nipples. Indignation had no time to form as the sharp pain turned immediately to molten desire.

"Again," she demanded.

As his nail rasped the hypersensitive bead, Sloan's entire body clenched. "Fuck." She cupped her breasts and pounded her ass onto Baine's dick. Her thighs screamed and her breath *whooshed* in and out of her lungs. The hard orgasm had her entire body throbbing. Heavy fingers bit into the skin of her butt as Baine followed. The muscles in his neck and chest tensed, forming a road map across his body. His hips slammed into her once more and his seed warmed her core.

He dragged her down, soothing a hand over her back. Below her ear his heart thundered inside his chest. "I thought you could multi-task," he said. One or two of the words panted from his throat.

Only her lips moved on her reply. The rest of her lay slack, like an overcooked noodle. "You interrupted me."

"Can't say that I'm sorry."

"Me either."

After three more fortifying breaths, Sloan propped her chin amid the light dusting of hair on his torso. "We've established I'm observant."

"Mmmmhumm."

"The codes we need are precious to Devereaux because they hold the means to his wealth and business. Most code producers are small. Small enough to keep with him at all times." Baine raised his head from the bed and met her gaze. "Have you ever noticed the way he rubs his chest?"

"Son of a bitch. I always hoped it was the warning signs of a heart attack. I never thought..."

"Yeah, I'd bet my life he carries the codes around his neck. Someplace he could always touch, someplace no one would search."

"You are amazing."

Talk about a blow to the solar plexus. The reverence with which Baine gazed upon her knocked her hard.

"I love you." She said it before the words stuck in her throat.

Baine's mouth moved as though about to speak, but Sloan placed two fingers over his lips.

"No. You don't have to say anything. You don't owe me anything. I just want you to know, before all this goes down. I love you." It came easier the second time. Warmed her. "When we were young I loved you as a friend. As hope. When I grew I fantasized about you, us. What would've happened, if we met again. You coming to rescue me from the loveless hell of my childhood. Stupid girl stuff I never shared with another soul, and hardly with myself.

"I always wondered what'd become of you. Then when I was briefed on you before the D.C. mission I almost threw up." He cradled her hands. "Then I saw you and unbidden, unwelcome even, my fantasies changed explicitly.

"There are things you can't say. More than your average person, I get that. And I have a pretty good idea of why you can't talk."

He flashed that devastating smile. "Atta girl."

"And," she continued, "I've never been more pleasantly surprised in my life. No matter what happens in the next few days, thank you for sharing yourself with me. It has meant more than you'll ever know."

Baine sat them up and crushed her in an embrace, for a long minute. Then he levered back and framed her face in his hands.

"Sia, Sloan, you are my love. You are every good thing in this world wrapped into one exquisite package. Everything I hope to be is for you. Because of you. As much as I saved you all those years ago, you saved me.

"I kept track of you through the years, but never contacted you because I knew it wasn't safe, even before I knew what my father did and especially after." He rubbed the side of her head. "When you were sprawled on the floor in D.C. it took every ounce of strength I had to walk away, but I had things I needed to get done first. It put my gut in knots to crack your head. And I killed my father's men because they wanted…" he sighed.

"To kill me," she supplied.

"After," he said, working his jaw.

A memory darker than the pits of hell and the shipping container she'd been locked in knotted her gut. She knew first hand what Devereaux's men did to women before they killed them. Her father got a bullet in the head trying to stop the five men who took turns raping her mother.

Baine settled her head in the crook of his neck. Only then did she notice the tears soaking her cheek and his broad shoulder.

"I love you, Sloan."

Her arms tightened around Baine. "Now how are we going to get this fucker?"

Chapter Twenty-six

"As much as I hate putting you in danger, I know you can handle yourself. So, we armor up and go hot. Form a plan. Take the fucking castle. Rip the codes off my father's neck and slap some nice bracelets on his wrists." Baine's hands bracketed her shoulders. All glimmer fled his eyes as he talked business. "I'll order us *room service* for lunch. That way we can all be on the same page."

"I finally get to meet your man?"

"Oh, he's definitely nobody's man, more like a beast." Baine chuckled "It tickles me to death to see him so placid. He'll be thrilled with the turn of events. Since we arrived, I've had to threaten physical harm to his Harley to keep him from blowing the lid off this place."

"How long ago was that?"

"Two years."

"My Lord."

"Yeah, it's been an exercise in self control." He leaned in, planting a kiss on her cheek. "But you've proven it didn't help my restraint one bit."

Sloan smiled, but would be distracted no longer. They stood on the precipice of downing the biggest arms dealer and mass executioner since Hitler, and they had shit to do. "So, we know the who and the where, or at least we think we do. Now we need to determine the when and how."

"Let's get dressed and get serious. I can only think of one thing with your caramel breasts staring at me. It's a tactical invasion, but not the target you have in mind. It'll take me five minutes to shower. Fifteen, if you come with me."

He stood and offered his hand, but she threw hers up to ward him off. "As much as I'd love to, I need clothes, a toothbrush, and a few minutes to think." When his brow rose she added, "Not about this." She swung a finger between the two of them. "About the logistics of our mission. The pitfalls and dangers we may overlook. It's my thing. A few minutes of quiet, before the craziness of duty."

Baine nodded. "I get it."

He pulled her up and wrapped her in his big arms. Though she wasn't slight or in need of comfort, she felt small and safe in the harbor of his embrace. And at the exact same time, immensely powerful.

"Hurry back. We have a shit ton to figure out."

"I will," she said, slipping back into her dress. Shoes in hand she walked to the door, oddly at peace.

"Be careful. Try to avoid—"

"I know and I will."

He stood and watched her go.

Sloan daydreamed about his beautifully naked body, the last image before she'd closed the door, all the way to her room and through her shower, somehow managing to keep her hands from wandering into warmer, wetter territory. The moment she reached her closet all notions of romance and Baine's body vanished.

Snatching a cotton day dress off the hanger, Sloan slipped the powder pink fabric over the strapless bra and thong she'd grabbed from the dresser. She slipped on sandals while yanking her bag of tricks from the top cedar shelf. Just like it should, the white leather hard-case appeared empty. For good measure and to keep from having to come back before dinner, she cluttered the bag with cocktail attire and all the cursed make-up she'd need to play her part. After snatching underthings from the drawer she snapped the case shut, careful not to turn the combination on the locking mechanism, and headed for the door.

Oddly enough, she didn't need the run through she'd always demanded before going into hot zones. Quiet and calm didn't call her. Baine did. She wanted him, not solitude. His calm reassurance. His apparent insight into the compound and Devereaux. His loving gaze.

Bag in hand, Sloan strolled down the corridor. As she neared the main junction of hallways and staircases she heard the rhythmic *slap* of dress shoes coming from the front foyer. Her pace slowed to a near stand still, as she waited, and hoped the man she knew was coming from the pace and force of each impact would pass.

Too bad she and luck weren't on speaking terms at the moment.

The steps grew louder, headed for the back door, she supposed. Glancing back, her bedroom may as well have been on the moon, because in the seconds she had to move undetected, it was unreachable. The door to her left belonged to Lana, the last lady she wanted to see right now. To the right? *Jackpot.* She leapt two giant strides on tiptoes to keep the low heels from striking the stone floor and eased the bathroom door shut as the footsteps pounded nearer.

Not wanting to raise suspicions by getting caught in the bathroom with the lights off, Sloan smoothed her hand over the wall until she found the panel. One. Two. Three. She swallowed hard. Three switches. One, obviously a light. Two, noise makers of the vent and fan varieties. *Damn it.*

With no time to screw around, she made a choice. Hoping these were wired like the ones in her bathroom, she flipped the left switch. Sloan closed her eyes against the blinding light and strained to track the footsteps through the thick door.

They stopped what sounded like a few feet from the back door, nearly dead center to the connecting rear corridors. After a pause they passed the bathroom and quieted again in front of her room. She cracked the door open enough to see Kobi's lightning fast B&E before he slipped into her room. In less than a minute he was out, and Sloan closed the door, listening as he retraced his steps.

Until they came even with the bathroom.

Sloan inhaled easily through her nose and let the breath go quietly through parted lips. Silence screamed on the other side of the carved oak for three long breaths. There hadn't been a shuffle, squeak, or even a tap dance to perk her ears.

Gooseflesh waved across her back.

What was he up to? Did he know she was in here and why was he looking for her? Sloan ignored the lurch and shimmy in her stomach. No time to borrow trouble. Time to move.

She straightened and studied the bathroom.

Eight by ten room. Toilet. Column sink. Interior walls. No windows. Fine art. And one small linen closet.

Thank heavens for oiled hinges. They glided like eagle's wings over the plain as Sloan swung the small door wide, carefully stuffed her carry-on into the shallow depths, and closed the latch. The whisper of footsteps neared the door, but she didn't squander a second by staring at the oak.

Instead, she faced herself in the mirror, dabbed her middle finger against the nozzle of the liquid soap, pulled back her left eyelid and rubbed the detergent against her smooth cornea.

Whoa. Desired affect achieved along with an unpleasant sting of pain. Sloan blinked wildly and tears cascaded over her cheek. She broke the silence barrier, turning the water on and cupping a few handfuls into her abused eye. After a blot she considered the bright red veins polluting the white of her sclera and smiled.

Sloan squared her shoulders and reached for the knob.

With arms crossed over his torso, Kobi glowered at her from the center of the corridor. He made no move to explain his presence, only stabbed her with his glare.

Refusing to be trapped in the tiny confines of the restroom with the letch, Sloan closed the door behind her and took one decisive step toward the foyer.

"Leaving so soon?" he asked. The words muffled through his clenched teeth.

Sloan struggled for meekness in her expression, squinting her brows and quivering her lower lip. "I'm sorry. I didn't mean to be rude. I thought you were waiting for the bathroom and was only getting out of your way."

"Nice try." He laughed, but the sound turned into more of a snort. The huffing bull before its charge. "I think you were hiding from me."

She tilted her head to the side and pointed for emphasis. "Hiding? No, I had a lash in my eye."

His face drew in a sneer. "Did it hurt?"

Oh, shit. She knew where this was going. *Unoriginal asshole.* And still she couldn't stop it without giving something away more precious and deadly than her body. "Yes, a little," she heard herself say.

"Well, I'm going to make you hurt a lot." His arms shot out as he lunged.

Unable to move with her normal speed, she still managed to stumble into view of the grand entrance in hopes someone would happen along and dissuade Kobi's attack. His grip clamped around her throat and she squealed, her eyes wide in feigned shock.

"Shut up," he growled. "Baine can't save you this time."

He drove her into the wall. The smack of her head against the unmoving surface echoed in the entryway. She cried out with what air remained in her lungs.

"I said, 'Shut up!'"

Those damn crooked teeth hovered directly in her line of sight as Kobi bore most of his weight on her windpipe. Had she not been trained to tighten her neck muscles and remain calm in every situation, she'd have already passed out. As it was, only a tiny percentage of the air she needed seeped through her forced pants.

Silver spots appeared like shooting stars above Kobi's head. Sloan had to do something fast or pass out and be at the mercy of this sicko. She went basic, flailing her arms out wide as if in search of a weapon. A way out. Automatically his eyes followed her hands and she kneed his balls into his stomach.

Kobi doubled over with a guttural moan.

Honey-sweet air burned her lungs as she coughed and heaved. Still sputtering, Sloan ran for the front of the house.

Before she rounded the staircase Kobi's body slammed her to the ground. They slid a good five feet and Sloan's head collided with the massive front door. Things tunnel-visioned while Kobi flipped her over and crawled up her body. The world refocused on his mean mug and thick arms as they straightened and strained. Both his hands cinched down on her already sore neck.

"I've never been into necrophilia, but I'm willing to give it a try this ti—"

A fancy shoe cut off his ugly tirade. It connected with a loud snap of bone and sent him careening.

Relief washed over Sloan like a renewing waterfall. The throb of her brain and the sting in her lungs eased with the return of air and blood flow. Plus she had the satisfaction of watching Kobi land in a heap again. Not unconscious this time, but not on top of her either.

When he levered up on his hands and knees, her rescuer bellowed, "Stay down, dog."

Well, the voice held no Brit. Her relief was doused in flames.

Devereaux.

Chapter Twenty-seven

The man in Sloan's every nightmare stepped over her, advancing on Kobi. "It seems pussy's made you doubly stupid. So, let me make things simple for you." Devereaux pulled a silver pistol from the small of his back. He cocked the weapon with a smooth hand and ground the muzzle into Kobi's temple.

Sloan scrambled up the door, her heart forgoing all training and beating wildly, unsure whether this was the end for her and Kobi both. She should run, but the scene unfolding before her made it impossible to look away. Side-stepping, she shrank into the corner.

Kobi's gritted moan filled her ears and for some screwed up reason reminded her of her father's pained cry before Devereaux's men ended his life. Sloan blinked the memory away, unable to spare any brainpower for the side trip at the moment.

Devereaux's hand flexed and Sloan braced for the *pow*. But the senior's voice rang out instead. "Do not lay a hand on this woman again. Don't even look in her direction. She is mine. Everything is mine. You are nothing. A mangy dog, not suited for my table scraps. Know your place. Remember it or I will end you here and now."

"Yes, sir," Kobi choked.

After a weighted pause Devereaux spat, "Now, out of my sight, filth."

Sloan nearly vomited as Kobi hung his head like a good little slave and slunk away. No, she didn't like him, didn't feel sorry for him, but no man or woman should be made to feel inferior. No matter what.

The master watched, gun in hand, until Kobi disappeared around the corner, and then turned his dark eyes on her. Sloan hoped the rage vibrating her entire body would be mistaken as fright, but right this second she didn't much care.

Absolutely nothing stood between her, Devereaux Kendrick, and the codes. They called to her from beneath his shirt and tie. She could snap his neck before he even realized he was in danger.

So, what's stopping you? Do it.

He stalked closer, crowding her personal space.

Sloan screamed at herself. *Do it. Kill the man who took everything from you and so many others.* But her hands hung leaden at her sides. They had no plan of escape or attack. If she got caught moving Devereaux's body, she was unarmed. If she got shot or captured she'd lose the codes before she had a chance to use them. And most terrifying of all, if Baine got hurt trying to protect her she could never live with herself.

No!

A finger skittered across her collarbone. Sloan couldn't stop the tremor of revulsion. "Oh, don't fear me, beauty. Where Kobi wished to harm you, I only want to pleasure you. And have you pleasure me, of course."

His ruffly salt-and-pepper brows waggled. "You have both my son and my dog chasing your tail and I want to know what all the fuss is about.

Plus, if anybody gets the goods around here, it's me."

Her stomach curdled and churned.

He heaved a sigh. The fermented air from his lungs billowed around her face. Sloan held her breath, unwilling to share even oxygen with this devil.

"I can see we'll have to wait for our encounter. You're shaken up by that oaf." His knuckles caressed her arm and he smiled down at her. "Wear something extra special for me at dinner. Tonight, I'm claiming what belongs to me."

Chapter Twenty-eight

Baine tucked a Reeder at the small of his back the moment he heard the bedroom knob jangle. He shot from the bathroom, leaving behind a sea of weaponry, crossing the expanse on silent feet. By the time the door opened his body lay flat against the wall behind it. Ready for anything.

Having disconnected the main camera in the room after Sloan left, nearly an hour ago, he wouldn't be half surprised to see Kobi break in to fix his equipment. With the poor bastard's ears and one eye inoperable, he didn't know jack. That was likely enough to push him over the cliff of reason.

Through the gap at the hinge a dark shadow blotted the light as the person moved into the room. The tinny sound of china on silver relaxed Baine's stance as did the voice that accompanied it.

"Lunch, sir."

Baine kicked the door with his foot. "Isn't the help supposed to knock first? You almost got your dick shot off, mate."

Law turned. A crooked smile stretched his face as he ignored the deafening slam of the door and the edge in Baine's tone. Law's gaze catalogued Baine, then the rest of the room, before settling for a weighted second on the spot where he knew the tiny camera sat. He returned his emerald eyes to Baine, brows raised in question.

"He's deaf and partially blind. Stick to the left side of the room."

"Thank fuck." Law unceremoniously deposited the tray on the nightstand and gnashed his head this way and that against the constraint of his black tie. "You can get your own damn tea...sir," he added with an exaggerated bow.

"I don't give a shit about tea. Have you seen Sloan? In the hallway? On your way here?"

Both his friend's palms came up. "Take a breath, big guy. No, I didn't see her. When was she supposed to be back?"

Baine moved toward the bathroom, careful to stay out of the camera's line of sight. He pulled Law along with a nod. "Didn't set a time. Damn well should have. I don't know if it's been too long or if I'm just on edge because this shit's about to get serious."

When they crossed the threshold of stone and granite Law groaned through his fat grin at the arsenal. "Is it Christmas? Because I've been very good this year." He palmed an Enfield assault rifle, running his hand along the barrel as though it was the most beautiful woman he'd ever seen. "It's been too damn long." Then he went bug eyed over a stack of C-4. "I know the perfect places for that."

"Good. We'll talk about it when you bring back the wine and dessert you forgot in the kitchen. Take this. It should fit pretty well under your coat, not that I expect anyone to take time scrutinizing the help, except for the blond and redhead that came from Walters. And the only bulge they'd notice is the one in your pants."

Law tilted his head. "You checkin' out my junk, McCord? I mean we're pals and all, but—"

"Shut up and put the blasted thing on," Baine barked. While Law shrugged off his suit jacket and put on the tactical vest loaded with enough guns and ammo to add forty pounds to his frame, Baine pulled on his own. "I don't give a fuck about wine or dessert, it's your excuse. We're going to find Sloan."

As if bidden by his words, the bedroom door flew open and Sloan marched in before either he or Law had time to take up a defensive position.

Good thing she was friend, not foe.

Baine watched her lock the door and stalk toward him. The elephant standing on Baine's chest levered a foot onto solid ground. *Thank God.* She moved with such determined strength and grace he caught his jaw before it hit the ground. She was gorgeous. Upset. No, pissed. And was that a hand imprinted in red and light blue around her throat? The elephant collapsed on his lungs while the beast inside him raged, scraping and snarling to be released.

He shoved Law out of the way and went to her, but her halting hands stopped him short not two feet outside the bathroom.

What the hell is it with these two and the calm-down palms?

Seeming to sense his agitation, she inhaled to speak, but stopped without a word. Her eyes widened at a spot behind him then looked toward the camera.

"It's disconnected. He can't see this side of the room," Baine said in as calm a voice as he could rally.

She nodded, her tousled hair brushing her bare arms and the pink of her dress. "Another reason Kobi was pissed."

Baine's teeth gritted and his fists clenched at the name. "He hurt you?"

She smiled, but no joy brightened her face, which was drawn in tight lines of fury. "He tried. Your father stopped him. I thought he was going to kill Kobi." Her fists clenched. "I don't know what stopped him. The chance at continued humiliation at the guy's expense, maybe. But I don't have to worry about Kobi touching me again, unless he plans a coup to take power."

Sloan's lower lip trembled and her eyes welled with tears. She jutted her chin and breathed deep. "Devereaux claimed me."

Someone ripped Baine's bowels from his body and jump-roped with them. The pain her words wrought inside him were that acute. "What are you saying, Sloan. Did he...?"

Her head recoiled, rejecting even the thought of the act. "No."

He hadn't realized he'd bowed his head until her cute sandaled feet met his leather shoes toe-to-toe. Sloan pulled his gaze up with the gentle cup of her hand.

"He didn't hurt me. Neither of them did."

Baine traced the brutal outline on her neck. "This bruise says otherwise."

"I've had worse."

"Sure know how to make a guy feel better," he puffed.

Those pretty lips of hers pursed. "Look at me. I'm whole. Totally pissed. And ready to rage."

Baine itched to pull her into his arms and cradle her there forever, but this wasn't the time. So, he stepped aside and tried to sedate his primal furor. After a deep breath he gestured between the two. "Sloan. Law. Law. Sloan."

His friend crooked his head then straightened, giving Sloan a wink. "You're a down-right scrapper. Knew it when you stepped off the plane, even before you tried to take Dev out with a butter knife."

"Yeah, not my best move, but I'd have gotten him," Sloan said. She stepped into the bathroom, offering Law her hand. Baine didn't miss her sigh of appreciation as she perused the weapons display.

Law agreed. "You'd have taken the two guards and The Devil, but there were, and still are, fifteen other guards and Kobi to deal with. How about we coordinate our attack this time and get rid of these sons of bitches?"

"Dog's bollocks," Baine mumbled.

Sloan whipped her head around and squinted at him. *Oh right. They spoke the same language, only not so much.*

"He thinks it's a blasted great idea," Law offered.

He'd say it a million times over, if it always had this affect. Her shoulders shook and her little nostrils flared as she fought back giggles. With emotions running high his daft comment provided a break. A release she could deal with in front of them. She covered her mouth with the back of her hand.

"Did you say, 'Dog's bollocks'?" she laughed.

Baine smiled. "Where I come from it's a rather common saying."

"Common?" She quirked a brow.

Law backed him up. "It's common. In bars."

She nodded. "If you two say so. It's a new one for me, but yes, I'm ready to plan. But I get Devereaux." Finality sealed her words and her suddenly stern gaze swiveled from Law to Baine, daring them to challenge her.

Baine found his hands on his hips and his spine straightened a degree more.

Sloan's eyes glinted golden. "Devereaux told me to wear something special for him tonight. He'll bring me to his bedroom, which is attached to his office. I'll wear my leather garter and double steels. They're extra special."

Baine wanted his father. He wanted to see the chav's face when he realized everything he'd killed for was being ripped from his fingers. Moreover, he didn't want Sloan anywhere near that man, especially since he knew what the demon planned to do with her. But she, more than even him, deserved the closure.

In a whisper of authority, Baine said, "Don't kill Devereaux. Extract whatever kind of information from him, however you want to do it, but you can't kill him."

Her jaw worked on that for a minute while Law's brows arched. Apparently, neither agreed with him.

Tough shit.

Chapter Twenty-nine

"You have no idea what you're asking me to do." Sloan's voice didn't pitch or rise, but the tremors shaking her body said she clung to her resolve with white knuckles.

Baine ignored her and pulled the trashcan out from below the sink and dumped several errant tissues into the washbasin. He collected the C-4, detonators, and wire into the metal bin, placed the garbage on top and foisted it into Law's hands. "You know where to put it. You've got the exterior guards. I'll take Kobi and the interior mob. She's got Devereaux. We move five minutes after Sloan and Devereaux leave the dining room."

Sloan barked. "Thirty."

"Ten," Baine countered.

Law stuffed one more pistol into the garbage can and headed for the door. "Move ten after they leave the dining room. Got it." He turned back and touched his index finger to his brow. "You two be safe."

The angry lines that marred Sloan's delicate features softened. "Thanks, Law. You be careful too."

His friend smiled, turned, and from the noise beyond, collected the tray and left the room.

Sloan and Baine squared off, both silent and still before the metal click of the bedroom door-latch. Then Sloan snatched one of the Sigs from the counter, holding it out to him in an open palm.

"In my mind, a part of it, I know I shouldn't kill Devereaux. The line I've lived by is clear, and if I kill him I know I'd be crossing it in the most egregious manner." Her head shook slowly back and forth. "But every time I clean a gun—which is a damn lot with what I do—when I wrack the chamber and pull the trigger, every time, it's his face I see."

Baine placed his hand over the gun, holding hers around it while she continued.

"I want to kill him. I want him to look into my face. To see realization smack him between the eyes when he understands a little girl, a monster of his own creation, is about to end his life."

A single tear brimmed over onto her cheek and she swiped at it with her free hand. "I want him to beg and plead like my mother did. I want to hear him scream like my father. Then I want to pull the trigger. To watch the gnarled life leave his pitiful body. And spit on him when he hits the floor."

The gun slid from her hand and Baine set it on the counter. He interlocked their fingers and cupped the nape of her neck. "I know you want to. Believe me, I do too. I've daydreamed about taking his life in a hundred thousand different ways. But we can't become killers."

"I already am," she snorted.

He pulled her closer. "You know you're not. You just said it yourself. You've killed out of duty. For the greater good. Never out of hatred. Sloan, if you kill him, you'll hate yourself and be no better than he is.

"I won't let you do that to yourself. You have a future that doesn't include Devereaux Kendrick, and as hard as it is for me to see right now, so do I. I won't let him take that from you or me."

Sloan buried her face against his chest and screamed. The heat from her fury leaked through the vest and shirt, thawing the lump of ice around his heart. He loathed her pain, but knew her surrender now would hurt less than her regret later. Every muscle in her small frame contracted and the sound, though suppressed, rang in his ears like a screeching missile and devastating explosion.

Baine wrapped her in his arms. "Let it out, love. Let it go, so you can be ready. Your time has come. I believe in you. I know you can do this. No one else. You." He whispered the litany, finished and repeated it, doubting she could hear it over the din of her roar, hoping the entreaty took root in her heart and mind.

Finally she sagged against him, spent. He caught her and eased them both to the floor. The cool wood cabinets braced his back while his legs stretched the territory, nearly butting the bathtub. Sloan curled into a ball on his lap, fisting his hand to her chest like a security blanket.

Were he not already on the ground, she would have brought him to his knees. And not for the first time. Something about Sloan, Sia, humbled him. She stripped away all his walls. Every pretense of distance and protection. Leaving his soul bared. Leaving only one desire. One need.

Her.

When they were kids she'd brought him the first sense of peace he'd ever known and now she sent his body shooting in five different directions at once. Peace. Lust. Possessiveness. Devotion. Love. Each emotion wrestled for dominance in a cartoon cluster of chaos.

He hugged her to him so tightly he feared he'd crack a rib, but she didn't complain. She wound an arm around his neck and squeezed him just as fiercely.

As they relaxed, only because they needed to breathe, Sloan warmed him with her expression. Her whiskey eyes softened and smile lines creased. He didn't know what it meant, but it made his already goopy heart melt a bit more. She looked upon him as though he was the only thing in the world that mattered. Lord knew there wasn't much he cared about outside the circle of his arms.

The silk of her cheek glided over his palms as he framed her face. Unable to stop himself any longer, Baine lowered his head. His lips hovered over hers while he drank in her heat, breathed her air, soaked in the aura of the woman he loved. Then he grazed his lips over her parted mouth. He swallowed Sloan's exhale and concentrated on her upper lip. His tongue licked the fine edge where rouge met caramel.

Baine planned to savor her, take care and time to bring her from heartache to desire. Sloan, apparently, didn't need time. While moving his seduction magic to her supple lower lip she attacked. Sloan threw her entire tiny, but surprisingly formidable, weight into the kiss, fusing their mouths together by force. Her hands weaved into the knit of his hair and latched on with bite.

Sloan raised herself, straddling his lap in a graceful swing of her leg. Her knees hugged the outside of his thighs while he craned his neck to keep their gazes level. She stared down into his eyes, an unusual feeling for a six foot five man. But with the jolt of lusty steel it sent rushing to his cock, he could get used to it. Ardent lips coaxed his mouth open and Sloan's tongue dipped into his warm depths.

So used to dominating where bedroom activities were concerned, this bit of domination *his woman* displayed thrilled his pants straight down to his ankles. Sliding his hands from her full bottom to the front of his pants, Baine planned to show her how much he enjoyed her display. Before he reached his mark, however, he found his forearms pinned to the cabinets by her knees.

"Control yourself, big guy. I'm running the show right now," she whispered.

"We sure do ask a lot from each other," he near panted.

"Mmm," she moaned into his mouth.

He took a mental breath and concentrated on relaxing and enjoying Sloan. Yep, his inner He-Man longed to plunge his sword deep into her slick body, but he could wait. Hell, he'd once waited fourteen hours laid out on the ground, looking through the scope of a sniper rifle, to get his target.

He could do this.

Baine thought that until she maimed his control with one zealous mingling of tongues. Her entire body got into the exchange, rocking against his chest, rolling against the tip of his pulsing erection. Sloan pulled his tongue into her mouth and worked it like a dick from base to tip several times before sitting on his lap and smiling.

"Woman, you're tempting the beast."

With one raised brow and that damn sexy smile, she said, "Good." Her gaze sharpened. "What was it you said to me? Oh, I remember. 'I was about to release your hands, but that look says you can't be trusted.'"

"Risk for reward," he answered.

"So right." She eased off his arms, but pinned him with those lion eyes. "Control, remember? It's my turn."

"Yeah, right."

As Sloan unfastened the sleek buckle at his waist and snapped the leather from its loops, Baine held tight to his tattered restraint. Holding onto a tree trunk in a hurricane might've been easier. When she spread the fabric of his slacks the broad head of his cock peeked out through the slit in his boxer briefs and she moaned. At the sound, sweat beaded on Baine's forehead and his hands fisted at his sides.

Sweet Lord!

Her cool hands wrapped around his hot girth as she guided it from the soft cotton to the silk of her mouth. He watched his mushroomed tip disappear between her red lips and his rod stretch her sweet mouth wider to accommodate. All ten of her fingers cloaked his base, working in tandem with her lips and tongue as she bobbed up and down his length. She set a grueling pace for the start.

The sight of her, the feel of her, the contented moans emanating from her throat and the vibrations they wrought all combined to snap his reserve. His hands gripped the edge of the counter as his hips jerked, shoving him into the back of her throat. She swallowed him down. Once. Twice. The third time he barked a curse at the intense pressure building in his balls. He did not want this to end. Then again, he did not want to waste a good orgasm in her mouth. Shit, as wild as he was for her he'd be in danger of piercing her brain. He wanted to pierce her womb. Come deep inside her, looking into her flushed face and loving eyes.

"Straddle me, Sloan," he demanded. "Ride the fuck out of me. But I want to look in your eyes when I come. When you come."

She popped off the head of his dick and pouted. "Thought I was calling the shots?"

"You were. Now I am."

He slipped the gathered sundress up over her hips, plunged his finger inside her nude thong, dragged them across her swollen pussy and positioned her over his cock. With a firm grip he wrenched her down his rod, until her ass grazed his balls.

They both cried out at the exquisite pleasure and slight pain of the joining. Baine wound his hands up her back and gripped her shoulders for leverage as he pulled out then rocked back into her. The weapons and ammunition clipped onto the vest chaffed the cotton covering her breasts. He smiled when she leaned into it, increasing the friction on her beaded nipples.

Sloan brought her knees up on either side of him, allowing better access. Her gaze seared into his as they rode each other like desperate souls contented only by the other. She wrapped her hands around the nape of his neck and arched into him. He nipped her breasts through the slight material.

Sloan bit her lower lip and her head lolled back. Fresh moisture coated his already slick cock as Sloan groaned her orgasm. Her body rolled with the gratification of climax. The sensation overcame him and Baine let her wring a fierce ejaculation from his body. He went tight all over, straining against his own skin until he went slack, completely sated.

His love nestled onto his chest. Amazingly, he found the strength to wrap her in his arms.

"And you said we couldn't make love on the bathroom floor."

"That was too primal to be called love-making."

Sloan nuzzled his neck with her cheek. "Thank you."

"Thank me? Love, you never have to thank me for that."

She giggled. "Not that. But yes, I, along with entire cultures, should thank you for that demonstration." Baine cupped her hand in his. "Thank you," she continued, "for making me see the ugliness in my hatred, for stopping me from doing something I would regret, something that would destroy the person I am, who I want to be.

"I love you," she whispered.

The words should have made him smile. But the way she said them twisted his gut. Because they sounded a lot like *goodbye*.

The best laid schemes
Of mice and men go often awry.
And leave us nothing but grief and pain.
For promised joy!

Chapter Thirty

The food, though gourmet as money could buy and a personal chef could prepare, rolled around Baine's mouth like pub peanuts scraped from the floor weeks ago. Where Sloan was concerned, each task associated with the magnificent woman ratcheted up a notch in difficulty.

First, he'd been unwilling to contact her because of his father's psychotic tendencies. Locked into a life of emotional solitude, guessing and wondering how Sia fared in this world for years, had been difficult. He'd nearly broken his promise to keep her safe and out of his life after a night of pub-crawling the first semester of his freshman year at Cambridge.

Baine had been practically on his own since the age of five, when his father fired Nanny Pat. Independent. Self-sufficient. Yet, that day, restlessness wriggled through his body from the early morning hours and didn't let up through his first or second classes. By the third he shifted so often in his seat the professor actually asked him to leave. He hadn't known what he'd been looking for when he fled campus, but he didn't find it in the bottom of his many pints or in the blue eyes of a barmaid.

So, he gave up, deciding Sia's voice was the only thing to give him peace. As luck would have it, he bumped into Law on the way to the bar phone to track her down. The big guy'd been a little miffed about wearing his beer, and Baine had been more than happy to oblige him with a fight. He'd woken the next morning in his London house propped in a wingback with a bloody headache, busted lip, and the chap snoozing on his couch.

He hadn't found Sloan that day which was best for her own safety. Surprisingly, he'd found a friend to carry him through the next miserable years of his life.

The second task, and slightly more difficult than the first, was cracking her on the head in D.C. to save her life. Third, trying to control his impulse to fuck her like a crazed animal. *Fail.* And now, watching while his father devoured her from across the table with his eyes, and not being able to do a damn thing to stop it.

More and more difficult. No doubt.

To her credit, she played Devereaux like Jimmy Page played the guitar. The man hung on her every glance, the rise and fall of her chest, the curve of her smile. And it was hard to blame him. Sloan, like Pages' textured notes plucked from the string, mesmerized.

Too damn bad he couldn't kill the man.

If matters weren't bad enough, Kobi fed the combustibility of the room by sending *fuck you's* with his darting glances. Sloan was the object of Kobi's sharp gaze through the first round of drinks and appetizers. Now, finished with the main course and with a few more drinks down his gullet, he spread the hateful glare between Sloan and Devereaux, though never making his disdain for either too obvious.

Baine knew the guy had plenty of hostility for him. The run-in earlier must have ignited his disdain for his master, as well as added to his raging obsession with Sloan, making Baine yesterday's headache.

Time to draw that attention elsewhere.

One more minute of Kobi's snarled gaze on the mocha skin that rocketed him to the moon with one touch, and Baine would blow the whole half-cocked plan to shit by ramming his thumbs into the man's eye sockets.

Try ogling her now, asshole.

With a finger, Baine signaled Law. His friend, the last guy in the world to be wrestled into a suit, straight-backed his way across the room like a professional butler. One hand tucked behind his back while the other he held in a stiff L before his middle, complete with a crisp, dangling, stark-white towel.

"Yes, sir?" Law asked with a slight incline of his neatly quaffed dirty-blond mop.

Law had to buy a brush and *hair* products for this gig and clean shave his perpetual stubble. A smile threatened Baine's lips. Hell, he was all over the place today. Gooey happy. Pissed. Smiley. Scared, for the first time in a long time. Since he now had something to lose.

Head in the game, McCord.

"Scotch straight, for me." He motioned toward Kobi. "And a vodka martini for him. Apple. Yep, an appletini for my friend."

"Right away, sir," Law replied.

As Law turned away to fulfill the request, Baine met Kobi's glower with a smile. "Something to brighten your mood a bit. You seem glum. We can't have that, now, can we?"

Bingo.

The sorry excuse for a barroom bouncer ground his teeth like an angry animation, flexing the muscles in his neck.

Baine knew the guy came from screwed up beginnings, but shit, these days who didn't. Baine certainly had. He looked across the table at the guy who'd profited from death and destruction, oftentimes orchestrating it to turn a nickel into a quarter. In spite of his father—or maybe to spite him—Baine had chosen a different path. Kobi, on the other hand, had chosen the path to hell, and boy was Baine going to enjoy helping him complete that journey.

A server entered from the butler's pantry carrying a tray of fluffy confections. Baine breathed through the spike of adrenaline in his veins, knowing the time grew nearer. No sugar for him. His nerves already vibrated.

Across the table Devereaux declined his finisher with a wave of his hand. The man's eyes, the ones Baine thanked his mother everyday he didn't see when he looked into the mirror, zeroed in on Sloan. "I have something much more delicious in mind for dessert tonight."

Yeah, me too. Your balls roasted on a spit.

Beside him Sloan bowed her head as if shy, but offset the move by smoldering the man with a come-hither gaze beneath her thick fan of lashes. What no one else in the room saw, except Baine, was her fisted hand in her lap, the way the veins in her small hand bulged and her knuckles whitened.

Devereaux stood, dropping his burgundy napkin into the seat. "Jesus Christ, Abram! Elbows off the table."

The room stilled and the thick man at the other end of the table straightened. "Sorry, sir," Abram said, returning a fork-full of soufflé to his plate. Nena's mouth hung open expectantly while her wide gaze jumped between Devereaux and the dessert. Thoroughly chastised, the chap's hands disappeared under the table. As though pulled by an unseen magnet, all eyes in the dinning room shifted back to Baine's father.

Conqueror of all, Devereaux smiled and met Baine's gaze while holding his hand out to Sloan. Baine didn't swallow the rock in his throat when his father said, "Come dear. I'm ravenous."

Now, why the fuck did he look at me when he said that?

Based on the report he'd falsified and placed on Devereaux's computer, and by Sloan's description of the confrontation between her, Kobi, and Devereaux earlier in the day, the old man should have needled that comment at Kobi. The hair on Baine's arms and neck all stood at attention.

Son-of-a-bitch.

He hadn't expected warm fuzzies when he watched Sloan leave the room hand in hand with the rat bastard. But every battle-honed instinct screamed inside his head as the last of her mocha skin vanished behind the double doors—because something was wrong.

As Baine replayed the meal in his head his heart did a S.O.S. against his sternum. His father had been unusually quiet. Not berating or saying a thing to Kobi, when even on the best of days the chav became the target of at least two back handed comments.

Baine shifted in his seat, ready to make a break for the double doors, when Law's penguin chest blocked his view.

"Sorry for the delay, sir. It took me a moment longer to *place* the apple." Law set his scotch in front of him and proceeded around the table to Kobi where he deposited one thin-stemmed glass of green appletini.

Kobi's face reddened, but Baine ignored him, instead snagging Law's gaze. "*Go ahead* and bring me another. It took long enough to get this one. I may die of thirst by the time you get back with the next."

Law gave an exaggerated nod, showing he got the intended message. *Get the fuck ready because shit's about to happen.*

"Another for you, sir?" Law asked Kobi.

"Fuck you." The chappie growled.

"Yes, sir," Law said. Then left the room.

A moan from the opposite end of the table snagged Baine's attention.

Yeah, if Devereaux didn't like elbows on his table, he might not be too wild about the half-naked ass on it either. Since he wasn't the one to put it there.

Abram, Nena, Josh, and the blond escort—Baine couldn't remember her name—tangled tongues and limbs in the beginnings of what looked to be a lively orgy. Abram, the bigger of the two lug heads, steadily eased Nena's skirt up her body, revealing quite a bit of pale porcelain skin. Too bad for them the party was about to get shut down.

But before he gave voice to his thoughts, a streak of movement brought his focus front and center just in time to meet the cold smack across his face. Fruity vodka dripped down his cheeks and around his lips.

Kobi stood across the table, chest puffed and chin high. His fists rested on either hip, but Baine noticed he listed ever so lightly to the right. Most likely the work of dear old Dad. The wanker snarled, wrinkling the wide nose under his beady eyes, and showed off a set of teeth that would make a proper Brit cringe.

Next to Kobi, Lana gasped and the room stilled. Even the orgy.

Without a word, Baine slid his drink across the table. The dark liquid seesawed in the glass before coming to rest several inches from Kobi.

The man's head jerked back in confusion while he stared at the glass as though it were a puzzle to solve. A really difficult puzzle...like why mass existed. When his gaze poked Baine again, he nodded toward the liquor.

"Mind tossing that one? I like to taste pussy, just not pussy drinks."

Kobi's yell split the air and ricocheted off the walls. Still no one moved until he pulled a gun from his shoulder holster.

Fuck you very much.

As if Baine's concerns about Sloan weren't high enough already, Kobi had to add to the cluster. Because no matter what happened to Baine, if that gun fired it could compromise Sloan's mission, or worse, get her killed.

The room came to life as the two female orgy participants shrieked. Bare ass flew off the table and ducked behind Josh. She pulled the blond with her as they scrambled for the door. Lana didn't scream, but hot heeled it out through the butler's pantry while the chaps stared big eyed and goofy jawed at the drama unfolding.

Kobi's hand gripped the gun like a little kid did a balloon that might be carried off in a swift breeze. His wrist quavered from the effort. Through gritted teeth he spoke. "One bullet'll wipe that smug look off your face, boy."

Boy? What the hell? Kobi had ten years on him, maybe.

"Stand up. Keep your goddamned hands where I can see them. Push your chair back and move that way." He motioned toward the head of the table with the barrel of his gun, away from the other men.

Having little option at the moment, Baine complied.

Kobi met him at the end of the room, leaving the table's width between them. "Kneel."

Again, what the fuck option did he have? None. So, he eased himself down until the hard wood greeted his knees. The weight of the weaponry under his vest embraced him, but did not a damn bit of good. He flicked a glance at the ornate wall clock. It had only been five minutes since Devereaux and Sloan left.

Too early to move. Calm. Control.

The silent mantra worked, centering his thoughts and relaxing his body. He could do this. He had to do this. For Sloan.

Chapter Thirty-one

Devereaux's hand pressed against the small of Sloan's back as he ushered her into his suite. The man had been quiet during the meal, but grossly intent on her. On her breasts, throat, face. She'd been thankful for the table between them, blocking his view of her lower half. Too bad only air stood between them now.

Air and opportunity.

Ryan's words echoed in her head and she smiled.

"You find the accommodations to your liking I see. Good." His hand coasted up her spine. "I want you comfortable. Totally relaxed. It won't hurt as much."

A chill ran the course from his touch and spread throughout her body.

"Hurt?"

Sloan heard the fear in her voice and was both repulsed and relieved. She despised the effect his words had on her, but knew her unease would satisfy the sadistic man, tranquilize the rage she'd seen bubbling in his gaze, first in the foyer this afternoon, then again during dinner.

He turned her to face him, the firm grip on her shoulders agreeing with his words. If she struggled in his grasp like a normal woman would, the pressure of his fingers would bite into her skin.

Crevasses lined the old man's forehead as he filed his gaze at her to a sharp point. His brown eyes hosted splotched scleras, like someone had taken an ink pen and doodled on the white surface. He smiled. The truly sinister expression carved quotations on his clean-shaven skin.

"You see, I like it rough. No chains or handcuffs necessary. I'll hold you right where and how I want you."

"I like it rough too," she breathed.

"Good. Then relax and it won't hurt a bit."

No, it's going to hurt quite a lot. Going to hurt you.

Devereaux released her and flipped his hand in a shooing motion. "Go sit on the sofa and wait for me."

Sloan nodded and turned away.

The twenty-by-thirty room held a massive four-poster bed that looked like something out of a castle, carved out of dark wood and gaudy as hell. Beyond the bed a wide archway revealed a white stone bathroom. Happy to ignore that side of the room, Sloan walked toward a large seating area nestled around a fireplace, above which Elizabeth McCord's painted eyes stared. Down from the painting and parlor area a closed door called to her. The red wood appeared thick and imposing. She smiled.

Office entrance.

After preparing two drinks at the sideboard, Devereaux sauntered over. All the confidence of an emperor bloated his chest as he neared her seat on the couch.

Half of Baine's DNA came from this inferior specimen, but when compared to Baine the man was less in every way, except evil. She could see no resemblance to the man she loved in the one before her. *Thank goodness.*

He downed the dark liquor in his glass then sat the other on the small table between them. When he remained standing Sloan crossed her legs and smiled.

"Thank you."

Devereaux stared at her for a long minute not saying a word. Silence danced between them and a warning bell sounded in Sloan's head. When the sound reached a fevered pitch, he spoke.

"I love women. Their hair and soft curves. The sweet scent of their throat and the valley between their breasts. I love their lips. High and low." His gaze narrowed on Sloan's crossed legs, and he smiled. "I said, 'Relax.'"

Sloan uncrossed her legs and sat straighter near the edge of the cushion. She breathed through the urge to attack and waited patiently. She had time.

"Better," he nodded.

"I love women," he continued. "But women get in the way." He let that hang in the air before stepping closer.

"Spread your legs," he demanded.

The braised lamb she'd eaten came to life in her stomach, wriggling and bucking, looking for a way out. But no way in hell could she get sick. She was a professional, if not escort, a professional undercover agent. A professional killer. She had to lure the prey in somehow.

Get over it. You have panties on.

Inch by vomit-worthy inch, Sloan spread her legs, and watched as Devereaux took another step closer.

"Hike your skirt," he practically panted.

Fuck!

Sloan wriggled the tight white material up her hips, focusing on the distance the pervert closed between them rather than the stomach acid in her throat.

Devereaux tilted his head for a better view of her crotch.

"Too bad you're wearing panties. I need to see what all the fuss is over your vagina. Is it magical? It certainly mesmerized Kobi and my son. Drove them to fight over you."

The man straightened and his jaw went to work. He sneered and shook his head.

"My son. I had such high hopes for him." Sloan's heart frosted. "Seems he has poor judgment where pussies are concerned. I tried to teach him they were only for play, but he was thinking with his dick when he tried to take what's mine and frame Kobi.

"My loyal dog. He would never bite the hand that feeds him. The hand that scooped him from the slums of Cape Town. He's forever loyal."

He took another step closer, leaving four feet between them.

A little closer.

"My son...what a disappointment. He's greedy like I was. Guess I should have expected it. After all, I killed my father and took what was his."

Devereaux shucked his suit coat and tossed it onto the chair beside him. His hands went to his fly and the zipper groaned open.

"It's time you show me what's so special about your cunt."

Chapter Thirty-two

Abram spoke. "Uh, Ross? What the hell are you doin' man? That's the boss's so—"

"Shut up. I know what I'm doing. He's a traitor. Killed our guys. Your friends." Kobi's neck muscles bulged and the visible pounding in his veins increased. He pointed with the gun barrel toward Baine's head. "Now it's his turn to die."

In his periphery Baine saw Abram and Josh look back and forth at each other in a pingpong match of *what the fuck*. Clearly, neither were going to be any help.

The corners of Kobi's mouth turned up. "They're not gonna help you. Daddy's not gonna help you. You're all mine."

"How sweet."

As if someone had slowed an old movie reel, Kobi moved with deliberate and easy pace in the next few frames. Kobi closed the chasm between them with one large step. His pistol hand drew back. Baine turned his head a quarter-inch to minimize the damage as he let the barrel slam into his skull.

One hell of a way to buy time.

The thud reverberated through dense brain tissue, making Baine's ears sing soprano. He righted himself and looked at the clock again. Blood tickled the corner of his left eye. The long and short hands bobbed in a sea of red. After several blinks, finally the numbers found dry land.

Two minutes left.

"Your gun," Kobi demanded, one hand outstretched.

Mindful that he'd only used the singular, Baine slipped one Reeder from its holster and handed it to the chav, barrel down. Seeing the beauty in his inept hands, Baine's insides twitched. And ever the smart mouth, he couldn't stop himself. "You sure you know how to use that thing?"

The black gun disappeared behind Kobi's back as he shoved it into his waistband. "Oh, I'll show you just how well, fucker." Kobi stood over him now. So close Baine could vise his balls in a blink. The man laughed. Oblivious to the danger or so caught up in the high of Baine Kendrick kneeling before him, he neglected all the possibilities.

He just had to be patient and keep the wanker from pulling the trigger. Because as ignorant as Kobi was, Baine couldn't ignore the precariousness of his situation. At this range the bullet would leave the barrel and impact his skull in about one-sixth of a second. For a big guy he was fast, but not that fast.

"What's your play here, Ross? Shoot me, then what? Take out my father? You'd have to. I doubt he'd take too kindly to the fact that you killed his only heir."

The kick came from a mile away with a slow wind-up. Baine forced himself not to block the tugboat-sized foot that sailed toward him. It made contact just below his tact vest. The air evaporated from his lungs like a waterhole during the dry season. Will to stay upright and maybe loads of experience getting the wind pummeled out of him were the only things that kept him from assuming the fetal position at Kobi's feet.

"That rat bastard deserves to die," Kobi spat. "He can't see how valuable I am. How loyal I am.

"He doesn't value you either. Does he?"

Air was required to speak, but Baine assumed Kobi wasn't talking to him. So, he concentrated on calming the spasms in his chest.

"No, he doesn't," one of the dopes still hanging at the other end of the room said. The other echoed the sentiment.

"It's time for new leadership," Kobi bellowed.

Yeah's and *wohoo's* chorused.

Baine braced his palms on his thighs and blocked the black tactical knife he slipped from his vest. His head hung between his shoulder blades as, incrementally, oxygen returned. He shook his head and wheezed. "Mutiny doesn't sound very loyal."

Cold fingers locked around Baine's throat and Kobi jerked his head up. The man couldn't get much closer unless they were going to kiss. Baine looked into the wild eyes only inches from his face and smiled.

"What do you have to smile about? You're about to die."

"I have this," Baine answered. Before Kobi could blink Baine rammed the blade into the man's gut. With his other hand, Baine latched onto Kobi's wrist and twisted heavenward. The pistol clattered to the floor. And without discharging. Always a plus.

Using every bit of strength he possessed, Baine rocketed off the floor and led with his shoulder as he battered Kobi against the wall. The wanker slid down the white paint, wide-eyed, clutching his gut. Before he could check for any other weapons, clopping footfalls captured his attention.

Baine turned to see Abram running at him, gun drawn. He dove for cover behind the dinning room table as a rapid succession of shots split the air above his head. The bullets chunked holes in the wall, then floor. Splinters of wood broke free as the table took several hits. Baine landed on his side, his second Reeder already drawn. He rolled to his belly, exhaled, and fired. One. Abram's shin bone. Two. Josh's foot. Three. Abram's forehead. Four. Josh's temple.

Baine pivoted his aim to finish Kobi. Only smears of red remained on the wall. A large crimson handprint decorated the corner door.

Damn.

He had four more interior guards to take out before he could get to Sloan and now he had to track that weaseley fuck, Kobi. Baine tucked and rolled up to the balls of his feet. With brain-matter covering the floor behind him there was no need to check Abram and Josh. Baine shot through the pantry door then snuggled against the far doorframe and scanned the expansive kitchen.

The staff had evacuated, leaving piles of dirty dishes in their wake. A tray of desserts met a tragic end on the grey and white checked floor. From his vantage point Baine could see no one in the room, but the outside door gapped open several inches.

Kobi could have hightailed it out of the house, but where would he go in the middle of the African wild? Baine heaved his body across the open space, crouched down, and slid on his knees to the far side of the island. All remained quiet as he crept to the door, constantly scanning the area for Devereaux's men. At the edge of the cabinets

Baine swung around the corner near the back door, leading with his Reeder.

The coiled breath he'd held seeped out through his lips. A bloody arm lay lodged between the door and frame attached to an exterior guard who didn't quite make it to safety.

Nice job, Law.

Baine stood from his crouch, refreshed his clip, and returned the gun to its holster. He shrugged out of his restrictive suit coat before continuing down the rear corridor, following the intermittent drops of Kobi's life force.

A footfall whispered in the distance and Baine flattened against the wall at the opening of the foyer. Soon enough the barrel of a fully automatic machine gun slowly drew into his line of sight. Baine balled his right hand, pushed the gun toward the ceiling with his left, and connected his fist with the guard's jaw. Immediately, the man slacked like a marionette with no puppet-master, capitulating his weight forward into Baine's arms, which hadn't been the plan, but worked to his advantage when his gaze met with the second guard, who was far better in stealth mode than the first.

It took most people a third of a second to think *shoot that S.O.B.* and actually pull the trigger. Sneaky Feet wasn't one of those people. As soon as their gazes met he began spraying bullets. The body in Baine's arms jerked once, twice, three times as bullets assaulted his flesh.

Baine fell to the floor, thrown off balance by the tremors. But he had zero time to think as Sneaky Feet advanced, never letting off the trigger. Effectively trapped by the dead weight and pelting bullets, Baine couldn't reach his gun. After one-hundredth of a second of *oh shit,* calm regained control.

Cold metal brushed his left hand. Without looking, only feeling, Baine found the trigger of the dead guy's gun, pointed toward Sneaky Feet, and held down the squishy trigger. He took out the guy's legs then peppered the rest of his body with twenty or so rounds.

He felt pretty damn lucky as he hefted the dead guy off him and stood. Then he heard a single pistol shot echo down the staircase and his heart crawled up his throat, trying to go to her.

Sloan!

Chapter Thirty-three

Devereaux pulled his semi-soft dick from his pants, but Sloan averted her gaze and her vomit reflex. She needed him close. As if sensing her wish, he closed the distance between them, palming his penis all the while, trying to get it to do something. He leaned over her and she fell against the cushion to keep from coming in contact with his lips.

His free hand latched onto her throat, pushing her windpipe so hard it brushed her spine. She could hold her breath for nearly two minutes. The pressure hurt, but she'd felt worse.

"What'd your father do to you to turn a nice girl like you into a whore?"

"I'm not a whore," she croaked.

"Right," he nodded. He sneered down at her. "You're Julia Roberts in Pretty woman and my son is Richard Gere." A deep chuckle varied the force he applied to her airway.

"No," Sloan growled and gasped.

"What was that," he asked, lightening his grip enough that fresh air reached her lungs.

"I said, 'No.'" She swallowed past the pain in her throat. "I'm not Julia Roberts. I'm Samuel L. Jackson."

His eyes narrowed in confusion then widened as the first hint of uncertainty flashed across his features. Devereaux cinched his grip around her neck, abandoning his dick to use both hands.

Sloan tightened her neck muscles and laughed. It sounded wicked even to her own ears.

Devereaux's face reddened and he doubled his effort.

Sloan's knee connected with Devereaux's soft, dangling balls. A small pop said she might have ruptured something important. As the man fell to the floor and curled into a gagging, hacking, sobbing puddle, Sloan's smile widened.

"There are rules in America. Unwritten, but strictly adhered to. Never talk about someone's momma. I think we should add another. Never talk about someone's daddy."

Sloan stood, smoothed out her dress, grabbed Devereaux's tie, and dragged him across the floor by the silky scrap.

"My father left behind a trust fund and one of the richest families in the States to teach impoverished children in third world countries, build schools, and help structure an education system. My mother also taught school. She cooked the best cassava rolls I've ever put in my mouth."

The knob turned easily as Sloan opened the door to reveal Devereaux's office. The idiot should've kept it locked or coded. She would've enjoyed torturing it out of him. With another wrap of the silk, Sloan heaved her live catch to the middle of the office. A few feet through the doorway Devereaux roused from his cocoon. His flailing arms and legs made dragging him more difficult. Each time she planted a stiletto-covered foot on the wooden floor, she lost a good inch or two to his antics.

Sloan turned on Devereaux and planted her heel into his gut with such force she was honestly surprised, and disappointed, the white spike of her shoe didn't come away red. The piece of crap folded like a fitted sheet. Ugly. Disheveled. Totally unsuited for company eyes.

The nagging tailwind subsided. Still, by the time she stopped in front of the wide desk, sweat dripped between her breasts and beaded on her forehead. She released his tie and ignored the red and white indentions circling her hands. With her left hand Sloan snatched Devereaux's hand from his chest, braced his arm straight, and bent his wrist in the most beautifully unnatural angle. His scream sang in her ears like music—the really good kind felt deep down in the center of the heart and mind.

Finally, Sloan found the sweet spot and Devereaux flipped to his belly in search of relief. He didn't find it. She pinned his elbow with her knee and with her free hand pulled a Smith & Wesson 9mm from its holster at the small of his back. After a quick check of the chamber and mag she released him and stepped back, gun by her side. Ready for anything. She honestly didn't know if she had the wherewithal to point the barrel at him and not empty the magazine into his head.

Devereaux rolled to his side and sat, listing to the side, careful not to put pressure on his left arm or his nuts. His gaze narrowed on her, and in his eyes flashed fear, anger, and confusion.

"Who are you?"

"I am a girl whose mother was raped, tortured, and killed while she watched. I am a girl whose father took a bullet in the head trying to stop the horrors befalling his family. I am one of thousands unfortunate enough to stand in the destructive path of your greed.

"I am a former slave in your house. I cleaned the fine china you ate off of while I ate from a ladle with twenty others. I washed your bed linens and slept on the dirt."

Her tears fell in earnest and her grip on the gun tightened so much she thought it might be crushed in her hand. She took a decisive step forward and smiled when he flinched.

"I, Devereaux Kendrick, am a monster of your making. You've taken so much from so many. Today is judgment day—and I get to pass down your sentence."

"Fuck you," he spat. "You're just a whore."

The sound of rapid gunfire carried from behind the office door. Sloan's heart squeezed as thoughts of Baine in harm's way assailed her, but she schooled her features. Devereaux, on the other hand, did not. He grinned.

"If you're going to kill me you better do it now because my men are going to shoot you between the eyes."

The sound of a machine gun carried up the stairs followed by hollow screams and then silence.

Devereaux's eyes bugged. He looked at her. Back at the door then lunged for his desk.

Her bullet landed in his shoulder and he howled. That fetal position was becoming popular. He assumed it and grabbed at his lower arm.

"You bitch! Forget a quick death. My men and I are going to run a train on you for weeks and you'll beg me to kill you."

"Nice try," Sloan said. "Stand and move to the back of your desk." He glared and groaned. "Does your shoulder hurt? I hope not. We're just getting started and I don't want you to pass out and miss the fun. Now move."

He did as she instructed a little too eagerly which made her giggle. "Go ahead. Press your panic button. No one's coming to help you.

"You really shouldn't have killed Baine's mother. Check your cameras. I'm sure by now he's taken out most of your men."

The man actually teared up. Sloan guessed it was from rage and a sense of helplessness. Regardless of the reason it sent a euphoric shiver though her entire body. She added to it by stepping closer, raising the gun, and aiming it between Devereaux's eyes.

The culmination of her life's work was about to be achieved. The Devil of her every nightmare was about to get his comeuppance. She was about to be free.

"With your right hand use two fingers to remove the necklace holding the code key. Then place it on the center of your desk and take two steps back."

At the words, "code key," the almighty Devereaux Kendrick blanched, turning as white as her cocktail dress.

Yep, it's there all right.

He'd just raised his quivering hand from his side when a series of shots resonated in the hallway outside the door.

"Hands by your side. And don't you move. I'm not the one who wants you alive. So don't push me."

Sloan moved around the desk, prodding Devereaux ahead of her. Behind the thick wooden workspace she faced the door with his body in between. She kept the gun trained on his head, but her heart wrenched itself out of her chest and flew to the door, ready to help Baine any way she could.

Her grip on the pistol tightened, as did the pull on her heart. Stay and deal with Devereaux or go help Baine? There had never been an easier decision in her entire life.

Chapter Thirty-four

Baine followed his heart up the steps, gun drawn, ready to walk through the fiery pits of hell for the woman he loved. Adrenaline rode him hard, a jockey relentlessly cropping his ass, insisting he reach his goal. But before he got his butt shot off, he took over the reins of his own body. One deep breath eased the hitch in his chest. Another full inhale quieted the roaring pump of his blood and calmed the rapid cadence of his heart.

His steps slowed at the top of the staircase, imitating Sneaky Feet. As he reached the apex not even a tiny rasp of fabric could be heard. Baine flattened himself to the wall and waited. He strained his hearing for any movement or talking beyond his location.

Nothing.

His left foot rose to move, but a sudden churning in his gut told him to stay put. The quiet was unnatural. Static. Baine eased a tiny mirror from a pocket of his vest and crouched low. At the corner of the top stair he adjusted the reflective surface to the correct angle then edged it toward a view of the corridor.

Close McCord. Too close.

Had he catapulted to the visceral need to reach Sloan as quickly as possible and leapt into the hallway like a crazed fool, he'd have been creamed. Two guards, one closer than the other, stood statue-still at the end of the hallway, subs at the ready. He had not a freaking clue what they were doing. Waiting for him? Kobi?

With no time to waste Baine exchanged the mirror for a flashbang, pulled the pin, and tossed the stun grenade around the corner. About a second after the sound of its landing livened the silence its *boom* discharged. Before the reverberations died down, Baine uncoiled his muscles, planning to take the guards out as he steered directly for Devereaux's bedroom three doors down across the hall.

Plans often have a way of falling apart.

As soon as Baine rounded the corner, revealing his entire body for target practice, he keyed in to three alarming facts. One, the fucking banger had rolled into the second open doorway. Two, only one of the guards blinked and swatted at his eyes like they were on fire. Third, the barrel of the other man's sub aimed somewhere between Baine's gut and kneecaps.

He hadn't even fully flatfooted it in the hallway when he threw himself toward the closest bedroom. About the time he became horizontal in the air the sound of automatic fire spat. Searing metal slammed into his body. The damn thing brought tears to his eyes.

When he landed, his Reeder kept sliding across the varnished wood and disappeared under a large canopy bed. Too bad Baine didn't follow it. He stopped with a thud, half in and half out of cover.

Down the hall he heard Kobi scream, "Finish him!"

Where the bloody fuck had that prick been hiding?

Move it, McCord! End this shit and get to Sloan.

His left leg didn't seem to hear the order. It just lay there. Numb as an Eskimo's tit. Baine used his elbows and right leg, snaked into the room, and slammed the door behind him.

The room was smaller than most in the house. He'd been in it for recon once before and knew the door to his left led to a Jack-and-Jill bathroom. The door to the right went to a small walk-in closet. Above the bed a long window stretched up to the ceiling, the only one in the room.

Baine glanced down at his leg. A small hole in his slacks showed at the side of his quad. No direct hit to the bone. Not much blood, yet. He'd live, if he could get the hell off the floor and finish asshole one and asshole two before they finished him. Then he had to get to Sloan.

With gritted teeth, Baine stood using a bedpost and his good leg for leverage. He hobbled toward the twenty decorative pillows littering the bed. Shoving them aside, he climbed onto the soft down, unlatched the window, and swung it wide. There was no place to go. Except thirty feet straight down. But they wouldn't know that.

He retreated to the V of the room sandwiched between the hinges for the bathroom and hallway doors. With no chance at retrieving his gun from under the bed, Baine pulled the last blade from his vest.

Baine had no gun and jack to hide behind. Nothing to stop another bullet. All he had was hope. That vicious bitch.

About ten seconds had ticked by when the bathroom and hallway knobs turned. In sync, the men moved into the room at the pace of a grocery store clerk. The short barrels peeked around the dark wood door. Then their hands came into view.

Baine aimed high on the bathroom door. As soon as the dark hair and skin of a forehead showed, Baine launched the knife. It caught the man in the temple and he slumped to a heap on the floor. The sound of collapsing bone and flesh called the other guy's attention. His head turned toward the commotion. Thankfully his gun stayed pointing at the windows.

Pushing off on his good leg, Baine collected every ounce of his two hundred forty pounds and battered the door. The man groaned and the sub clattered on the floor. Baine and the guard fell in a tangle of arms and legs. Too bad the guard ended up on top. His knee connected with Baine's hamstring. Once. Twice.

Baine's eyes closed against the brilliant pain. When the man straddled his legs and clamped both his hands around Baine's throat, his eyes opened.

Sloan.

The pain dulled instantly. Thank fuck his wits didn't.

Looking into the eyes of his would-be killer, Baine memorized the sweat slicked ebony skin and white teeth that ground together. He smiled and the man's eyes grew wide.

Baine tossed the last flashbang a few feet above his head and clamped his eyes shut. Too bad he couldn't close his ears. After the blast, a mute scream escaped the man's wide mouth and his hands flew to his face, rubbing the tears that flowed in rivulets from behind his lids. Air raced back into Baine's lungs and he landed a jab to the man's protruding nose. The weight pinning Baine to the floor toppled off his chest to his legs.

He ignored the throbbing ache of his thigh and sat. The need to get to Sloan had been insistent since he'd lost sight of her in the dining room, but now that his road-blocks had been eliminated, the urgency to touch her, to rescue her from his father, itched so badly he could rip his skin off. He also had to find Kobi. With two well-placed hands Baine ended the guard's whimpers of pain with a quick snap. He shoved the sack of skin from his legs with a roar and scrambled under the bed to retrieve his gun.

A fresh magazine in the chamber, Baine ground a layer of enamel off his teeth as he stood and ran for the corridor. He cleared right then left. No sign of Kobi.

Where the hell...

Baine's eyes zeroed in on Devereaux's bedroom door and his heart plummeted. His body shifted into gear before his mind. Baine's hand reached for the doorknob.

Boom! The explosion originated outside, but the house vibrated around him. Then three rapid pistol shots rang out behind Devereaux's office door.

Chapter Thirty-five

"Take your tie off and toss it behind you," Sloan ordered.

Devereaux didn't budge. "So, you want to fuck after all."

Sloan slammed her foot against his kidney like a strike of lightning. The air wheezed from his lungs and he braced his hands on the edge of his desk to keep from hitting the floor. "Tie, now!"

The dark hair on the back of Devereaux's right hand danced as his fingers quavered. He reached for the tight knot. After two forceful tugs the fabric gave and slid around itself like a coiled snake until the end freed with a snap. A circle of red maimed Devereaux's neck. Knowing the mark would bruise, sadistic pleasure bloomed in her mind. But she wiped it away, snatching the tie from his hands. Sloan trained her eyes on the prisoner while she fashioned a slipknot with the skinny end of the silk.

"On your knees."

Outside the office door the machine gun fire died down. The unsettling silence that took its place frosted her from head to toe, causing her to fumble with the makeshift bond. Devereaux seized the opportunity, sliding the middle desk drawer open a quarter-inch before she stopped him with another kidney strike. Both his hands splayed on the middle of the desk as he struggled to breathe and stay upright.

"Knees," she demanded. He complied stiffly. "Let's get those hands tied before you get any more stupid ideas."

And so I can go find Baine.

Sloan flipped the safety on and stuffed the pistol in the cleavage of her low-slung dress. *Gawd, I miss functional clothes.* She grabbed Devereaux's left wrist from the desk and guided the loop over his thick hand below the wrist and pulled the end tight. Sloan watched as his opposite shoulder coiled to fight back, but she popped her fist against his ear.

Ring-a-ding.

His upper body weaved from the blow, but he remained vertical. Without delay, Sloan grabbed his left wrist, ready to complete the first part of a hogtie, but the quiet scrape of metal on metal brought her attention to the door. She dropped Devereaux's hand, snatched up her gun, slid the safety off, and planted it against Devereaux's temple in time to watch Kobi Ross slip into the office, machine gun at the ready.

"Thank God," Devereaux mumbled. "Kill her," he ordered in an angry garble.

Sloan crouched, shielding all but her head from Kobi's view with Devereaux's body. "Go ahead, shoot. I'll die happy, knowing my autonomic reflexes will take this piece of trash with me."

Kobi's face gleamed with sweat, and his normally pasty complexion looked two shades lighter. When he stepped closer, Sloan noticed the hitch in his step then the dark smear his ostrich loafers left on the floor. She followed the line up his body and found his dark grey suit oil-coated on the lower corner.

The man's crazed eyes bounced between her and Devereaux. Sloan's inner siren whooped to life. Gooseflesh rose along her arms and coursed in a wave down her body. Sweat formed a thin sheen on her upper lip, but she tamped down the fear that bubbled up from the recesses of her brain. She was not a child anymore. She was capable and trained by the best.

A hollow laughed emanated from Kobi's gaping smile. The sound froze the blood in Sloan's veins and even had Devereaux's frame jolt to attention.

Kobi raised and lowered the nose of the sub from her head to Devereaux's and back again. "What is it you always called me, sir? Loyal dog?" He paused on The Devil. "Dogs bite when they're mistreated. You should've thought of that while you were busy kissing your son's ass and kicking mine."

Before Sloan could react, Devereaux opened his pride-stuffed mouth. "Ungrateful filth. I scraped you off the street like day-old garbage and gave you purpose, fine food, and women. I know you want this one, but my equally ungrateful son stole her away."

Sloan wrapped her arm around Devereaux's throat and squeezed, but the son of a bitch continued, "I'll let you have her forever, and the take on the shipment, if you kill my son and stop this bitc—" Even though his windpipe squished under the weight of her arm, his words, though strained, wafted through the air like the stench of a dead carcass to a hyena, enraging the beast.

"Your son's already dead," he spat.

Kobi's words lanced Sloan's heart. She didn't for one minute believe Kobi had gotten the drop on Baine, but even though she knew they weren't true, they hurt worse than any pain she'd ever experienced. Worse than being stabbed. Shot. Electrocuted.

Without permission Sloan's arm eased on Devereaux's windpipe, but the man held still. Maybe in shock. More likely calculating his next move.

Kobi smiled. "You see, old man. No more blood heir. And after I kill you, and the slut here for good measure, I inherit the kingdom." He shrugged. "I was going to make it fast, but I love the shocked expression on your face so much, I think I'll take it slow."

Boom!

The flashbang popped in about the same place as the first and Sloan had to bite her inner cheek to keep from smiling.

Baine!

From recon Sloan knew the guards didn't carry the devices. They carried actual grenades. Not stuns. And she'd seen them on Baine's vest earlier. Heck, she'd felt them rub against her thighs.

Kobi didn't share her enthusiasm. His smug smile fell and he shuffled backward, locking the door he'd entered through without taking the gun or his eyes off her and Devereaux.

Boom!

Sloan half expected the windows to come raining down on them in crystalline shards. The floor shook beneath her feet, but she remained steadfast with her weapon and line of sight.

Apparently unaccustomed to combat, Kobi reached out to the wall with one hand and let the machine gun fall to his side as he tried to steady himself. With a smooth wrist flex and ease of the trigger, Sloan fired three shots into Kobi's chest.

As his body grew slack and fell toward the ground, that sharp pain she'd experienced when Kobi said he'd killed Baine returned...only a little lower.

Chapter Thirty-six

Baine ran through the open door from his father's empty bedroom into the office. For a moment the entire world stopped spinning. Gravity no longer held his universe together. Everything he held dear plummeted into the black abyss of space and he stood utterly alone. Lost.

Devereaux drew his bloody hand from Sloan's middle, a blade held in his taut fist. Red poured from its edges. Sloan's exquisite mouth hung open in surprise. Devereaux cranked his arm back to strike.

"No!"

Baine raised his Reeder. Devereaux's head turned at the roar. Shock etched in his features. Baine placed two bullets in his father's skull.

The man collapsed, folding over atop himself. Sloan caught herself on the edge of the desk. Her once pristine dress grew a red accent at her middle. Dread ripped its way though Baine's heart, leaving it in shreds at the bottom of his stomach.

Too late. You didn't keep her safe.

When she teetered, Baine ran like a ball player seeking home plate. He passed Kobi's corpse and the puddle of blood seeping from it. Sloan's legs gave out as he rounded the desk. He caught her in the cradle of his arms, her thick hair cascading over his arm, her precious brow knit in pain.

He lowered them to the ground, unable to stand, whether from the bullet in his leg or his shattered heart, he wasn't certain. His gun clattered to the floor at his feet as he pulled her against his chest.

Her tender smile nearly closed his throat with a thick lump. "I messed up. Knew he had a gun in the right drawer, but..."

Baine shook his head. "No. I put you in a bad situation. I should've let you kill that fucker straight away. Should've gotten here faster."

"You were right on time. I asked for more time, remember?"

His head still shook. He didn't know if the motion would ever stop. Like his reluctance to lose her would keep the reaper at bay.

"Hush now," he said. "I need to take a look."

When she nodded Baine eased her toward the floor, but her hands fisted his vest straps. Only hours before she'd gripped them in a lively show of passion. Now she clung in fear. Clung to life.

"Don't let me go."

His eyes burned, but Baine refused the welling emotions. "I'll never let you go." His left arm secured her to him while the fingers of his right hand ran down the curve of her waist in a careful caress. "Scream if you need to, love. This is going to hurt."

The warmth of Sloan's skin as she nuzzled her head against the side of his neck only made the ache in Baine's chest sear deeper into his soul. He had field training in first aid, but he was no doctor. Why couldn't he have been a healer? A giver of life, instead of a killer?

Because there was no amount of miracle working to right his father's wrongs. He'd become a killer to stop his father, and he had accomplished his goal. But at what cost? Hell, even if he were a doctor, they were hours from the nearest hospital with no I.V., no supplies, nothing. In a house filled with weapons and whores, killers and con-men, the real possibility of losing Sloan forever set his hand shaking.

Baine steeled his nerves with a long exhale and slipped his index finger inside the frayed material of her dress, careful not to touch the wound. He made a claw with the digit, hooking the blood-soaked cloth, and pulled. It howled as it ripped horizontally across her stomach. The hole grew from two inches to nearly six in a second.

Sloan tensed in his arms.

"I'm sorry, love. So sorry."

She shook her head against his neck, but Baine's focus riveted on the pucker of gnarled skin that flayed her perfect belly. His gaze flew to the weapon used to inflict the damage. The fucking letter opener lay next to his father's body, all four inches of the hilt covered in Sloan's blood. Even the silver handle was smeared with her life force.

In a city this wouldn't be a mortal injury.

But out here...

Baine's jaw tightened against the negativity. She would live. She had to. And where he failed her before, he would not this time.

He pried her left hand off his vest, placed it over the wound and applied pressure. "Hold tension on that for me. I know it hurts. You're so damn brave, Sloan."

She peeked out from his neck and smiled, her bottom lip quivering. "I didn't get the codes from his neck. I was tying him up to come rescue you."

"Love, that was my job. Fat lot of good I am at it."

"Sexist. Sometimes men need rescuing."

Yeah, Baine could use a rescue right about now. Because if anything happened to her he'd...

Baine hugged her tighter then pulled his phone out of the back pocket of his vest and held the button for Law.

His friend answered. "Clear outside."

"I need a HELO now. Whatever you have to do to get one. Call in Devereaux's goons and we'll take em' out. Call in a favor. I don't care."

"Fuck! Is she okay?"

"For now. Hurry though."

The dead silence of a disconnected line hung in Baine's ear. His friend would do everything in his power to help. Now Baine had to contend with the impotence of watching Sloan suffer and being unable to help. He'd rather lose a limb than see her suffer. The sadness in her eyes when they were children haunted his dreams and now...

"Baine." Her scratchy voice yanked his attention to her face. He dropped the phone next to the gun and scooted the damp hair from her forehead. His thumb ran the ridge of her cheek down her jaw.

"I'm here and not going anywhere."

Her thick lips crinkled in pain and she breathed short rapid breaths.

Please God, don't let him have stabbed a lung.

"I'm sorry," she said. "I just..."

"Stop apologizing. You did, and are doing, nothing wrong."

A tear escaped, sliding down the side of her face before falling into her hair. "No matter what happens..."

Baine opened his mouth, but the look of wild desperation in her eye told him to shut the hell up.

"No matter. I want you to know I wouldn't change a thing about coming here, being with you."

A teardrop landed on her honeyed skin and it took him a minute to realize it had come from him. *Pussy.* She needed him to be strong.

The corner of Sloan's mouth curved. "I need you to promise me one thing."

"I'll have to hear it first."

"Why?" she breathed.

"You don't get a dying wish. Because. You. Are. Not. Dying."

Her right hand released his vest and slid up to his face. Her cool hand cupped his rough cheek.

"Promise me you'll get all the assholes in that black book and make them pay."

"Done. But I want you to come help me when you're ready."

They both heard the *whop whop* of the whirlybird. And he wondered how in the hell Law had pulled that out of his butt so quickly, but he wouldn't complain one bit.

He leaned down and kissed Sloan's head. Her skin lacked its usual warmth and when he sat up he watched in stunned horror as her eyes rolled back into her head.

"Sloan. Sloan!"

With his hand cradling the nape of her neck he eased her to the floor. He ignored the scream of pain in his leg as he kneeled over her. Baine placed his left hand over her wound where hers had fallen limp at her side and with his right felt for a pulse.

Nothing.

He couldn't feel a fucking thing because he was totally numb. He readjusted his fingers and tried to calm the roaring ocean in his head.

After what seemed like a million years in suspended animation, a feint pulse caressed his finger.

He had to move. Now.

Baine bent to scoop her into his arms and heard footsteps, at least five sets, rushing down the hallway. The big desk wasn't the best cover, but these guys were coming fast and he didn't have time to move either of them.

Reeder in hand, Baine aimed at the door and waited.

Chapter Thirty-seven

Law opened the door with both his hands up where Baine could see them. Flanking and filing behind him were four men in brown tactical gear armed to the eyeballs with M-4's, side arms, grenades, and blades. Baine's gun didn't waiver. He only regarded his friend. Was Law a hostage? His hands were up like one. Then again, he could've presented like that so Baine wouldn't shoot him accidentally. The two in the front lowered their weapons while the two in back ignored him, scanning the hallway at the ready. One big mother in the front, as big as Law and not much off Baine, split from the crowd, stepping over Kobi toward him and Sloan. His blue eyes were wide as fucking dinner plates.

Baine zeroed in on him. "Don't take another step." The guy drew up, but stared at Sloan. "Who the fuck are you?"

"Is she..." The guy looked too pained to even finish the thought.

"Last chance. Who are you?"

That caught the blond's attention, drawing his sharp chin and narrow eyes to Baine for the first time. "CIA operative Ryan Noble. Sloan's partner. I know you as Baine Kendrick, son of that piece of rotting flesh. Who are you, really?"

US? It fit with the weapons and the type of chopper they flew, if his eyes and ears didn't deceive him.

"Baine Kendrick McCord. British Intelligence. Show me your creds."

The guy reached two fingers into his back pocket, took two measured steps forward, and reached his hand out to give it to Baine.

"Open it. My hands are full right now." No way was he taking his hand off the gun or Sloan before every doubt was erased from his mind. His gut told him the bloke was a friendly. The sheen of moisture covering the hard guy's eyes said as much. Then again, he could be one hell of an actor.

The eagle-emblazoned card read Central Intelligence Agency, United States of America, Clearance Code: 102708102412KDS, Issue Date: January 2010, Operative: Ryan Noble. Baine looked at the bottom right corner for the red BB that emblazoned his own credentials and found it. He, Ryan, Sloan, and Law were all Base Branch agents. The only difference was in what part of the world each was stationed. Policy mandated they identify themselves as Intelligence agents from their respective countries of birth. No one could know they were Branch operatives, but sometimes they needed to identity themselves with authority.

"What's her favorite color?" Baine couldn't be too protective of Sloan.

The guy's brows quirked. "Revenge. She doesn't give a shit about colors, unless they're vital to a mission."

Baine eased his gun down, but watched for any movement behind Ryan, who motioned one of the guys forward. "Get the I.V. in her and we'll book it."

A chappie with as many freckles on his face as Baine had hairs on his head stepped forward with a first aid kit, placed it on the ground near Sloan's feet, and got to work unloading the supplies he needed.

Ryan dropped to his knees across from Baine. He reached a shaky hand toward Sloan and Baine had to stop himself from biting it off at the wrist. When Ryan found her pitiful pulse his jaw tightened. "Damn it, partner, you hang in there." Then he turned to Freckles. "We gotta move fast."

A moment later, Baine and Ryan's gazes tangled as they spoke atop each other.

Ryan with, "What the fuck happened? Is it a shot or stab wound?"

Baine accompanied, "How the fuck did you know she was in trouble and why the hell didn't you draw on me?"

Both men's jaws screwed down as they sized each other up. Ryan gave first. "We've been three clicks east, hidden in the gorge, since Slo dropped. She sent the signal at nineteen hundred. We moved according to the plan, two hours after."

His bronzed fist clenched. "I tried for one hour. I talked her down from three, but there was no getting her to come off more."

Baine looked down at Sloan and smiled as an invisible band cinched a notch on his chest. "I know exactly what you mean. The damn woman's a force of nature."

"Didn't draw on you," Ryan continued, "because it looked as though you'd already been shot in the heart. And your partner sweet-talked us as soon as we touched down."

Baine eyed Law who stood quietly in the far corner of the room, face tight, but eyes sympathetic. "I failed her," he said in answer to

Ryan's earlier question. "Didn't get here in time. She got cornered and my...the fucking monster stabbed her with a letter opener."

"From the looks of the place and your leg, I'd say you had your hands full trying to get to her," Ryan said.

"Ready, sir," Freckles piped up.

"Let's move," Ryan barked.

Both Baine and Ryan bent to scoop Sloan. The pretty boy bit his lower lip and shook his head. "It'll be easier if we don't have to transfer her at the HELO."

"Then we won't," Baine growled. "I'm taking her all the way."

Still that blond hair flopped back and forth. "No can do. Against regs and about fifty other international laws."

"Fuck em'," he ground through clenched teeth.

"We don't have time for this," Ryan huffed. "If you want her to live, let her go."

It was a solid blow to Baine's head. Like a mallet met him center between his eyes, his hands slacked to his sides. Ryan hefted Sloan easily, murmuring in a calm, reassuring tone as he hurried from the room. The stampede of boots receded from the stairs, through the foyer.

Next the *whoop whoop* dimmed.

And still Baine stayed on his knees, collapsed back on his heels, paralyzed. The litany carried on. *Let her live. Let her live.*

Chapter Thirty-eight

Holy fuck on a fox. It'd been seven hours. Most broke within the first thirty minutes of his ministrations, but this chav showed backbone Baine didn't have time or any more patience to entertain. He needed to get this shit wrapped up so he could get to Sloan. It'd been two miserable months since she'd been wrenched from his life. He ached for her. Her touch. Her smile. He also hurt for sleep. For peace. But he wouldn't go to her without completing the task she'd asked of him. She deserved that much from him. A whole damn lot more. But at least that much.

He dropped the bloody pliers back on the metal table with a *clack*, dismissing his swollen knuckles and sore forearm. "I believe I've been going about this all wrong, Miguel." Baine stood in front of the man, zeroing in on the defiant gaze settled in his well-worn face. "You will tell me who bought the last shipment or you will regret it for the rest of your miserable life."

Baine turned to Law who stood guard at the door. As the words flowed from his mouth he hated himself a little more. "Bring the girl. If he doesn't care about his own wellbeing, perhaps he cares about hers."

Law nodded curtly, but his eyes glittered with rage. He hated what Baine had become too, but he obediently left the room. Baine turned to the master of one of Mexico's largest cartels and saw the first wave of emotion roll across his features, breaking the smug facade he'd hosted since they'd dropped in on his operation yesterday.

Miguel Castillo's lower lip quivered. "You call me a monster, but you are no different. You will hurt an innocent girl to get what you want."

The man was right. He was a monster, and he would.

What the bloody hell have you become?

No. He was better than Miguel. The man had slaughtered hundreds of innocents to get what he wanted. Drugs. Weapons. Money. All for Devereaux Kendrick. Baine was putting an end to that.

But at what price?

Law stepped inside the room with Rosanna Castillo. Both her tiny hands wrapped around the big man's forearm. She seemed totally at ease even as he led her blindfolded into the room. Law guided her toward the metal table behind Miguel. Every muscle in her father's body tensed. He thrashed against the bonds at his ankles and wrists, causing fresh blood to pool beneath his arms. Jaw working with fury, his head jerked left and right, trying to see what horror lay in store for his beloved, but the head restraints refused to give.

Baine smiled and walked around Miguel.

Quietly the man whispered through the saliva and blood. "Dios te salve, Maria. Llena eres de gracia: El Señor es contigo."

Baine chuckled and despised the sound.

The girl joined her father. "Santa María, Madre de Dios, ruega por nosotros pecadores, ahora y en la hora de nuestra muerte."

Her sugar-sweet voice raised every hair on Baine's weary body. His voice ground the word. "Amén."

Miguel drew a ragged breath.

Baine ignored Law's scowl, turning his attention to the little girl of maybe five or six years. "Hola Rosanna, me llamo Baine."

"Buenas noches Baine. Mi nombre es…" Her forehead creased behind the dark fabric. "Oop, sabes mi nombre."

He continued in her native language. "Yes, I know your name. I know your mommy's name, your daddy's. I even know little Nicolás." The girl smiled and Baine's stomach churned. Acid rose into his throat and for a moment he thought he would not be able to call it back.

After a full body shiver, he continued. "Would you like to play a game with me, Rosanna?"

"Sí," the girl giggled.

"Wonderful. Give me your hand." With a toothy grin she placed her tiny palm against his. "Great job, Rosa." Gently he placed it on the cold table next to the hacksaw, pliers, and knife. "Now, I want you to spread your fingers out wide, just like this and hold as still as you possibly can."

Her mocha hair swooshed as she nodded enthusiastically. "Sí, señor."

Baine grabbed the blade and began tapping a star pattern around the girl's fingers. "Very still now," he reminded.

Again she nodded.

The taps grew louder. Faster. The tempo rose. And rose. Until it sounded like an S.O.S. on speed. Baine nodded to Law who leaned close to the girl's ear. The pace reached a fevered pitch as drips of sweat rolled off Baine's nose. Three. Two. One.

The girl's scream ripped the room in two.

And Miguel Castillo screamed. "Cezar Vilaro!"

Rosanna clamped off her scream and tilted her head. "Papá, when can I see Uncle Cezar?"

Baine punched the man in the jaw and watched his body go slack. "Rosanna, you played the game very well. I think Law can find you a treat in the kitchen."

She squealed in delight. Her two perfect hands reached toward Law. Clamping him around the wrist she hurried him toward the door, listing all the toppings she wanted on her ice cream.

As soon as the door closed behind them Baine collapsed to his knees. His sob split the room nearly as loudly as Rosanna's scream had. He hung his head as his shoulders shook and his chest heaved.

I have turned into the very thing I hate most in this world. My father.

Baine only had one more bastard to deal with before he could go to Sloan. Cezar Vilaro. But how could he go to her as this monster? She would hate him. Hate what he'd become. His entire body hurt from wanting her, but better him hurt than her.

Chapter Thirty-nine

Sloan winked at Ryan as she tightened the straps of her overnight pack and adjusted the waist of her loose fitting khaki's. In the dull light of the Blackhawk's belly she watched Ryan's glare intensify. If the last week was any indication, the mean squint of his brow was permanent. It hadn't let up since Commander Tucker briefed him on his current mission.

Ryan turned away from her with a dramatic snap of his body. He huffed like a petulant child before catching the latch in his grip and wrenching the heavy hatch back.

Her fist met his shoulder in a solid knock and she hollered above the whirling blades of the HELO. "I'll be fine. See you tomorrow at twenty hundred."

She sat gingerly on the metal floor. Each day she could do more and more. No thanks to Tucker or Ryan, who'd practically taken up residence in her crappy apartment and hovered at the office. When they weren't mother-henning, she'd jogged short distances and lifted with her legs and arms at the Branch facility. She could even tighten her core, but it hurt like a mother if she twisted or slumped. Yep, abdominal exercises were still a month or so off. If the infection hadn't set in, she could've been operational by now. But she shouldn't worry about that and just be glad to be among the living.

Sloan waited for her shoulder bump from Ryan and one final comment about how crazy she was for dropping into Sierra Leone alone and in her "condition." Even Tucker thought she was nuts, but had okay'ed the personnel and supplies for her journey. He, more than most, understood her need to confront the past and release the demons that had lived inside her for the better part of twenty years.

When Ryan's fist didn't come she looked up. He stared intently at her, his face an unreadable mask. Her breath stilled in her chest. She'd always been able to read Ryan. It made them perfect partners. In the field they didn't need words. Just a quirk of a brow. A shift of the eyes.

But now his eyes bore into hers with a depth she'd never before seen. His hand nestled under her jaw at her pulse, which beat like a tribal drum. He held her loosely as his head dipped low, then stilled, his thick lips only an inch from her own. She tried to swallow, to speak, but hell if her mouth hadn't gone dry as the ground of Namibia.

Ryan's eyes never hid behind his lids, not even to blink. At this lover's proximity Sloan noticed the near white-flecks fracturing his pale blue eyes. The sheer opposite of Baine's steely blue. His face drew nearer and his warm lips brushed over hers then back again in the most painfully sweet embrace.

Sloan's heart shivered. Not in love or anger, but sadness.

His lean body withdrew from her space, a small smile playing across his mouth. "I love you, Sloan."

Sloan swallowed the clump of sand clogging her throat. "I love you. But I'm in love with Baine."

That beautiful smile didn't falter. "I know."

"Then why..." Her head shook, unable to form a coherent though with the structure of her world shifting under her feet yet again.

He chucked her shoulder with his fist. "I've always loved you as a partner and friend. Then I almost lost you to that." He pointed toward her stomach. "And I'm losing you to Kendrick, McCord, whatever the hell you wanna call him."

Ryan chuckled but the sound sailed away in the whir of propelled wind. "You've been my center point for a long time. I got scared, and figured why not go for broke."

For some reason she wanted to cry. The fear of the unknown. The changes she hoped were on the horizon. Sloan hugged Ryan's face in her hands, ignoring the well of moisture in her eyes.

"You're not broke or broken. You just need to kick your mommy's handpicked harem of socialites, along with her ass, to the curb, and find your own center. Not hers. Not theirs. Not mine." His brow quirked. "You always worry about doing the right thing. Being the Boy Scout. Screw the right thing," she laughed, "or maybe the wrong thing for once, and find something worth fighting for."

His index finger tapped her nose. "Is that an order?" His tone downplayed the emotions and seriousness of the subject matter, but the corners of his mouth turned down and his lips pursed like they always did when he was trying to figure a complex tactical problem.

"No, just something to think about," she said, throwing her arms around his neck. She squeezed him as hard as she could without rupturing an intestine and he hugged her back. His strong arms gave her the courage to let him go.

He held her shoulders at arm's length. "If you come back in one pretty piece, I'll think about it."

"Done. Anything to get your mother out of your ear. She spews slow-acting neurotoxins. I fear for your health."

Ryan's hand dropped to his side as his shoulders shook with laughter. His genuine smile lightened Sloan's sadness. *Everything will be okay.*

Ryan's hand went to the Sig at his waist. "Since you aren't going to let me whisk you off your feet and out of this place or let me go with you, at least take my side arm."

Sloan slid to the ground. "I'll see you tomorrow. Twenty hundred hours."

She turned to Ryan and waved. He just stood there, feet spread wide, one hand on his hip and the other on his gun, shaking his head at her.

From the tree line she watched the lights of the HELO rise into predawn ink and set out south to Liberia. When they became a distant twinkle, Sloan, with her civvies and overnight pack, set out north toward the Moa River, or Makona as she'd called it in her youth. The boarders of Guinea, Liberia, and Sierra Leone converged about six clicks ahead. She set an easy pace, partly due to the dark, the nearness to a rebel stronghold even ten years after the war, and her physical limitations. Mostly though, she strolled along taking in the smells and sounds of her homeland for the first time since she'd left in a small crate on the back of a supply truck nearly twenty two years ago.

As planned, she made it to the river's edge just south of the village at dawn, without incident. Too early to roam the main dirt path through the heart of the small town before its resident's daily routines beat the town to life, Sloan eased from the thick foliage down the steep embankment to the flat bar below. The rich tan sediment jutted about five feet into the river then curved back to the shore.

Shucking her pack, Sloan's shoulders relaxed from the release of pressure and sank an inch more as the view eased the small rattle of nerves she'd carried with her since she decided to return.

The golden sunlight rose from behind the trees, bathing the water and brilliant green leaves in unadulterated hues of yellow. Up the river the forms of a carved out canoe and petite man showed black against the splendor. He cast a net into the dark water. The scene warmed Sloan from deep inside and had her unlacing her calf-high hiking boots with rapid flicks of her fingers. She rolled both pant legs before toeing off the ten-pound boots and pulling off her plush socks.

A smile stretched her face as she burrowed her feet against the cool sand. Bits of rock pricked her skin, but she only wiggled her toes and sank deeper into the earth. She filled her lungs so full of the clean air her ribs would give no more. At the point of bursting she held her breath and turned her face up to the sun. Now heated from the inside and out, with her eyes closed, Sloan stepped into the water. A swarm of prickles enveloped her feet and the chilly water set off a wave of gooseflesh through her body, but she had never felt such peace.

In a rush of air, she released into the wind every haunting thought, every heartache Devereaux Kendrick had ever given her. The next breath came more easily and the next easier still. Sloan opened her eyes to the beauty of her home, forgetting the one day of horror she'd endured, and remembering the love this place cultivated for the first five years of her life.

After her feet were properly pruned Sloan replaced her shoes and backpack and set out for town. The fisherman, a young man of maybe fourteen or fifteen, traced her movement up the bank. He waved as she passed. His eyes were bright and smile wide. When she returned the wave he hid his smile with the back of his hand. The shy gesture tickled her belly and had her giggling all the way to a broad dirt road at the main corridor of the town.

Sloan stopped dead at the expanse of red clay. It had only been a donkey trail when she was little. From the columns of varied tire tracks she could tell it was well used. She didn't know why the sight of it surprised her so. Things changed on a daily basis. Worlds progressed. She'd been gone for a long time. She shouldn't have expected things to remain the same. The road was a great thing. A sign of growth and good fortune.

She slipped back into the brush and changed her pants for a patterned wrap and swapped boots for sandals then added her tracks to the carrot-colored dirt. As she walked, the roadside changed from rambling greenery to sporadically-placed one-room clay homes with thatched roofs and some tin. Closer to the center they multiplied, filling the space at the street edges. A scooter putted past carrying a man with a toddler wrapped to his front in a *mei tai* cloth. After a minute a large truck rumbled in his path, carrying what looked to be jugs and barrels of water.

Up ahead the street was congested with pedestrians. *The market.* Her mother had traded schooling for food and other necessities in this narrow strip. On one side of the road the old cement building stood proud, still the cerulean blue of her childhood on its doors and roof, but the exterior hosted a fresh, as in the last five years, coat of orange. Across the street, vendors set up their goods, while others, older children mostly, walked about the bazaar, carrying baskets of merchandise on their heads or propped in their arms.

She garnered only mild curiosity from the merchants as she mingled in the crowd. The children didn't gather around her in interest. The men and women offered easy smiles, but no one questioned her presence. She'd planned it that way, wearing well-used clothing with vibrant colors and patterns to mimic the women of the town. In a weird way she felt as though she belonged. As though she were one with the strong woman who had given her life.

Past another clump of homes Sloan reached her destination. The place that changed the course of her life forever. No longer a clay shack and tin roof, the cement building sat where the old school house had burned to the ground with her parents' bodies inside. Its clean cream lines stood proud against the green forest. A tear fell. Then another.

The school was more beautiful than the pictures had shown. It was more worthwhile than a D.C. home or pricey car. More precious than a twenty-carat diamond from the pitted earth of Sierra Leone.

Sloan swatted the tears away and hurried toward the building. When she rounded the final home she saw another building across the street from the school. It mirrored the structure in shape, material, and color. And like the first it held children. Sloan heard the joyous voices of young people singing.

"We pray that no harm on thy children may fall, that blessings and peace may descend on us all..."

Her throat tightened in recognition and at their sweet pitch. Quietly she sang along. "So may we serve thee ever alone, land that we love, our Sierra Leone."

Without instruction, her feet carried her to the corner of the schoolhouse. She hung back from the door, unwilling to interrupt the beginning of class, but realizing she might very well draw attention in her current position. Still, there was nothing she could do to stop herself.

Sloan placed her forehead on the rough exterior. *Thank you Momma and Papa for peace. Thank God.* She actually stretched her arms out wide and held the structure in her embrace. *Life again.*

Smooth metal caught her right hand and she stepped back in surprise. A placard embedded in the cement read: Cabanos Pre-School Built January 2010 *In Loving Memory of Elizabeth McCord by The BKM Foundation.*

The air whooshed from Sloan's lungs. *Baine.*

She turned toward the other building and zeroed in on its relieved metal plate, but didn't go to it. From the pictures Head Mistress Sienna had sent Sloan knew it read: *Cabanos Primary School Built January 2010 In Loving Memory of Sylva Kolat Johnson and Daniel Johnson by The SKH Foundation.*

Sloan loved Baine, was in love with him, but had never yearned to throw her arms around him more than she did in this moment. She didn't need a night here to expel her demons. Her eyes were open and staring straight ahead. No looking back. It was time she looked toward the future.

Chapter Forty

Though Baine couldn't see the mug in his hand for the sloe of his home, he had no problem guiding it to his mouth and finishing the cold beer in one gulp. Now, if only Easton were here. He didn't like being served. He did, however, like cold beer. And in order for him to get more he'd either need to turn on a light or trip over himself trying to find it in the buttoned down cave of his home.

He set the empty glass on the side table and slumped back in the chair. The squeak of leather sang through the hollow room, hitting the high ceiling before carrying up the grand mahogany staircase and batting around the wall of stained glass at the landing.

On second thought, thank goodness the butler wasn't here. The man would worry him to death with lights and drink. He'd insist on feeding him like he weren't a man capable of taking care of himself. Then he'd most assuredly insist on talking. As the closest thing Baine had to a father, he knew enough not to ask many questions about what Baine did or where he did it. But it sure didn't slow the rattle of his old mouth. Thank goodness he had a lady friend to keep his mouth busy these days.

Before Ruth, Baine's off-duty days had been brutal. With Magdalena gone away to school, it had just been he and Easton rattling about the old estate. And it didn't matter how many times he dismissed the man to go about his life as he chose. His reply was always the same, "Ah-ah, your grandfather commissioned me to this house and to you, you ungrateful brute. So, until you burn the place to the ground, I'll be about my duties."

Now, if only Baine could be about his duties. He wouldn't be sitting here in the dark, pissed at the world.

No, not the world. Only at himself.

After years of his father beating the same message into his skin, it had apparently only taken the man's death for the directive to commence. *You're such a failure. Whack. Nice doesn't get you anywhere in this world son. Whack. Get mean. Whack. Don't be a cunt. Whack. Take what you want. Whack. Fuck everyone else. Whack. You're the son of Devereaux Kendrick. Whack.*

The beer sloshed in his belly despite the fact that he hadn't moved an inch. He scrubbed both hands over his face. *How dare you make him proud?*

God he wanted to go back three or four months. To put his finger on the point where everything inside him went berserk and erase it from the pages of history. He didn't want to be a monster. Never wanted to be anything like his father. But bloody tosh if he knew how to make things right.

Which was why he sat here with the drapes shut tight, instead of finishing the last barmy slime tied to his father. He'd never quit before completing a mission. But he'd pulled himself off the job after the shit with Rosanna. If he'd hurt that little girl he'd have been staring down a BritRail. At a hundred plus miles per hour he'd be a human pancake spread out on the front of the red train in no time at all.

"Fuck!"

A sound caught his ear. Not the echo of his own roar, but a tiny drawl of breath.

Baine was up with his Reeder in hand in a blink. He turned and swept left then right, sure the sound had come from behind him. Only black greeted his eyes. He pricked his ears for any whisper, but only the hum of household appliances filled the air. His shoulders should've relaxed. He should've returned to wallow in his self-loathing, but his feet carried him forward.

He moved through the living room and into the kitchen, clearing the space as he went. Well, the little bit he could see. At the back door he peered out the clear glass panes at the vacant gravel drive and the guest house which remained devoid of life with Mags at school and Easton at Ruth's. Law occupied the east half of the main house's upper floor, but wouldn't come home tonight. He currently avoided Baine like the monstrosity he'd become was the latest flu epidemic.

Maybe the shit was catching.

Good thing he was alone. Alone. He'd never cared much about being alone. Usually liked it better. There were only a handful of people he could tolerate and he lived with all of them, except one. The one that made his solitary status lonely for the first time.

Sloan.

As if conjured by his thought, the scent of verbena wafted across his face, knotting his gut in desperate need. He should have gone to her straight away. Screw revenge. Screw justice. But wishes wasted effort on things that would never be. With a huff, Baine tucked his sidearm and headed for the fridge. Since he was already up...why not have another?

Jeez. The light from the appliance was bright enough to call all the battle ships to shore. He squinted against the headache the illumination triggered and grabbed a bottle of...*son of a bitch.* All his Newk Browns were gone, leaving only Law's Old Tom. He hated the stuff on principle. It had a cat on the label and he hated cats. *Screw it.* Baine grabbed a puss beer, twisted the top, and took a long pull.

"Wouldn't have pegged you for a pussy beer drinker."

Chapter Forty-one

Baine's beer spewed from his mouth. Most of it. The rest he coughed and sputtered on for a few seconds. It gave her more time to look at him in the light. His blue eyes hollowed into his sockets and were punctuated with shadowed circles. The center of his cheeks sank in shallow pools of despair. The demons she'd released had flown with the fury of hell on the African wind and settled in the soul of her beloved.

After pulling a steady breath, he abandoned the beer to the counter and stepped toward her around the refrigerator door. When the door closed they were plunged again into total darkness. Though she knew Baine hadn't left the dark in many weeks, if not months.

"Sloan."

Pain. The word, her name, on his lips sounded like a plea for help, a broken wail. *Oh God.* She hurt for him.

She also cursed her feeble body for taking so long to heal. So long to get to him.

"I'm here." She reached out her hand and her fingers met his wrist. They walked to his palm and curled around his immense hand. He squeezed hers in return and the longing to be encased in his arms and wrap him in return jumped eagerly in her chest. When Baine didn't pull her close a sense of dread crept into her psyche.

"I...how are you?" He stumbled over the words.

"I'll be cleared for duty in two more weeks."

Their words sounded so cold and distant. She needed to see him. To gauge his reactions, so she knew how to advance. "You do have lights in London, don't you?" She tried for lighthearted and failed miserably, if the silence across from her was any indication.

The dread turned into a bold bitch, forgoing the gentle creep for an all out attack on her nerves. It hacked and trampled over her zen in a matter of seconds. So much for subtlety. Sloan squared her shoulders and kicked her fear square in the ass.

"Turn on a light."

"I can't." He inhaled like he was going to say more, but didn't.

Sloan yanked her hand away and moved to the wall, feeling around for a switch. She hit metal and a pan clattered to the floor, shattering the silence.

"Unless both your hands fell off in the last two seconds, I suggest you turn on a light now, or I'll rip this place apart looking for the damn switch."

His shoes scuffed the hard ground and before she could tell which way he was going, he was on top of her. The sun may as well have risen in the kitchen because its overhead light had the same blinding effect. Sloan blinked Baine into focus and wanted to weep at the haunted features that stared back at her.

"What happened, Baine?"

When he met her gaze a tiny bit of the horror in his eyes faded. He clamped his arms around her shoulders and buried his face in her hair. She wrapped her arms around his middle and held on for dear life. One hand fisted in his shirt while the other latched onto the muscles of his back. His warmth seeped into her bones and she molded to his body.

But all too soon he pulled away. She fought to hold him, but he took her arms in his hands and disentangled her. Her gaze zeroed in on his massive hands cradling her wrists. The size difference seemed comical, but she couldn't laugh. She couldn't bring her gaze to meet Baine's for fear of what she'd see. Detachment. Rejection.

Well, screw fear.

If she'd learned anything in her life, it was that fear only controlled you as far as you let it. Sloan raised her gaze to Baine's in challenge.

He dropped her hands and straightened. "I think you need to leave."

Sloan laughed. "Not a fucking chance."

That earned her a double brow raise before they knit together in an expression of pure determination. "I'm no good for you. You deserve better than me. Better than what I am."

"I know you, and I know I deserve you."

His head shook, and his hair, longer now, bobbed about his forehead. "No."

"What happened while I was...away?"

"Away," he scoffed. "Try *fighting for your life.* I should've been there for you. With you."

She stepped closer to him and placed her hand over his heart. "But I saddled you with my baggage, making you promise things I shouldn't have. And from what I've heard you've done a hell of a clean-up job."

He turned away and stalked to the window.

"I'm here for you. I'm not going away. No matter what comes out of your mouth. You're stuck with me, Baine. Like it or not." But her words didn't move him. "Look at me, damn it." Her voice rose. "What happened?"

He gripped the sink and pinched it between his palms. His forearms bulged. Veins rose like ripcords across his heavy muscles. Baine hung his head between his shoulders and his teeth bared as a growl of anguish tore through his chest.

Sloan went to him and cloaked his back with her body. Heat and rage radiated off him in waves so powerful she wondered if he'd break the counter. Still she hung on, willing him to expel his demons. To give voice to the pain and lessen its power over him.

After what seemed like an eternity he freed the counter and stood, but she didn't let him go. Sloan hugged him until her weak muscles shook. His hands wrapped around hers and she braced her heart for a cool dismissal that didn't come.

"To get what I wanted I became the monster I've always hated and feared. I hated it because it hurt people. I feared it, not because it hurt me, but because it was in me. In my blood."

His head shook and one hand left hers to scrub over his face, but he didn't pull away. He drew in a deep breath and continued, "We never talked about birth control..."

Out of left field, because she'd never thought about having children, a smile spread Sloan's lips at the possibility of one day being pregnant with Baine's child.

Only to be wiped away.

"...because I had a vasectomy shortly after I found out about my father's legacy. I never wanted to give a child my tainted blood. My ruined name."

She couldn't think about children when the man she wanted to share them with hurt so deeply.

"Oh, Baine. You are not your father. You are not a monster."

He stepped from her grasp and turned to face her. "I tortured people to get names that weren't in the book."

"You collected information to stop an illegal ring of gun smugglers, drug dealers, murderers, and rapists."

Baine took her face in his hands and bent so their gazes were level. "I used a little girl to get information out of her father when he didn't crack after I'd beat him to hell and back, cut off three of his fingers, pulled six teeth, and cut off his blasted ear."

His gaze searched her face, but her expression didn't falter. She'd heard and seen plenty worse than that. Heck, she'd done some of each on various missions. Sometimes the greater good outweighed the welfare of the scum of the earth.

"Did you hurt the girl to get your information?"

"No. But—"

"Did she see her father battered and bloody?"

His jaw worked for a minute before he answered. "No."

"Was she afraid of you?"

"No. How the hell did you know all that? Law called you, didn't he?"

She smiled. "I know what's in here." Under her hand and the solid breadth of his chest, Baine's heart knocked frantically against her touch. His lids shut. The skin at the corners of his eyes wrinkled with the fierceness of his denial. A denial of the truth in her words. "Besides, Yannick Bakou was elected by his people last month. Only a month after he'd come out of hiding without a scratch. You did that. You made the world think he was dead to trick your father when it would have been a hell of a lot easier and safer for you to have put a bullet in Bakou's head."

When his features refused to lighten, she continued. "Did you torture people to line your own pockets?"

He clamped his lips together in defiance, but she waited for his gaze to return. When it did, she needled him with her amber stare until finally he spoke. "No."

"Did you enjoy hurting those people? The murderers? The rapists?"

"No."

"Are you your father?"

"No."

"Are you a monster?"

The hard lines of his face softened and he lowered his head. His lips attacked her mouth in firm strokes. Sloan's nerves washed from her body on a wave of love and arousal. They would get through this. Together.

Her tongue invaded his mouth and she kissed him with matched fervor. Her need became a pant of desire, but she pulled back, needing him to answer her last question. Baine pulled a ragged breath into his chest then her against it. He pillowed her cheek against his frame.

"Answer the question, Baine."

"Only if you answer one for me."

She comforted him with steady brushes of her hand over his back. "Fine, but mine first."

Her head bobbed with his breath. "No, I'm not a monster."

She crushed him in an embrace. "You don't believe it yet, but you will in time. Two weeks and three days, to be precise."

His thumb turned her chin up to meet his gaze. One bushy brow rose in question.

"I'm cleared in two weeks and we have one more mission left to wrap up the disaster that was our childhood." He shook his head. The man had to have a headache he did it so much. "It's done. The mission is set. We're going to finish this thing. Then you'll see you're no monster because we'll lay the last of the real ones to rest together."

"I love you," he said.

"And I you, Baine McCord." She stood on tiptoes, stretching out her body, and kissed him on the forehead. Her lips trailed down his cheek, across his stubble, to his ear. "Now the only question is, how are we going to fill the two hours until go time?"

"Not the only question," he growled. Baine set her at arm's length from him and gave her a hard stare, searching her face. He took a deep breath then dropped before her onto one knee.

"Sia Kolat. Sloan Harris. The love I don't deserve. Will you marry me?"

JUSTICE MINE
A BASE BRANCH NOVEL

For justice. For country. For love.

After witnessing her friend's sexual assault, seven-year senior Magdalena Wells escapes an attack with a few bruises and a thousand questions. As a journalist in practice, if not in pay, Mags vows to utilize the skills she mastered in the Democratic Republic of Congo and answer every single one, just as soon as she gets the hell out of town.

Law Pierce's aim is rest and relaxation after two years undercover in South Africa on an extended Base Branch mission, but restlessness puts him in trouble's path. As a servant of justice, Law will do everything in his power to keep trouble safe. The fact that trouble's petite stature and luscious curves stir his every primal instinct is a massive inconvenience he struggles to ignore.

Together Magdalena and Law uncover a web of corruption and dirty lies that could set their country's top official ablaze, if the inferno doesn't consume them first.

STRANGER MINE
A BASE BRANCH NOVEL

One takes control. One finds balance in letting go.

Base Branch operative Ryan Noble is accustomed to taking orders whether from his commander or his overbearing mother. His best friend urged him to take control of his life, but the only thing worse than an angry woman is a teary one. He has no desire to upset his mother's fragile emotions. Losing his sister was hard enough; his mom couldn't bear losing another child. Even if it is to the other side of D.C. It's a damn good thing she doesn't know what he does for a living.

On a routine mission to destroy a cargo-free human-trafficking facility and exterminate its operators, Ryan blows his extraction to rescue a woman he finds chained inside.

Piper Vega is caught between metal and a hard place. She needs information and it has taken far too long to cull it from her leads—also known as her captors. She finally has the facts she needs to complete her task, but it'll take a miracle to set her free and see it achieved. Santo Padre knows she never expected her good favor to come in the form of a man.

Through intense battles of will, Ryan takes the reins of life in his sturdy grip while Piper discovers balance in loosening hers.

Megan Mitcham was born and raised among the live oaks and shrimp boats of the Mississippi Gulf Coast, where her enormous family still calls home. She attended college at the University of Southern Mississippi where she received a bachelor's degree in curriculum, instruction, and special education. For several years Megan worked as a teacher in Mississippi. She married and moved to South Carolina and began working for an international non-profit organization as an instructor and co-director.

In 2009 Megan fell in love with books. Until then, books had been a source for research or the topic of tests. But one day she read *Mercy* by Julie Garwood. And oh, Mercy, she was hooked!

Megan lives in Southern Arkansas where she pens heart pounding romantic thriller novels and window-steaming erotic romance. For information on releases and giveaways subscribe at meganmitcham.com!

Facebook: @MeganMMMitcham
Twitter: MeganMitchamAuthor
Pinterest: MeganMitcham5
Goodreads: Megan_Mitcham
Website: www.meganmitcham.com

FOR INFORMATION ON NEW RELEASES &
GIVEAWAYS, SIGN UP FOR MEGAN'S
NEWSLETTER AT WWW.MEGANMITCHAM.COM.